ALL THAT REMAINS

LIAM HANSON

CRIME PRINTS

Copyright © 2024 by Liam Hanson

All rights reserved.

No part of this publication may be reproduced, distributed, or transmitted in any form or by any means, including photocopying, recording, or other electronic or mechanical methods, without the prior written permission of the publisher, except as permitted by U.K. copyright law. For permission requests, contact author.

The story, all names, characters, and incidents portrayed in this production are fictitious. No identification with actual persons, living or deceased, is intended or should be inferred.

Published by CRIME PRINTS

An Imprint of Liam Hanson Media

ISBN-13: 9798320011523

For my wife and children

Current Books in the Series

Current books in the series:
_____

DEADLY MOTIVE
COLD GROUND
KILLING TIME
CHASING SHADOWS
DEVIL'S BREAD
ALL THAT REMAINS

ALL THAT REMAINS

Chapter 1

EDWARD COLLIER PACED THE room like an expectant father. The rug in front of the open fireplace and the writing bureau against the opposite wall, his markers for each about turn. He gave his aching right hip a rub and stared at the corded telephone while the carriage clock on the mantlepiece counted time.

On his next circuit of the living room, the mounting urge to make the call overwhelmed him. He grabbed for the handset and dialled a number from an address book held open in front of him.

'Hello,' he said when the ring-tone finally gave way to a woman's voice. 'Hannah. Is that you?'

'Ted?' Hannah Oakley sounded unsure of her assumption. There was a brief pause on the line, followed by an unsettled: 'Is Mum okay?'

'What time did she leave Aberystwyth?' Collier asked. 'Only, she wasn't there at Cardiff Central when I went to pick her up.'

'What makes you think that Mum's been here with us?'

Collier placed his hand on the table and leaned some of his weight on it. His hip was playing up like a bad case of toothache. 'She arranged it with Mark. Didn't she?'

'Mum and I haven't spoken since . . . Not since . . . You *know* we haven't.'

Collier straightened slowly and drew a sharp intake of breath as worn cartilage let bone grind against bone. He easily recalled the events of that afternoon of the summer barbeque. As would most of the neighbours and the local police, if asked. 'Mark wanted the three of you to sit down together and sort things out, once and for all.'

Oakley managed little more than a deep sigh in response. 'I think that's highly unlikely, don't you?'

'That's what your mother told me. Why don't you ask Mark?' Collier suggested.

'I would, but he's gone to the gym and won't be back for another hour, at least.' There was the sound of Hannah Oakley pulling a wooden chair across the surface of a tiled floor. Then a huff as she dropped onto it. Followed by a sudden and loud exclamation: 'Hang on a minute! I'm only just back from a few nights away with some work-friends. Why would he invite Mum here? He'd be stuck with her until I got back. One of them would wind up dead, for sure.'

Collier used the back of his hand to wipe perspiration from his clammy brow. 'So, where is she? Where did she go?'

'How should I know?' Another deep sigh. 'When exactly did she leave Cardiff?'

'A week ago today. Tuesday morning, first thing. She'd booked into an Airbnb, in case things didn't work out. Mark was going to pick her up when you were both ready to meet.'

'Give me the address for the Airbnb.'

'I've no idea where it was.'

'How can you not know?' Oakley's tone was harsh and accusing. 'Ted?'

Collier's response was defensive. 'Your mother insisted I didn't get involved. She and Mark made all the arrangements. I did as told.'

Oakley mumbled something that Collier didn't catch. He let it pass unchallenged. 'But you did take her to the station and put her on the train?' she said. 'And saw it leave for Aberystwyth?'

'Not exactly. I had a hospital appointment that morning. My hip's been playing me up something rotten lately and—'

'Mum used a taxi then?'

'No,' Collier said sheepishly. 'Nathan took her.'

'Nathan?' Oakley's chair did the same scraping thing against the tiled floor. She repeated the name.

'It was no bother for him to do it. Never is. Not where your mother's concerned.' Collier coughed. It was a poor attempt at dealing with the awkward direction their conversation was travelling in. 'But you'd know that already.'

Oakley didn't commit to an answer either way. 'Mark couldn't have been aware of Nathan's involvement. He'd have gone mental if he'd even suspected it.'

Collier sat on the arm of the sofa, listening to the carriage clock count time. 'I've no idea who knew what. You and I appear to be the ones kept in the dark.'

'You know a damn sight more than I do,' Oakley countered. She snatched a breath. 'As always.'

'Meaning what?'

'Let's not go there. Not today. You've tried ringing her, presumably?'

'Not before yesterday. She asked me not to. In case I interrupted something. She sent me three or four texts during the week, saying things were good there. *Better than expected* was the term she used. But beyond that – nothing.'

'This makes no sense at all. Why would Mum claim to be here with us, when clearly she wasn't?'

Collier shrugged, puffed his cheeks, and exhaled slowly. 'I really don't know.'

'Any contact from her today?'

'Not even after her train came and went. That's when I rang her. And not just the once.'

'And?'

'My calls kept going to voicemail. I left messages urging her to call me back, but . . .'

'What the hell is she playing at?' Oakley asked.

'I think we should call the police,' Collier said. 'If only to raise our concerns.'

'I don't know about that. Not yet, anyway.'

'She might have had an accident, or fallen ill on her way home. They could make enquiries on our behalf.'

Oakley disagreed. 'Let me get hold of Mark first. I'll find out what they've both been up to.'

'No police, then?' Collier asked.

'Don't you dare. I'm not being made to look like an idiot.'

Collier shut his eyes. He was breathing heavily. 'Are you not at all worried for your mother's wellbeing?'

'Worried?' Hannah Oakley forced air through her front teeth. 'You know Mum. She'll surface soon enough.'

Chapter 2

MILL STREET, CARDIFF.

DETECTIVE CHIEF INSPECTOR BRÂN Reece waited with his hands buried deep inside the pockets of his black trench coat. He'd only an hour earlier received a telephone call alerting him to the discovery of human remains beneath the road in Mill Street, Cardiff.

Control had despatched a pair of uniformed officers to attend the unusual find, and following a brief assessment of the situation, decided it warranted the presence of a detective. With foul play not yet ruled out, the most appropriate person to have on scene would be someone senior from the Regional Murder Squad. Hence DCI Reece's presence.

He raised his collar and used the front overhang of the nearest building to shelter from the latest downpour. He was fighting a losing battle. The wind must have realised what he was up to and drove the cold rain towards him at an almost horizontal angle, and with little care for his wellbeing.

He went and found himself another spot—it was no better there—and finger-combed a length of wet hair from his line of sight. A droplet of water ran along the bridge of his crooked nose, swelling to a fair size. He shook his head to get rid of it, then repeated the finger-combing process until he had full vision of his surroundings.

Detective Sergeant Elan Jenkins stood with her leg bent at the knee and the sole of her shoe pressed against the wall of the building. She looked as wet as Reece did, but was shivering more than he was. 'Wish I was a librarian,' she said, checking the sky for any hint that the latest deluge might be the last of the day's quota. The briefest of glances confirmed her fears that it wouldn't be. 'I'd have a warm and dry place to work in, and a nice mug of hot coffee whenever I fancied one.'

'You couldn't shut up long enough to be a librarian,' Reece said, walking towards a pile of excavated earth. '*Oi!* I thought I told you to get out of that hole,' he told a burly man wearing orange coveralls and a white hard hat. 'If this turns out to be a crime scene—' He paused to check in all directions. 'Where have that pair of uniforms gone?'

'To dry off, if they've got any sense,' Jenkins said. 'They were both soaked to the skin when I last saw them.'

'I told you I was on my way.' The man in the hard hat was wading through a puddle that was almost knee deep. 'I was saving my torch from drowning. I'm assuming you'll be wanting to use it when you get down here?'

Reece went to the edge of the hole and saw three mud-stained shovels and a solitary pick leaning against the dirt walls. 'Hurry up,' he said, shaking himself off like a wet dog. 'You're giving me vertigo.' He came away from the hole and tried to stamp warmer blood through his cold feet. It wasn't working, and in many ways, might have been making things worse. He could do with a hot shower and that coffee Jenkins was banging on about.

'Huw Jones,' the man said, joining him on the rain-soaked pavement. He wedged the torch between his knees, removed a pair of filthy gloves, and proffered a hand in greeting. He took it away again when Reece made no attempt to accept.

'No offence, but I've seen healthier offerings during my trips to the morgue.'

Jones took a moment to study each hand in turn, before putting them away again. 'Water gets inside the gloves,' he said, stating the obvious. 'Makes the skin go all wrinkled and white. You should see my feet.'

Reece had no intention of doing any such thing. 'Can we move away from this generator?' he asked. 'I can't hear myself think.' He turned his back before Jones could reply, the new focus of his attention being DS Elan Jenkins. 'Move those rubberneckers and get uniform to cordon off the area while you're at. Come on. *You* should be kicking their arses, not me.'

'Boss.' Jenkins stepped off the wall and soon had the pair fighting to stretch blue-and-white tape from one side of the road to the other. It broke in two, leaving both officers staring at her for further instruction.

Reece swore under his breath. 'They shouldn't be allowed to breed.'

'I've got a pair just like them,' Jones said. 'Even when you put a shovel in their hands, you've still got to tell them to dig.'

'I'm surprised you're allowed to bring them out in the rain,' Reece replied with lashings of sarcasm. 'It's only a matter of time before someone claims it's an infringement of their human rights. Anyway. Enough of that. What have you found in that hole of yours?'

Chapter 3

Reece hated heights and had done ever since a childhood incident on a quarry back home.

In the scheme of all things short and tall, the drop to the foot of the hole from the pavement above wasn't much of one. Top to bottom of the aluminium ladder measured a little less than twelve feet, give or take a few inches. Still enough to earn him a broken leg, or worse, if he didn't get it right. Dressed in the appropriate work-clothing, including a hard hat which he couldn't get to sit right on his head, he gripped the uprights of the ladder and descended its treads without daring to look down.

'Watch your step,' Jones said, steadying the ladder with his boot resting on the lower rungs. He led the way through the mud and water, calling to Reece over his shoulder. 'It's treacherous underfoot. You could snap an ankle as easily as that,' he continued, clicking his fingers.

Reece's borrowed wellies rubbed the backs of his heels, but kept most of the water out. He couldn't help but give thought to all those men and boys terrorised in the trenches of the First World War. They'd endured what must have seemed like an eternity of mortar shells raining down on their positions, with no way of ever knowing when the bullet carrying their name was winging its way across the smoky battlefield.

He was humbled by their selfless sacrifice and gave himself a good telling off for having moaned about his current predicament. 'Is that it?' he asked, pointing towards a waist-high cavity in the dirt wall ahead of them. It was the size and shape of a car windscreen.

Jones confirmed it was with a solemn nod of his head and came to a halt next to it. 'We clocked the bones as soon as we had our first look inside,' he said. 'That's when I knew we should call your lot.'

Reece didn't think the water level in the hole was going down by much, despite the generator-aided pump working overtime up at road level. He suspected it wouldn't until the weather front had cleared the area for several days. 'I can hear running water,' he said, craning his neck towards the cavity. 'Sounds like a river.'

'That'll be the underground canals,' Jones told him. 'Cardiff's riddled with them. St David's Shopping Centre is built over what used to be the Glamorganshire Canal. They're under Queen Street.

Greyfriars Road. You name it and there's probably a tunnel or canal under it.'

'I've read about them,' Reece said. 'Didn't they once find an opening to a water-filled tunnel running from the basement of the Angel Hotel, right across to the castle?'

'Aye. In the early fifties. Most of these waterways would have served the docks during the industrial period. The majority were filled in over the years, but there's bound to be some we haven't found yet.'

'And what is it you're doing here?' Reece asked.

'It's all this rain we've been having.' Jones checked the sky. 'Those underground canals swell and spill their contents into the drains. All sorts get washed along in the torrent. Some of it gets stuck, causing a dam effect and *heave* of the ground above. Plays havoc with the foundations of buildings. Or breaks up the road, as it did in this case.'

'You're here to fix the road?'

'To sort the blockage underneath it,' Jones corrected with a shake of his head. 'Someone else will do the resurfacing once we're done.'

'Right.' Reece was beginning to get some idea of what was happening. 'And no one's been in there except you?' he asked, wanting to be sure.

'And two of my crew. We went *tools down* as soon as we saw it.'

'You did the right thing,' Reece said, crouching to get a better view inside the cavity. 'Let me have that torch.' He swung the beam of light along a wet stone wall and low archway. A person couldn't have stood upright in there. An icy draft from within caught him unawares, like the breath of something evil watching his every move. It unnerved him. He shifted the torchlight; saw a dark and fast-flowing body of water, and something small and furry scurry away. There were fallen stones and mounds of earth. And there, among it all, an exposed ribcage.

Chapter 4

The ribs stuck out of the ground like the exposed timbers of a shipwreck at low tide. A jarring contrast in form and colour against the backdrop of darkness and muck. There were more bones lying alongside them; tangled together as though Mother Nature had woven them into the fabric of the earth. There was no clothing that Reece could see. No personal effects such as shoes or a bag.

He moved his arm to the left of its current aim; the puddle of torchlight dutifully following his every command. There was a human skull—now lit up like a stage prop from a Shakespearian play—casting a shadow several times larger than itself on the stone wall behind it. Reece's breath condensed on the cold air. 'There's no doubting it being human.'

'A murder victim?' Jones asked for a second time. 'Dumped somewhere else and washed down here by the rain?'

Reece didn't answer. Now wasn't the time for speculation, or sharing opinions with members of the public. He studied the skull. It lay on its left cheek, open-mouthed, as though its owner had died mid-yawn on a soft pillow. Now it rested on a mound of mud that was riddled with worms and crawling insects. Even when held captive in the stark white torchlight, it possessed a yellow hue that had him thinking its owner hadn't died recently.

'What do you think now you've seen it?' Jones asked, still fishing for something juicy to retell down his local that night.

Reece's mind was working through several potential scenarios. The age of the remains didn't rule out the possibility of a crime having been committed. That said, he was well aware of the city's past and knew this could represent a historic find. 'Can you make that hole big enough for my forensic team to have a proper look around?'

'I could have lobbed a stick of dynamite in there and made less mess,' Reece said, watching the workman hack at the wall with a pick. 'Did I forget to mention that this might be a crime scene?'

The man took a breather and glared at him. 'Be my guest,' he said when able, and offered the tool.

Reece kept his hands in his pockets. 'Just get on with it.'

To be fair, the dig wasn't an easy one. The walls were peppered with stones, and the ground beneath the waterline so slippery that every time the workman twisted to swing his pick, he was fighting to maintain his balance.

'Are you still okay down there?' Jenkins shouted. 'Want me to go get you a coffee and a hot corned beef pasty from Greggs?'

Reece came across to the centre of the hole. Looking up at her was difficult, given the amount of rainfall coming his way. He put his arm across his face in an attempt to shield his eyes. 'Why the hell would I want a pasty when I'm stuck in a sodding sewer?'

'I thought it might warm you up.'

'Nice try.'

'What do you mean by that?'

'If I'm out in this, then so are you.'

'Please yourself,' she said above the noise of the generator, and promptly disappeared from view altogether.

He couldn't blame her for chancing her luck and wanting to get out of there. She'd likely have been the focus of abuse from people whose commute had been disrupted by the roadworks and crime-scene tape. 'Any journalists yet?'

Jenkins stuck her head over the hole. 'A few. They'll be swarming like flies soon enough.'

'Don't say a word to them. Not until I'm with you.'

'What do you think I was going to say?'

'I wasn't having a go,' Reece said, rolling his eyes. 'I'm just saying – you haven't been down here.' Someone tapped him on the shoulder.

It was the workman wielding the pick. 'That big enough for you?'

'Yeah. That'll do.' Reece was slipping and sliding his way over to it when Jenkins called for his attention again. He turned to face her, lost his balance, and was saved a near-drowning only when the workman grabbed him by the coveralls and pulled him upright. 'Look what you've done now!' He raised a leg and almost toppled over. 'My wellies are full up with water.'

Jenkins didn't appear to have heard him. Either that, or she had bigger things vying for her attention. 'Boss. This lady needs to talk to you.'

Reece couldn't see anyone from where he was. 'Who wants to talk to me?'

'You're to stop digging,' Jenkins told him. 'And right away.'

Reece removed his helmet. 'Last time I looked, I was in charge around here.'

'Not any more, apparently. She wants you out of the hole.'

'*Whooo* does?' he screamed, bent at the waist. How difficult could it be to get an answer to such a simple question?

A second face appeared above him. Bespectacled and with flyaway red hair. 'That would be me, Detective Chief Inspector.'

'And who the hell would *you* be?' he asked, wading through the water, still weighed down by the contents of his wellies.

'I'm Doctor Ruth Ellis,' said the new arrival.

Reece's mood suddenly lightened. He didn't recognise her from the mortuary, but the staff there had a habit of changing without warning. 'The on call pathologist?' he wondered out loud.

'Forensic anthropologist,' Ellis said. 'At the university.'

It took him a moment to recall what one of those was. There had been a discovery of bones. The arrival of a specialist in that field made sense. 'Who sent you? Chief Superintendent Cable? ACC Harris?'

'Cadw.'

Reece's understanding of that particular government service was it belonged to the *Tourism and Culture group*, and had been formed to keep or protect historic buildings and land sites in Wales. It had nothing to do with murder victims. 'I don't get you. Where's the pathologist?'

'I have no idea,' Ellis said apologetically. 'But I must insist that you stop what you're doing. This area needs to be mapped and documented for historical purposes.'

'Hang on a minute.' Reece reached for the ladder and began a slow climb. 'You and me need to talk.'

Chapter 5

Reece stepped off the ladder and wobbled onto the pavement with a sloshing sound coming from within his wellies. His knees felt like they'd seized through lack of proper use. He straightened with a muted groan and addressed the newcomer. 'What did you say your name was?'

'Ruth.' The woman had one hand on top of her head, taming her unruly hair. The other clung to a multi-coloured neck scarf that was making a good go of getting away. 'Doctor Ruth Ellis.'

'From Cadw?'

'That's right. And Cardiff University.'

'How did you hear about the find?' Reece glanced at the crowd, and members of the assembled press in particular. 'Did one of that lot give you a call?'

Ellis let go of her hair and was immediately hidden behind it. 'One of my post-grad students got wind and came over to see what was going on.'

'And I bet Jones's lot weren't shy in telling her everything they knew?'

'Something like that,' Ellis said. 'Can we get out of this rain and talk?'

'There's the back of the forensic team's van,' Reece suggested. 'It'll be a squeeze, but they won't be pitching a roadside tent any time soon in this weather.'

Ellis nodded. 'Even the back of a van has to be better than this.'

The CSIs were not overly happy with Reece's request, but gave in on the promise of him sending for hot coffees all round. He introduced everyone and asked that they listen to what the forensic anthropologist had to say.

Ellis began by asking if anyone present knew the history behind the Greyfriars area of the city?

'This'll be right up your street,' Jenkins said, glancing at Reece. 'Just take notes.'

She produced her pocketbook and pen and nodded at Ellis. 'Ready when you are.'

'The area is named after the colour habit worn by the Franciscan friars who worked with the town's most destitute,' Ellis said, going on to explain that Cardiff hadn't always enjoyed city status. 'They built a great friary in the thirteenth century. When Owain Glyndŵr burned the town and castle in the fourteen-hundreds, he spared the friary on account of the good work done by those living there. It was on the orders of King Henry the Eighth that the building was torn down during his reforms of the church. Henry sent his soldiers to Cardiff and cut down anyone who refused to conform to his will.'

'Didn't many of the friars go underground to avoid the king's men?' Reece asked.

Ellis looked impressed. 'They dug several tunnels and lived down there until it was safe enough for them to return to the surface.'

'But the friary *was* demolished?'

'Sadly, yes. The Herbert family bought the land in the late sixteenth century and built Greyfriars House on it, using some of the old stones left lying about.'

'Where's the house now?' Jenkins asked.

It was Ellis who answered. 'When the family ran out of male heirs, it fell into a state of disrepair. The Marquis of Bute had the site excavated in the eighteen-eighties. And in the nineteen-twenties, there were further excavations that uncovered five hidden vaults – some of them containing full human skeletons. The Capitol Tower building marks the position of the original friary.'

'And you think this might be a similar find?' Reece asked. 'We're nowhere near Greyfriars Road.'

'We don't need to be,' Ellis said. 'The history here spans more than six thousand years. Even Emperor Nero posted a Roman Legion where the castle is now.'

'*Nero*. Doesn't that blow your mind?' Reece asked the team.

'Totally,' Jenkins said, clucking her tongue. 'Roll on the next pub quiz.' She quickly stepped out of reach when he swung a playful slap at her. 'I'm just saying.'

'Well, don't. This stuff is wasted on you. You're a bloody heathen.'

'Sticks and stones,' she teased, still keeping out of his way.

'I'll need to examine the remains and their surroundings,' Ellis told them. 'When would that be possible?'

'Just as soon as the pathologist gets here,' Reece said. 'Once I know we're not dealing with a crime scene, it's all yours.' He climbed out of the van, alert to raised voices coming from the hole in the ground. 'What the hell's going on now?'

Huw Jones came wading away from the chamber with a hand clamped to his open mouth. The workman with the pick was already ahead of him and fighting for first turn on the ladder. Jones left him to it and promptly vomited into the water.

Reece heaved at the sight and only just managed to keep his stomach contents south of his diaphragm.

Jones wiped his mouth on his sleeve and hooked a thumb over his left shoulder. 'There's a—' He burped loudly and vomited for a second time. 'There's another head in there. I swear to God.'

Chapter 6

REECE HAD JONES REPEAT himself. He could have sworn the man was claiming to have found a human head and not just the bare skull and bones they'd both laid eyes on.

Jones spat and composed himself. 'We were fetching our tools,' he said, swallowing bile. 'The thing was wrapped in a black bag and stuck on a bit of a ledge next to the running water.' He put his hand to his mouth and screwed his eyes shut. 'I should have left it where it was.'

'And what *did* you do with it?' Reece asked, losing patience with the man.

'I opened it,' Jones said apologetically. He looked up quickly. 'I didn't move it. The thing stank worse than a dead cat.'

'And you're sure it wasn't a dead cat?' Reece asked. There would be plenty of those tossed into local rivers on their meandering journey to the sea.

'I know a face when I see one. It was staring at me.' Jones shuddered. 'That thing's gonna give me nightmares for years.'

'Serves you bloody right,' Reece said, turning his back on him. 'Next time you'll listen to what you're told.' He went over to the CSI's van—still sloshing a small amount of water in his wellies—and knocked on its metal side panel. 'Me again. There's been a development.'

'Something for us to get our teeth stuck into?' one of them asked.

Reece repeated his conversation with Jones. 'We'll get some better lighting set up down there and have a look for ourselves.'

The nearest CSI pulled a face and shaped her mask to the contours of her face. 'A rotting head? Great. You sure know how to show a girl a good time.'

'The duty pathologist should be here any minute,' Reece said, checking his watch. 'I want you both to join him and report on what you find. We'll take it from there.'

The CSI hugged herself. 'Okay, boss. Understood.' Her colleague answered with a thumbs up gesture.

'This won't be a pleasant one,' Reece told them. 'If you need more support or advice, then phone Sioned and ask for it.' Sioned Williams was a very capable crime scene manager and a well-respected colleague. She'd be back at base, waiting to coordinate things her side whenever called upon to do so. To Doctor Ellis, Reece said: 'I guess this changes things?'

'Perhaps. But not necessarily.'

'Jones said his new find has hair and flesh. If he's right, then it couldn't have been down there for very long.'

Ellis didn't look so sure. 'There have been numerous finds of people buried hundreds, or even thousands of years ago, with some of them in remarkable states of preservation.'

Tollund Man was one such example that Reece could recall from his reading. Hanged some three-hundred years before the birth of Christ, he was found buried in a peat bog in Denmark, Scandinavia. So well preserved was he, that the local police believed him to be the victim of a modern-day murder. 'Those bodies were mummified by their environment,' Reece said. 'This is nothing like that.'

'Decomposition will begin only when the specimen is exposed to air and moisture,' Ellis argued. 'It might have lain in its own tomb, protected from the environment until the recent rains flooded everything and washed it out from wherever it was.'

Reece scratched his whiskered chin. 'I'd like you to go down and take a look at it with the pathologist. Are you okay with that?'

'Of course.' Ellis smiled at him. 'There isn't much I haven't seen over the years.'

'It's going to get complicated if this turns out to be a mix of both modern *and* historic,' Reece said. 'A murder investigation carries the trump card.' He was establishing boundaries. Setting out his game plan.

'True,' Ellis conceded. 'But I'm hopeful we'll be able to work something out between us.'

Reece liked the sound of that. 'I'm sure we will.'

'I'll need to contact the Ministry of Justice,' Ellis said. 'To obtain a licence to remove human remains.'

Reece didn't require any such paperwork for his side of things. 'How long does it normally take before you hear back from them?'

'I know someone there who owes me a favour. More than one, actually. I'll lay it on thick and get things moving.'

'Do you need anything else from me?' Reece asked.

Ellis handed him her empty paper cup. 'Another coffee while I wait would be very welcome.'

Chapter 7

THE HOME OFFICE FORENSIC Pathologist had arrived. Reece could see him quick-stepping down the street with his medical case held as an umbrella above his head. The rain was pounding off the top of it, but didn't seem to be getting him down like it was everyone else. He wore a broad smile and was whistling a merry tune as he drew up next to them.

Reece had always been suspicious of overly happy people. It wasn't natural for a person to be smiling all the time. It had to be forced, and therefore, false in most cases.

He recognised the pathologist as one he'd recently worked with on a fatal arson case in the docklands area of the city, and hadn't forgotten the deeply irritating *snort, snort,* that accompanied most things the man said. But annoying habits aside, Reece had found him to be perfectly competent in his work, and timely in both the verbal opinions and written reports he provided when tasked to do so. Reece extended a hand in greeting and reminded the pathologist of his name and rank.

'Call me Gareth,' was the reply. 'No need for formalities. Not when we're batting for the same side, eh, Chief Inspector?' Snort, snort.

Reece kept his mouth shut and directed the man towards the gaping hole in the road.

The underground cavity was now far better lit than it had been during Reece's first visit. Accompanied by Dr Ruth Ellis, Dr Gareth Bagshot, and a couple of CSIs, he suggested they begin with an examination of the rotting head.

Jones hadn't been wrong about how bad it smelled, and five people vying for space and breathable air wasn't helping the situation.

Reece repositioned his facemask for a second time, but it didn't help much. 'There's no obvious sign of any other body parts,' he said, scouring the area.

'Could be stuck upstream, or already washed further down?' one of the CSIs suggested.

'Or floating in the bay,' Bagshot said. 'That would certainly ruin someone's morning walk.' Snort, snort.

Reece checked his phone. No signal. He made a mental note to request a boat to recce the man-made lake and the sluice gates of the barrage system.

'We can also use ground-penetrating radar to survey this area,' Ellis said. 'If there's anything else buried out of sight, it'll show up.'

'You've got that with you?' Reece asked.

'There's a research team on the way.'

'Good. But I want them working under the guidance of the CSIs.'

'Understood,' Ellis said. 'I'll make sure they wait until you're ready for their input.'

Bagshot was squatting over the head. If he was bothered by the smell, he wasn't showing it. Years of working in the cutting room of the mortuary obviously had its benefits. 'This is a recent death,' he said, unprompted. 'Seven to ten days would be my best guestimate.'

'Can you tell yet how the killer removed it from the rest of the body?'

'With a sharp knife and a handsaw.' Bagshot got one of the CSIs to take photographs before rolling the head onto its side. 'You can see where the blade incised the soft tissues and the teeth of the saw went through the bone, just here.'

'And if we found the saw in question, would you be able to match those marks to it?'

'Probably. Although it's likely to be a brand common to most DIY stores.'

It was still something to go on. 'So our victim—' Reece paused. 'Male or female?' He couldn't tell for himself. The flesh was witch-green. Black in places. Absent in parts. The eyes had ruptured and collapsed in on themselves. And there was plenty of evidence of rodent and insect activity.

'What remains of the larynx suggests the latter,' Bagshot said. 'Although I'd imagine this isn't one of her best hair and makeup days.' Snort, snort. It was gallows humour. It got people like them through the day without completely losing their minds to the horrors of their jobs.

'So,' Reece said. 'She was killed, dismembered, and then dumped somewhere along these underground waterways.'

Bagshot nodded. 'There's every possibility of that being true.'

Chapter 8

It was early evening before the two of them climbed the steps leading to the front entrance of Cardiff Bay's Police Station. They were beyond cold, and in Reece's case, carried the lingering odour of decaying flesh.

His knees still hurt. As did his shoulder from the old gunshot injury sustained two years earlier. Even though he wasn't pushing the pace, Jenkins was making a fuss about the steps, like she always did. Inside. Outside. It didn't matter where they were – she hated them.

'All right, George,' Reece said, passing the front desk with little more than a glance and a courteous nod. The acknowledgement lacked any enthusiasm and was uttered only because he thought he should. George was a good friend and colleague. The pair of them made time to sit and chat most working days. Conversation about rugby, or whatever trouble Reece happened to be in with the chief super.

The burly desk sergeant poked his head through a small opening in the glass while nibbling on a sizeable pork pie. 'You two look like drowned rats,' he said with a hearty laugh. 'Been swimming with your clothes on again?' It was a reference to the time Reece had jumped—fully clothed—into the water at Mermaid Quay. During a long and hot summer, and against all warnings not to do so, local teenagers were tombstoning off the walls there. The cold sea, uneven sandbanks, and fast-moving tides conspired against anyone who got into difficulty. One youngster did and owed his life to the man who was willing to risk his own.

The mention of rats was enough to make Reece shudder. He'd seen first-hand the damage they could inflict on human flesh. 'Something like that.' He doubted he'd put George off his snack with an explanation of the afternoon's events, but left it anyway. 'See you,' he said, opening the door to the stairwell. It closed behind him with a click and a soft thud. He opened it again and said: 'Not coming?'

'Sod that for a game of soldiers.' Jenkins jabbed at the button to call the lift. 'You getting in?'

Reece wouldn't normally have entertained the suggestion, but on this occasion, he put up no argument and stepped inside.

Detective Constable Ffion Morgan was standing near her desk when the pair trudged into the Incident Room. 'Is everything okay?' she asked. 'You both look terrible.'

Jenkins took off her wet jacket and slung it onto the floor next to her desk. 'We can't all look like a model off the cover of a Vogue magazine.'

Morgan blushed. 'Still raining, is it?'

'Let me go see.' Jenkins went over to the window and squinted into the darkness outside. 'I think it is, you know.' She turned. 'Of course it is. It hasn't sodding stopped for the best part of two weeks.'

'I'll go put the kettle on,' Morgan said, making her way over to a corner of the room they jokingly referred to as *the kitchen*. 'The two of you must be freezing?'

'What are you still doing here?' Reece asked, checking his watch. 'I thought you'd have made a run for it by now?'

Morgan spooned coffee into three mugs. 'I got someone to go check the barrage sluice gates like you asked. They've only just got back to me.'

'I don't suppose they found anything over there?' Reece expected as much. 'When can they get a boat and divers on the lake?'

'Not before first light.' She stirred two sugars into Reece's coffee and handed it to him with a warning that it was scalding hot. 'The conditions are awful out there in the bay.'

'They weren't much better in Mill Street,' Jenkins said.

Reece brought the mug up near his chin, warming both hands before raising it that bit higher to take a sip. 'Ooh, that's good.' He looked for somewhere to put the mug and settled on Morgan's desk being as good a place as any. 'I need a shower before I do anything else.'

'You're not going to drink that first?' she asked with a look of disappointment. 'I can add some cold water, if you'd like?'

Reece grabbed another sip and puckered his lips. The coffee would be fine to leave for five to ten minutes before it was too cold to drink. 'I'll finish it when I get back,' he promised.

'I think I'll have a shower too,' Jenkins chimed in. 'Otherwise I'll never warm up after the day we've had.' She reached under her desk for an overnight bag kept there for *emergencies*.

'I was the one in the hole,' Reece complained. 'All you did was skive off to Greggs every time my back was turned.'

'Don't listen to a word of it,' she told Morgan. 'He's only going off on one because I got a bit of mud on his car seat.'

'A *bit!*' Reece's lower jaw dropped open. 'It looks like I've given a couple of sheep a lift home.'

Jenkins wagged a finger in warning. 'I'd be careful if I were you. That's how rumours start.'

Chapter 9

REECE WAS SURPRISED TO learn that Morgan wasn't the only member of the team to have stayed behind. He was keen to get everyone home to their families, suspecting the case might drag on for weeks, or months, even.

Showered and *"smelling bloody lovely,"* as Jenkins had put it, they all sat down together for the final briefing of the day.

There was usually a *golden hour* following the discovery of a crime. Murder, especially. A precious window of time when police gather as much information and evidence as possible. With Dr Gareth Bagshot's estimate that the head had been separated from its owner somewhere in the region of seven to ten days ago, there was little point in him deploying helicopters and road blocks. The perpetrator would long ago have returned to their everyday lives.

But the scene *had* been secured. And the head transported across the city to the mortuary at the University Hospital of Wales. There, it would be cooled in an attempt to slow any further decomposition. They might still get some DNA evidence, if they were lucky. Reece had his fingers and toes crossed on that one.

Doctor Ellis's team would be back in the morning to complete their survey using ground penetrating radar equipment. Reece would remain on call overnight, ready to respond to reports of more body parts turning up in the city. His coffee had gone cold. Rather than get himself a fresh one, he pinged it in the microwave for fifty seconds. It did a fair job.

'Did I add enough sugar?' Morgan asked. 'It was a slightly smaller spoon than the usual one.'

Reece nodded. 'It's perfect. Thank you.'

Morgan rose from her seat. 'I'll get you some more, shall I?'

Jenkins stopped her. 'Sit down. You're going to rot his teeth with this sugar thing.' She turned to Reece. 'Seriously, boss. You could give yourself diabetes at your age.'

'What do you mean, *at my age?*'

'Well, you're not getting any younger. How much sugar do you think is in all that apple tart and custard Doris in the canteen keeps feeding you?'

'Look—'

'I read an article in a magazine,' Morgan said. 'It was about conspiracy theories involving government and the food industry. Did you know that—?'

'Okay! I get it,' Reece interrupted. 'I'll stop using added sugar. Happy now?'

Jenkins swung on the back legs of her chair. 'I'll believe that when I see it.'

'I'll put a forfeit box on my desk,' Morgan said, clearing space. 'Just there. And every time we catch you putting sugar in your coffee, you stick fifty pence in it.' She frowned at her own idea. '*Ooh*, he has two sugars. I'd forgotten that. Do you think a pound is too much?'

Reece held his head in his hands. He opened his eyes and looked up slowly. 'Are you two doing this on purpose?'

'We could give the money to charity.' Morgan said, oblivious to the tension building in the room. 'Or use it to get a new toastie maker for the—'

Jenkins made eyes at her and winked when she took the hint.

'Sorry, boss. I got a bit carried away.'

Jenkins lowered the front legs of her chair onto the carpet tiles. 'Do you want to tell the others about the monks?'

'Friars,' Reece corrected.

'What's the difference?' Morgan asked. 'Both of them are blokes with dodgy haircuts.'

Even Reece chuckled at that. '*Monks* lead solitary lives involving plenty of prayer and self-contemplation. Whereas the friars were often out and about, helping local people.'

'Does the skeleton belong to a friar?' one of the team asked.

'It's definitely not a recent death,' Reece said. 'But we'll have to wait until Ruth Ellis and her team get a proper look at it.' He explained about the request for a licence to remove the remains. 'Our pathologists at UHW will be dealing with the head. Obviously there's no licence requirement there.'

'Why the difference in approach?' a uniform asked. 'Surely human remains are just that, regardless of the age?'

Reece was happy to explain. Any find thought to date back more than seventy years is classed as archaeological. Anything thought to be less than seventy years old is dealt with by the police and considered suspicious until proven otherwise. Archaeologists require a licence from the Ministry of Justice before they can excavate and remove human remains. Our rules of engagement are different, this being a murder victim.' He stood and massaged his aching shoulder. It was difficult to believe that two years had elapsed since the bullet ripped through it in Billy Creed's basement. Recent x-rays had shown that arthritis was starting to take a hold on the joint.

He'd now said all he intended to and rechecked his watch. 'I want you back bright and breezy in the morning. Go on, get out of here.'

Chapter 10

Reece watched them get up and collect their things. Some made it out of the door quicker than others – pounding across the landing towards the lift and stairs with only one arm shoved inside the sleeves of their coats. They were like school kids. *His* pupils. The sight made him smile.

A few of them stopped behind to chat together, or to return items of paperwork to their desks. At least one officer paused to make a telephone call; no doubt to somebody waiting at home. A police officer's life could often be a lonely one, especially for partners and spouses. It was no wonder that relationship breakdowns and full-on divorce rates remained so high.

Jenkins and Morgan were among those who stuck around for a short while longer, making sure Reece needed nothing else from them before they left. He said that he didn't and bid them a safe journey home.

When alone, he went around the table, repositioning the chairs, clearing away empty coffee mugs and sweet wrappers. The night-shift cleaners had enough to do without having to tidy up after a bunch of detectives who should have known better. He turned off most of the lights and went to collect his coat from his office. It was still wet enough to suck the heat from his body if he were to put it on. He'd have to hold something over his head and make a run for the car once he got outside. His leather satchel would do. That or a newspaper. He went searching for one in the bins and was rewarded for the hunt.

He took the stairs down to the foyer and exit. Chief Superintendent Cable was near the front desk, in conversation with someone he didn't recognise. He was reversing through the door to the stairwell, intending to hide there until she'd gone, when she looked up and saw him.

'Chief Inspector,' she said, quickly apologising to the other person. She made her way over to where he was standing and placed her case on the floor at her side. 'Don't look so worried.'

He wondered what restrictions top brass were going to impose on him this time. There was usually someone they didn't want him going near in the course of his investigation. 'Ma'am. I was on my way home.'

'I was hoping for a brief catch up before you left,' Cable said. 'I've been stuck in a divisional budget meeting most of the afternoon.'

'I'll need plenty of people on overtime for this one,' Reece replied. 'Don't be pulling the plug on that.'

'How did that thing in Mill Street go?'

She'd ignored his overtime comment. That wasn't a good sign. He recounted most of the day's events, all the time wishing he didn't have to. 'Look, Yanto's dropping the dog off at the cottage. I really need to be going.'

'Humour me for two minutes.'

'I've told you everything,' he said, trying to pass. 'We'll know more tomorrow.'

Cable sidestepped and blocked his way. She was only five-feet and three inches tall, but carried herself with the presence of someone with a far larger stature. 'Is everything okay with you?'

Reece's eyes narrowed. He shuffled awkwardly. 'Why shouldn't it be?'

'Relax. It's just that I was talking to Miranda Beven earlier. She was at Headquarters.'

'No more counselling,' Reece said, waving both hands in front of him. 'I've moved on.'

'I didn't say that you hadn't.'

'Then why were you talking about me?'

'We weren't. Not really. Miranda asked after you and I said she should give you a ring – socially, not professionally.'

'I bet you didn't tell Harris what you were up to?'

'ACC Harris,' Cable corrected. 'And I wasn't up to anything.'

'Yeah, right.'

Cable lowered her head and changed the subject. 'They said no to filling Ginge's vacancy. They'll take a look at it again in the new financial year, but I'm not holding out much hope. Everyone's been told to do their bit in minimising an overspend.' She sighed. 'It's the world we now live in, I'm afraid.'

Reece spun one way and then the other. 'I told you, didn't I? That lot would have me run this department on peanuts and good will.'

'Keep your voice down.' Cable checked the foyer behind her. 'It's the same for all organisations, not just the police.'

'We're the Regional Murder Squad, not a sodding pizza delivery chain.'

This time he managed to barge his way around her and stormed towards the exit. 'It's like an episode of the Muppet Show with that lot.' He fully expected her to come chasing after him. She didn't. So, off he went, newspaper overhead, dashing into the evening rain.

Chapter 11

Yanto wanted a takeout curry. Reece seldom had any issue with that kind of request. Even the grizzly sights and smells of the day couldn't put him off a lamb bhuna with all the trimmings. He'd made it clear that alcohol was out of the question and not up for debate. Being on call meant him remaining legally capable of driving back to Cardiff should he need to.

The farmer told him he could please himself. He'd argued with his wife and wasn't going home until she'd apologised in person.

Reece thought that very unlikely. Ceirios wasn't the type. In fact, he couldn't remember her ever apologise for anything. Besides, these episodes did mostly turn out to be Yanto's fault. He'd have a drink and stay the night. Then return home in the morning with his tail between his legs and a bunch of garage forecourt flowers gripped in a grubby fist. He always did. The pair were schoolyard sweethearts. Reece doubted anything would ever change that. He envied them it.

The curry sat in a cardboard box on the front passenger seat, held there with the help of a fastened seatbelt. It tormented him for the entirety of the journey home. He drove, inhaling lungfuls of it, all the while fighting the almost overwhelming urge to pull over at the side of the road and get properly stuck in.

The Land Cruiser accelerated along the winding roads of the Brecon Beacons—Bannau Brycheiniog—National Park, its bright headlamps punching through the wall of darkness ahead. There were plenty of deep ditches and sharp rocks lying in wait on both sides of the road, for all but the most careful of motorists. There were floral tributes also—too many to count—and T-shirts daubed with the names of motorcyclists whose spirits would ride that very same route in perpetuum.

The rain drummed on the thin metalwork of the Land Cruiser's roof and the wind screamed like a banshee as it rushed down the slopes of the nearby mountains. Reece sped up the windscreen wipers and eased off the accelerator in anticipation of the bend he knew from experience was coming up ahead.

As he entered the tight turn in the road, a pair of startled eyes marked the exact spot where the white centre lines should have been. They belonged to a large and fluffy sheep. Something to steer well clear of if an expensive insurance claim and a visit to a vehicle body shop were to be avoided. He braked hard and felt the back end of the Land Cruiser twitch on areas of loose road surface. Applying a careful amount of opposite steer and less brake, he came to a full stop, resting almost diagonally across the narrow carriageway. For what seemed like an age, he sat gripping the wheel until he had his rate of breathing somewhere close to normal. Conscious of being a more substantial, and consequently dangerous, obstacle for any oncoming traffic, he straightened up and drove off, tooting his horn loudly at the stupid animal. The sheep offered no intelligible reply and disappeared into the wet night like a ghostly apparition.

When he pulled up outside his cottage, Yanto's white Land Rover Defender was parked near the back door. Its engine was making ticking sounds as several of its components cooled down and contracted. It hadn't been there long. Reece lay his hand on the warm bonnet, confirming his suspicion. He came away with the cardboard box and its contents held between his hip and elbow, drawn like a moth to the yellow glow behind the kitchen curtains.

Redlar, his New Zealand Huntaway, was barking loudly. It was an inescapable trait of the breed, used to drive sheep and cattle towards other herding dogs. The side door of the cottage opened, releasing a knee-high puppy that came hurtling towards him in a fit of excitement. Reece roughed the animal's neck. Barking and howling, it welded itself to his legs, almost making him lose his balance and fall over. 'Easy boy. In you go now.' Redlar cocked his leg over an empty flowerpot before scarpering back into the kitchen to do zoomies.

'Hang on!' Yanto wailed, trying to get out of the dog's way. 'Why do you always have to wind him up like that? He was quiet and lying on his bed a minute ago.'

'All I did was come home,' Reece protested. 'He's excited, that's all. Are you sure you've given him enough exercise?'

Yanto pointed a finger. 'Don't you start. He's been out with me for most of the day. He should be bloody knackered by now. I told you when you got him that those things need far more exercise than most breeds.'

'So you keep saying.' Reece dumped the cardboard box on the kitchen counter next to a crate of beers. 'I told you I wasn't drinking tonight.'

'Who said any of those are for you?'

Reece shot his friend a look of warning. 'You're not getting pissed. Not here.'

Yanto went over to the fridge and returned carrying two chilled bottles. He knocked the tops off both using an opener fixed to the thick cottage wall. 'You can have one, can't you?'

Reece took it. 'One only,' he said, slurping froth. 'And I mean it, so don't be going on at me later.'

Yanto took a gulp of his and promptly burped without apology. 'I lit the fire in the front room. It was colder in here than it was outside.'

'It'll warm up soon enough,' Reece said. 'Get a couple of plates and help me dish this up.'

'They're warming on the stove.' Yanto used the neck of his bottle to point across the kitchen.

'You'll make someone a great wife one day,' Reece joked.

Yanto fetched the plates and began spooning mounds of mushroom rice onto them. 'That's just as well, coz Ceirios reckons I make a *shite* husband.'

Reece chuckled. 'Come on then. Tell me. What did you do this time?'

Chapter 12

THEY WENT THROUGH TO the living room where the log burner was roaring and giving off the sweet smell of wood sap. The only light came from a couple of table lamps. It was restful and cosy-warm, and made Reece yearn to curl up on the plump sofa and enjoy a good nap. 'Come on,' he insisted. 'Tell me what you did.'

Yanto used his fingers to lift an onion bhaji from his plate, dipped it in a large dollop of mango chutney and bit it in half. 'That's the thing with women,' he said, chewing noisily. 'You never really know what you've done, coz you can't get a word in edgeways to find out.' He demolished the second half of the bhaji before continuing. 'And they can't keep it relevant. Always bringing up things that happened weeks ago. Months ago.' He licked his fingers and waved his spoon in the air, sending grains of rice onto the floor. Redlar was there in a flash.

'Watch he doesn't get any onion,' Reece said. 'It's poison for dogs.'

Yanto checked between his feet and nodded that all was good in that respect. 'How the hell are we supposed to keep up? It's like they write everything down as evidence to be used against you when it suits them.' He smacked his lips and reloaded his spoon. 'Could you remember some comment you made about a dress she was wearing ten years ago? Because she bloody can.'

Reece gripped his plate, trying not to tip any of his supper as he squirmed with laughter. 'But you must have done something? You always have.' Yanto went silent and pushed his food round his plate. Reece pressed. 'You must have done something to piss her off.'

'She even brought up the time I forgot her birthday. I was in hospital having my appendix out and she's still giving me grief over it!'

Reece doubled over. Redlar came to make sure he was okay. 'But what did you do *this* time?'

'Nothing.'

'*Yanto* . . .'

The farmer put his spoon down and took a deep breath. 'All I said to her was—'

'Here we go. Now the truth's coming out. I knew there'd be something.'

'All I said was: "*I preferred your hair the way it was before you'd had it done.*" It was meant as a compliment. Why do they always have to look for bad in everything a man says? Over fifty quid that mullet-job cost me.' He raised his eyes to the ceiling and cleared his throat. 'I could have put her in line with the sheep and done a better job myself.'

Reece buckled, his plate in danger of falling to the floor. He caught it in the nick of time and put it in a safer place on the arm of his chair. 'Please tell me you didn't say that?'

Yanto refused to look at him. He lowered his voice. 'Well – she'd pissed me off by then. What else was I supposed to tell her?'

'Not that,' Reece said, close to giving himself a hernia. He wiped his eyes with the back of his hands and immediately wished he hadn't. 'Shit,' he said, getting up. 'I've got chilli or something on them.'

Yanto watched him beat a hasty retreat to the kitchen. 'That'll start stinging in a bit.'

'It's stinging now,' Reece said, running the cold water tap.

'That's why they warn you to always wash your hands before you have a pee.' Yanto shuddered. '*Ooh*, can you imagine the pain?'

'I'm trying not to,' Reece said, splashing his eyes. He went back through to the living room, dabbing his eyes with a clean tea towel taken from one of the kitchen drawers. 'That's better,' he said, dropping into his seat. He ripped himself a piece of Peshwari naan and dipped it in the curry sauce, bringing it to his mouth with his other hand held under his chin to catch the crumbs. 'This was a good shout,' he said, reaching for his bottle of cold beer.

Yanto raised his own bottle in acknowledgement and gulped down a good measure of its contents. 'Not too shabby, if I say so myself. Want another one of these?' he asked, putting his empty to one side.

'What did I say earlier? I'm on call, remember?'

'Just being polite.' Yanto closed the refrigerator door and returned carrying two bottles. 'They're both for me. Saves having to get up again.'

Reece went over to the far corner of the room. 'Are you okay with me putting some music on in the background?' They shared the same taste in that department. Nothing modern was the strict rule. Nothing manufactured by computers or forced through an auto-tune device. Instead, they'd cut their teeth on real bands who travelled the roads, learning their trade the old-fashioned way. He selected an album by Jackson Browne and made sure the volume wouldn't intrude on their conversation. 'Have you ever come across buried bones on your farm? Human bones.'

Yanto lowered his bottle and stared. 'What do you mean?'

'You being a farmer. Always turning over the land. I wondered if you'd ever come across something that shouldn't have been there?'

Yanto's eyes narrowed. 'Why would I know anything about buried people?'

'Why are you being so defensive?' Reece asked. 'Plenty of battles were fought on this land. Romans. Saxons. It made me wonder, that's all.'

Yanto rested his plate on the arm of the chair. 'I need the toilet.'

Reece watched him leave the room. 'Don't forget to wash your hands before you get started.' The joke earned him no response. What the hell was going on?

Chapter 13

REECE WOKE TO THE sound of loud snoring in the living room. He opened one eye and saw the world through blurred vision. The other eye was stuck down, and for the most part, useless. He rolled a knuckle in the socket and tried again. That made it marginally better, though the darkness in the room wasn't helping any. He could just about make out the shape of Yanto, still fast asleep under a coat in the armchair opposite.

Redlar was spread out on the sofa—not somewhere he should have been—taking liberties and whimpering in his sleep.

Reece got up with a groan and rubbed his lower back. He'd noticed more and more of late that sleeping in chairs had him seize up like a piece of junk machinery. It was only a few years ago that he would have been able to spring out of that same chair and chase off an intruder. Now, he'd have to request they stay put until he'd completed his full stretching routine. His jerky movements woke the dog, but not Yanto.

The cottage was uncomfortably cold. Not fully winter-cold as yet. That would come in the months after Christmas. But cold enough for him to wish that he was wearing more than a thin shirt and suit trousers. His shoulder hurt more than his lower back did. Massaging it didn't help much. The x-ray hadn't been wrong in its assessment. The onset of trauma-induced arthritis was something he unfortunately couldn't escape.

He wandered into the kitchen in stockinged feet and opened the back door for Redlar to go out and do his business. Chilled air raced in through the narrow gap between the door and its frame. He closed it as much as he could while still keeping an eye on what was going on outside. Redlar was having a good sniff of whatever had wandered by the cottage during the night. Badgers. Foxes. The usual culprits.

Reece set a pot of coffee to percolate for when he got back from his morning run. He called Redlar's name, and to his complete surprise, the dog returned on the first ask. Yanto had obviously been working hard on recall. He gave the animal a well-deserved fuss and a small treat from a packet he kept on top of the fridge.

On his way through the living room, he woke Yanto with a gentle tap of the ankle and told him about the coffee.

Yanto sat up and got himself moving with the speed of a man well used to being in the thick of it by the crack of dawn. 'I'll take mine with me,' he said. 'Save me going in when I get back to the farm.'

'Promise me you'll sort things out with Ceirios.'

'Don't start.' Yanto ruffled his mop of hair with a pair of hands that looked capable of hammering nails into wood. 'She was in the wrong. Not me.'

Reece dwelled no more on the matter. He said his goodbyes to Redlar and went upstairs to get ready for his usual morning five miler.

He turned away from the cottage and began a slow jog before settling into a comfortable rhythm. His running shoes scraped across the gravel surface, disturbing the silence with a sound not unlike that of someone crushing eggshells. He wore a woolly hat and expensive gloves, but the cold still gripped him tightly and hung on for a free ride. It wasn't raining, but the ground was still waterlogged in places from the previous day's downpour. He leapt over a puddle and made his way along the potholed drive, with miles of undulating terrain lying open on either side of the wire fence. It went right up to the road and then well beyond. A thin veil of mist hung low on the fields, taking a lazy moment to decide in which direction it wanted to travel that morning.

Reece marvelled at the changing contours of the land and its rich palette of colours. There were deep crevasses and rocks of all shapes and sizes to negotiate. Green forests and smaller areas of woodland to enjoy. Mountains, lakes, and reservoirs. He'd seen them all a thousand times or more. In all of their guises, and never once had he tired of their beauty. People paid good money to experience what *he* had on his doorstep.

But he never took it for granted. Nor did he drop his guard in its presence. For all its natural beauty, Bannau Brycheiniog—the Brecon Beacons—was more than capable of chewing a person up and spitting them out, should they be foolhardy enough to underestimate it. The very reason why the British military still use the area for training of its Special Forces.

An adventure across the Beacons was as much a test of human endurance as it was a person's guile. A battle to be lost or won. Reece reined victorious. But then again, he and the land were boyhood companions.

His breakfast consisted of coffee and leftover curry and rice, eaten cold from the foil trays it was sold in. Following a quick shower and shave, he was almost ready to go. Dressed in a clean shirt and suit, he was dawdling in the middle of the kitchen, gulping a second mug of coffee, when his phone rang. 'Reece,' he said, wedging it between his good shoulder and chin.

It was Dr Ruth Ellis. 'Good morning Chief Inspector. I hope I haven't disturbed you?'

'Brân,' he insisted, and returned the greeting. 'What can I do for you? Did that radar thing pick up anything of interest?'

Ellis told him they'd only just restarted work, but the licence to remove the remains had already been approved. 'I was wondering if you'd be interested in seeing them?'

He'd very much enjoyed their conversations about history and the role anthropology played in deciphering it, but today was a new day, and there was a murder investigation to conduct. He took his empty mug over to the sink and gave it a quick swill under the hot water tap. 'I'd like to at some point, but I'm going to be busy with—'

'They'll be going over to the mortuary at the hospital,' Ellis told him. 'Until we get something suitable set up at the museum. You could always come and take a look while you're over there.'

'That's an idea.'

'And we could get a coffee, maybe?'

Anwen smiled at him from her place on the windowsill. He picked up the photo frame and stared at her. 'Would you be willing to help us get somewhere with that head?'

'I don't know,' Ellis said. 'In my experience, your average Home Office Forensic Pathologist doesn't take kindly to us sticking our oar in. Many of them see anthropologists as something of a threat.'

'Don't you worry about that,' Reece said, locking the kitchen door behind him. 'I'll have a quiet word in their ear.'

Chapter 14

Reece sat at his cluttered desk, tapping out a tune on its surface, waiting to be told they were ready for him over at the city's mortuary.

He'd already been warned of a delay caused by a shortage of forensic pathologists in the department. Something that was about to get worse before it improved, apparently. There was no more information on that. He'd made a fuss. Played merry hell. A murder investigation took priority over most things. Didn't it?

He took a Biro from a pot and drummed a new beat on his knee. He didn't do waiting very well and got up and started tidying his office. On the other side of the slatted blinds were detectives working diligently at their desks. His eyes were drawn towards Ginge's empty seat. He had mixed views on the incident that had culminated in the newbie's instant dismissal from the force. On the one hand, there would never be room in his team for anyone so easily influenced by corruption. But on the other, Ginge had shown himself to be a bloody good copper with prospects of a very successful career ahead of him.

A phone rang, bringing an end to Reece's daydream. Not his phone, but one somewhere in the Incident Room. An officer wearing civvies answered it, and following a brief conversation with the caller, went back to tapping at her computer keyboard. Another telephone chirped for someone's attention; this time at a different desk. Reece sighed and went back to tidying.

In front of him on the desk were several case files requiring his attention. There were numerous queries to answer. Overtime sheets to complete and forward to Chief Superintendent Cable for authorisation.

Reece didn't like paperwork. He was a *boots on the ground* kind of copper. Had no interest in driving a desk. Being stuck inside gave him the same heebie-jeebies it did a kid suffering with an attention deficit disorder. It gave him far too much time to dwell on things that were probably best left alone. Like images of his late wife dying on a cobblestone road in Rome, gripping her abdomen as blood soaked through her blouse.

'Coffee, boss?' Jenkins had taken the liberty of bringing two steaming mugs with her.

Reece took one. 'Ta.' He sipped and immediately pulled a face. 'There's no sugar in it.'

'Welcome to the future.'

'Not mine,' he said, opening one of his desk drawers. He removed a plastic pot and used the Biro to shovel sugar into his mug.

'You promised.'

'Like hell I did. It was the only way I could shut the both of you up.'

Jenkins sat down. 'Fine. Have it your own way.'

'I will,' he said, licking drips off the end of the pen. He took another sip. 'That's much better already.' He sat on the other side of the desk. 'I was wondering what Ginge was doing now.'

'Time, hopefully.'

'That's not nice.'

'It's what he deserves. The two-faced sod.'

'It wasn't all his fault,' Reece said. 'He was born into the wrong family.'

Jenkins was having none of it. 'He should have stuck up to them and broken the cycle.'

'That's easier said than done.' Reece put his coffee down. 'How are things with you at the moment?'

Jenkins gave the question some thought before answering. 'It's quiet without Mam being there. I don't know how I juggled her needs and kept working at the same time.' She caught him staring at her. 'Or didn't I?'

'You did brilliantly. Margaret was well looked after, and that was all down to you.'

For a while, Jenkins made no further comment, and sat there picking skin from around her fingernails. 'I've put Mam's house up for sale. Seems so final now.'

'There's a lot of memories stored in a family home,' Reece said.

Jenkins wiped her eyes. 'And in our case, all good ones.'

'Don't ever forget them.'

'I won't.'

'Any news from the search team on the lake?' Reece asked.

'Ffion's dealing with that. She's over there now, taking advantage of a break in the bad weather.'

'I don't hold out much hope of them finding anything,' Reece said. 'The rest of that corpse is probably caught up somewhere underground.'

Jenkins nodded in agreement. 'We were lucky to come across the head.'

'I don't think Jones would agree with you. I wonder if he's able to eat yet?'

'It didn't stop you,' Jenkins said. 'I heard you had a curry last night.'

'And for breakfast this morning. Don't knock it until you've tried it.'

'Each to their own.'

'I'm still working on that profiling secondment, by the way. You shouldn't have to lose out because the department is one detective down. Harris needs to fund us properly.' Reece's phone rang. 'Here we go,' he said, putting it to his ear. 'The call we've been waiting for.'

Chapter 15

'What's the matter with you?' Reece asked as they approached the sign for the mortuary. 'Anyone would think you didn't want to do this.'

'Who's the pathologist for this one? Please tell me it's Bagshot.'

'They didn't say, but there's not many to choose from.'

'Not Cara Frost, I hope.'

Reece slowed. 'Is there no possibility of the two of you ever getting back together?'

'Not a chance in hell,' Jenkins said, striking an indignant pose. 'She let me down. I can't forgive her for that.'

'Can't or won't?' Reece opened the changing room door. 'I'll see you on the other side.'

They met up again in the viewing gallery, with Jenkins looking no less anxious.

Reece led the way down the steps to the front of the room. 'Relax,' he said, looking over his shoulder to be sure she was following. 'What do you think she's going to do to you?'

'It's not what she can do. It's purely being in the same room as her that bothers me.'

The PA system crackled with static. Followed by tapping sounds, as Dr Ruth Ellis checked the mic was working. 'Sorry about that,' she said. 'Can you hear me?'

Reece confirmed they could with a thumbs up gesture.

'Come through to this side. You won't see much from where you are.'

'Suits me just fine,' Jenkins whispered.

The bright light in the cutting room bounced off the white wall and floor tiles, and every shiny metal surface reflecting the movements of the mortuary personnel. It was a stark contrast to the dark viewing gallery and made Reece squint until his eyes adjusted to it.

There was the smell of disinfectant and something far more organic in origin. Reece guessed it was coming from the decomposing head that rested on a tray like a Sunday roast waiting for the oven to warm up to temperature. He did his best to scratch that thought from his mind and swallowed a mixture of bile and spices. Curry for breakfast wasn't the best decision he'd make that day.

'I thought you might be interested in seeing this while we wait?' Ellis said. 'Doctor Frost is going to be another ten or fifteen minutes before she's able to join us. It's all go here today.'

Jenkins gave Reece one of her *get-me-out-of-here* looks. He turned away and offered her no such opportunity. It was important that she be there to witness the post-mortem examination first hand.

'I thought Doctor Bagshot was the pathologist for this one?' Jenkins said. 'He was at the crime scene yesterday.'

Ellis shook her head. 'I can only convey what I was told. I think he wears two hats. One for this department and another for the Deanery.'

On an extraction table towards the rear of the room was a full set of bones, positioned like a person lying supine with their arms held close to their sides. There was a more obvious yellow-brown tinge to the bones now they were out of the ground and clean.

'Would you like to take a journey back in time?' Ellis asked, like a hypnotist standing before a paying audience. She brought her hands together and wrung them as she spoke. 'Let's see if we can't find out who this person is while we wait.'

Reece caught Jenkins snatching another look over her shoulder. Cara Frost was nowhere to be seen.

Ellis went to the top end of the table, leaving the detectives standing on either side of it. 'Is this person male or female?' she asked.

Reece had nothing with which to make a comparison. There was a fifty-fifty chance of him being correct, whichever way he guessed. 'Female?' he said, agonising over his answer.

'And what makes you think that?'

He studied the skeleton from the crown of the skull to the tips of the toes. 'It's shorter than your average man.'

'It's male,' Jenkins said. 'You can tell by the shape of the pelvis.'

'I was going to say that next,' Reece joked.

Ellis took the skull in both hands. 'In addition to the pelvic differences, we have these brow ridges here on the forehead.' She traced them with a finger before turning the skull onto its side. 'And a large mastoid process, as you can see here. Well done, both of you. We've now established this being a man.'

'Can you tell his age?' Reece asked, getting closer.

'The teeth tell something of a story,' Ellis replied. 'The third molars—wisdom teeth—show very little wear, in this case. And the growth plates at the ends of the clavicles—she lifted the collar bones to better demonstrate what she meant—suggest this young man was aged somewhere between seventeen and nineteen years when he died.'

Reece watched her return the bones to their correct anatomical positions on the table. 'Was he killed? Or did he die from an illness or disease?'

Ellis leaned against the table. 'Timing of trauma can be classified as: *ante-mortem; peri-mortem;* or *post-mortem*. And the types of trauma as *ballistic or projectile; blunt force;* or *sharp force*.' She took the skull in both hands and presented the back of it to the detectives. There was a wide split in the bone, measuring the length of her index finger. 'This man's life was ended by a single impact with a sharp and heavy object. An axe or sword would be the most likely culprit.'

'Do you think he was a friar?' Reece asked. 'Killed by one of Henry's soldiers.'

'That would be a reasonable assumption,' Ellis said. 'We'll have to use radio-carbon dating and analysis of stabiliser tropes, to be sure.'

A door opened, bringing an end to their conversation. The overhead air-vents clicked with the change of pressure within the room.

Jenkins lowered her gaze to the floor and whispered: 'Beam me up, Scotty.'

Chapter 16

DR CARA FROST MADE her way across the cutting room floor with an attitude befitting of her name.

'Morning,' Reece said.

'Good morning, Chief Inspector.' Frost turned to Jenkins. 'Sergeant.'

Jenkins mumbled something but didn't look up.

'Doctor Ellis has been telling us about the skeleton,' Reece said. 'Definitely a cold case.'

Frost hadn't yet acknowledged the anthropologist. She approached. 'And you're here because . . . ?'

'*I* asked.' Reece said before Ellis could respond. 'We're going to need all the help we can get with this one.'

Frost looked from Reece to Ellis, and back again. 'As you wish.' She then addressed Ellis directly: 'I don't see too much of a problem so long as professional boundaries are established and maintained at all times.'

'I'm not here to muscle in on your case,' Ellis promised. 'Merely to offer assistance to the police, should it be required.'

'Anything to do with the severed head will go through you or one of your colleagues,' Reece assured Frost. 'But if I think there's something to be gained in asking the opinion of someone possessing a different set of skills, then I won't hesitate to do so.'

Several seconds elapsed before Frost responded. 'And the head is all you have so far? Nothing to go with it?'

Reece nodded. 'It is, yes.'

Frost circled the extraction table, studying the gruesome specimen from all angles. 'Doesn't smell the best.'

Reece gestured to Jenkins and tapped his pocket.

'I didn't bring it with me,' she whispered. 'It's in my desk drawer, back at work.'

'What was that?' Frost asked with a deepening frown. 'Speak up so that we can all hear you.'

'I usually carry something to help with unpleasant odours.' Jenkins offered a smile that lacked any warmth or sincerity. 'But you'd know that already.'

Reece gave her a look of warning. 'Suck on a mint instead.' He offered one. Jenkins accepted. Frost declined. Ellis came over from where she was and helped herself to two.

The examination of the head began with another walk around the table. This time, more slowly. Frost was studying it like she was buying a used car. Noting its good points as much as she did its bad ones. 'The process of decomposition begins within minutes of death,' she announced. 'Cells break down and bacteria invade. Many factors influence that process, notwithstanding the ambient temperature, soil acidity and moisture content.'

'The head had been immersed in water at some point,' Reece said. 'Then washed along before getting stuck on a ledge. It was cold in there too. More so than up at road level.'

Frost gave no indication she'd heard him and carried on. 'Typically, a body buried inside a coffin will start to break down within a year. And skeletonise within ten. Quality of the materials used in the manufacture of the casket will play its part,' she quickly added. 'A body that isn't so well protected will usually skeletonise within five years.'

'Gareth Bagshot estimated death being around seven to ten days ago,' Reece said, staring at the putrefying flesh on the face. 'Would you agree?'

Again, Frost responded as though she hadn't heard him. 'Within eighteen hours of death, the skin will sometimes turn green, or slip and blister as it detaches from the underlying tissues. The abdomen will bloat due to the release of toxic gases inside it. Marbling occurs within twenty-four to forty-eight hours. Eventually, the bloat will collapse in on itself and black putrefaction will ensue.'

That was the point at which Jenkins made a swift exit and could be seen on the other side of the glass, running up the gallery steps towards the exit with her hand clamped over her mouth.

'Was it something I said?' Frost asked with a wiggle of her eyebrows. 'I didn't have Elan down as the sensitive type.'

'Time of death?' Reece repeated. 'Would you agree with your colleague?'

Frost referred to Dr Gareth Bagshot's crime scene report before answering. 'It says here that the ambient temperature yesterday was as low as six or seven degrees Celsius. The underground cavity was a couple of degrees lower than that. The environment was, as you've said, a wet one. We now have the soil type and its acidity to consider.'

Reece curled his fists. 'And given all of that . . . Your best guess would be?'

Frost's head came up quickly. She lowered the report and stared at him. 'Chief Inspector, I'm not in the habit of entering into guesswork. This is science, not a conspiracy theory.'

Recce had had enough. 'Can we quit with all the points scoring and teenage attitude?' he said, locking eyes with the pathologist. 'I get that you and Elan didn't part company on the best of terms. But that's where it stays – between you and her. I'm the SIO on a murder case and your role is to assist me in getting justice for whoever that poor sod was. Do you understand?'

Ellis went over to her skeleton, leaving them to it. She had no idea of the history between them, and it wasn't her argument.

Frost lowered her head and spoke quietly. 'You're absolutely right. That was very unprofessional of me.' She came away from the table and took a moment to gather her thoughts. 'From the level of decomposition present, I too would estimate this individual's death being seven to ten days ago. Nearer the ten.'

'Thank you,' Reece said, relaxing his pose. 'Now let's talk about gender and cause of death.'

Chapter 17

On their way back to the police station, Jenkins apologised for walking out of the cutting room. It was the decomposing head and not the challenging company that was to blame. That's what she kept telling Reece. Regardless, he'd given her the same stern talk he had Cara Frost.

After the apology came an outpouring of emotion that couldn't be stemmed until Jenkins had fully vented it. There was so much playing on her mind. Another failed relationship. And her mother's recent death had rocked her far more than she'd realised. A blessing, it was. But not one she was yet coming to terms with.

Reece suggested that her return to work was premature and promised he'd square more leave with the chief super. Something Jenkins had turned down in an instant.

'It helps when my mind is occupied,' she told him. 'I couldn't imagine sitting at home, dwelling on everything.'

He knew where she was coming from and didn't argue.

They drove the remainder of the journey to the station in silence.

'For anyone who might be interested,' Reece told the team, 'our skeleton probably dates back five-hundred years and belonged to a male in his late teens.'

'That's way too young,' Morgan said, making sure she had her phone on silent for the briefing. 'Eighteen is when you should be out enjoying yourself with your mates.'

Jenkins pointed out that student pub crawls were probably unlikely in the Middle Ages.

'Life was cheap then,' Reece said. 'Not making it past thirty was commonplace. Women regularly died in childbirth. Men in wars and during violent disagreements.'

'Any idea how he died?' Morgan asked.

'Whacked over the head with a sword or axe.' Reece pointed to an area of his own head. 'A big split in the skull, just there.'

'Bloody hell.' Morgan grimaced. 'That's got to hurt.'

'Not for long,' Jenkins said.

'You might think that,' Reece told them. 'But it took days for some men to die. Lying in mud; bleeding internally from being run through with steel. Awful wound infections – especially when the sword cut through a loop of bowel on the way in.'

Jenkins raised both hands in surrender. 'Know your audience.'

Reece rolled his eyes. 'I'd forgotten how delicate you've become lately.'

'That head was hideous,' she argued. 'It's the only time I've had a problem with something like that.'

'Yeah, it wasn't pleasant,' he conceded. 'Not pleasant at all.'

Chief Superintendent Cable was sitting opposite and, until then, hadn't spoken. 'What do we know so far?'

'That our victim is female,' Reece said. 'Cara Frost was certain of that. In her late fifties, or more likely, early sixties.'

'And the cause of death?'

'Losing her head might have had something to do with it.' Everyone looked at Jenkins, who apologised immediately. 'Sorry, ma'am. I'm not feeling very well today.'

'Do you need to go home?' Cable asked.

'No, ma'am.'

'We know the head didn't come off with one clean strike,' Reece said. 'There's clear evidence of tooth marks left by a saw on the cervical vertebra.' He put his hand to the back of his neck to indicate where he meant.

'Find the saw, find the culprit,' Cable said, clasping her hands together.

'It'll likely be a bog-standard, off-the-shelf type.'

'It might still carry the killer's DNA.'

'I didn't say that we weren't going to look for it,' Reece said defensively.

'Are we still working on the time of death being nearly two weeks ago?' asked one of the uniformed officers.

Reece nodded. 'Give or take a day or two. But there's no way of us knowing when she was dismembered and disposed of.'

'How do you transport a head without someone raising suspicion?' asked the same uniform.

'In a sports bag,' someone else said. 'Pretend you're off to the gym.'

'What if it leaked blood?'

'You'd wrap it in something first,' another uniform said. 'Like cling film.'

'It was in a black bin bag,' Reece told them. 'Most of which was ripped off during the journey downstream.'

'So our killer would have needed access to an opening in the underground waterways?' That got people talking. Everyone seemed to have an opinion on how the head got to where it was found.

Reece agreed with some of them. 'Ffion, find out who's responsible for those tunnels and waterways. I want the names of all employees working in them within the last two weeks. Better make that three, just to give us a margin of error.'

'Right you are, boss.'

'Anything of interest turn up over on the lake this morning?'

'The divers are still looking,' Morgan said. 'They're going to ring when they're done. Nothing from them yet, though.'

'I want someone checking all MISPER calls received within our timeline,' Reece said. 'You never know, we might get lucky.' He got up and went over to the window; drawn there by the sound of voices rising from the road below. 'There's a scrum of journalists out on the steps.'

Cable checked her watch. 'Ah. Yes. That'll be for the press conference. Get yourselves ready.'

Chapter 18

THE STEPS OUTSIDE THE police station were soaking wet. The sky hanging low and foreboding over Cardiff Bay. There was the briefest glimpse of sunlight off in the distance and out to sea. It showed little prospect of returning.

Reece, Cable, and Jenkins were hunched under a single umbrella, shivering despite their heavy coats.

Their umbrella wasn't nearly as colourful as those belonging to members of the press, who'd turned out en masse. They too waited in a tight huddle—umbrellas permitting—blocking both the pavement and one lane of the road. Several motorists sounded their horns as they crept past the gathering. Not that it did any good. The journalists were there to stay.

Reece gestured for the crowd to come forward a few paces and sent a pair of uniformed officers onto the road to direct the traffic and keep the peace. Then he called everyone to order. 'I'm Chief Inspector Brân Reece. Lead detective for the Regional Murder Squad here in Cardiff. This is Chief Superintendent Cable. And standing to my left is Detective Sergeant Jenkins – also from the Regional Murder Squad. In a moment, I'll be issuing a very brief statement, but I won't be answering questions at this time.'

A series of groans rose from the pavement below. 'Come on. Do you know how long we've been stuck out here waiting?' someone asked.

'Freezing our nuts off,' moaned another.

'You think it's any warmer for those of us without nuts?' Maggie Kavanagh called to him, prompting another wet coughing fit on her part. She winked at Reece and prompted him to get on with it.

He acknowledged the gesture and watched Kavanagh light up another cigarette, provoking a brief argument between herself and those standing close by. The woman was like a Victorian chimney, spewing clouds of smoke with little to no regard for the consequences. He imagined her airways being just as caked in soot and tar as those narrow brick passageways. 'Shall I continue?' he asked once the fracas had mostly died down. If they didn't shut up soon, he'd go back inside and leave them out there with nothing to show for their day.

Once there was quiet again, he repeated the introductions and began the press release. 'South Wales Police were yesterday called to the discovery of human remains beneath the road in Mill Street, Cardiff. Following careful examination by experts in the fields of anthropology and forensic pathology, the following conclusions were made: A skeleton likely dating back to the sixteenth century is now in the possession of Cadw. It being linked to any modern-day crime has obviously been fully ruled out. The partial remains of a second person were found in the same area. These remains are thought to belong to a female, aged late-fifties to mid-sixties. Death is estimated to have occurred within the past seven to ten days, and circumstances of the find point to this being an act of foul play. For that reason, my team and I have now been tasked with conducting a full and thorough murder investigation. Thank you,' he said, turning away as the questions came thick and fast.

'Do you have any idea who the victim might be?' shouted a journalist from his position at the foot of the steps.

'Is it true that only the head was found?' shouted another.

'Where's the rest of the body? Do you have that information yet?'

'Are we looking at a serial killer here?'

'What about it being a gangland hit?'

Someone else pushed their way up a few of the steps before a uniform could stop them. 'Have you arrested anyone in connection with the find?'

And so the questions continued.

Reece wasn't at all surprised by how much information the press had already. They'd have greased someone's palm. A copper at the station, or one of Huw Jones's construction team. It was the way these things worked. Always had been. And it wasn't going to change anytime soon.

'We'll be issuing a more comprehensive statement within the next forty-eight hours,' Cable told them. 'Once we're in possession of additional information.'

'Do you know where the rest of the body might be?' a reporter asked for the second time. 'What was the method of dismemberment?'

'That's all for now,' Cable repeated, and turned her back on them. 'Let's get inside.'

'What additional information are we expecting?' Reece asked as they walked through the foyer. Cable stopped in front of the lift and called it. Reece resigned himself to having to get inside for the second time in as many days.

'Progress with the woman's identity,' Cable said. 'Can't Doctor Ellis help us with that?'

Edward Collier was chopping an onion when he heard the news broadcast start up in the other room. He swilled his hands under the tap and wiped them dry on a clean tea towel. He limped through to the living room and sat on the arm of the sofa, watching a group of police officers talk into a camera. Reaching for the remote control handset, he turned up the volume and listened more intently to what they had to say.

It was the male detective doing most of the talking. A short woman, wearing a senior rank uniform, rounded things up at the end. Collier had missed the detective's name. It was no bother. It would be all over tomorrow's newspapers, and repeated on television for weeks to come.

The victim was female. Late-fifties to mid-sixties. Collier's stomach turned over. Not his partner, Janet, surely?

Chapter 19

Jenkins settled at her desk and was reluctant to remove her coat for a good ten minutes or so. 'It's freezing out there,' she said, slouching with her legs stretched in front of her. She folded one leg over the other and examined her wet shoes. 'I'll have nothing dry to wear at this rate. My house looks like a Chinese laundry – there's stuff hanging everywhere.'

Morgan volunteered to go make everyone a coffee. Reece was working them hard, as he always did with any murder case placed in his charge. He could be one hell of a taskmaster, but his results spoke for themselves. A detective didn't become lead for the Regional Murder Squad by sitting on their hands, and Reece had been in charge for the past ten years, warts and all.

Jenkins declined her colleague's offer. 'Too much caffeine,' she explained. 'I'm like the Duracell bunny if I drink it too late in the day.'

'There might be decaf there.'

'Nah, you're all right. What have you been up to while we were outside?'

'Looking into who has access to those underground tunnels and waterways.'

'You don't sound like you're having much success?'

'There are so many,' Morgan said. 'Some were built over with roads, hotels, and shops. Others—like the canal behind the castle—weren't. The local authority is responsible for most, but not all. Those friars even dug a tunnel running through Bute Park.'

'Bloody hell. Busy boys. weren't they.'

'And then there are the more recent tunnels. Like the ones built in the seventies by British Telecoms, to carry cables through the city.'

'Rather you than me.' Jenkins's attention was taken by her phone flashing and vibrating its way across the surface of her desk. She sat up straight and moved away from it. She could have sworn she'd deleted Cara Frost's number. Clearly not. Her ex's name was displayed in white lettering. There was no mistaking it. The call rang off unanswered and the phone went still – not that she'd made any attempt to reach for it. 'What the hell?'

'Talking to me?' Morgan asked without looking up.

'No.' Jenkins was now thinking that she should probably have answered. What if Cara was ringing with new information relevant to the case? She'd have contacted Reece, surely? And then the phone rang for a second time. Again, displaying Cara's full name. Jenkins took a deep breath. 'South Wales Police. Incident Room. Detective Sergeant Jenkins speaking.' She had no idea why she'd answered in such a fashion, it being her own personal phone and not the official one belonging to her employer. She put a hand over her eyes.

Frost was momentarily thrown by the opening dialogue. There was a brief silence on the line, followed by: 'Elan, it's Cara.'

'I know who you are,' Jenkins said, making no attempt to hide her worsening mood.

'Then why such a formal introduction?'

'Is there a reason for this call?' Jenkins checked Reece's office door was still closed and lowered her voice even though it was. 'Because I'm busy right now and don't have the time to be—'

'And that's why I thought we should meet tonight. Somewhere neutral where we can talk things through.'

Jenkins gripped her phone. 'Are you for real?' She was about to follow that up with something far more acerbic when she realised how loudly she was speaking.

'Someone giving you the runaround?' Morgan asked.

Jenkins waved her off. 'It's nothing.' She ended the call with a tap of her thumb and rose from her seat. 'I'm going for a walk.'

'Fancy company?'

'You're all right,' Jenkins said, grabbing her coat and making for the landing. 'I won't be long.'

Morgan reversed with only three of the four castors on her chair working properly. She jerked herself away from her desk. 'Are you sure?'

'I said I'm fine.' Jenkins's system was flooded with a cocktail of hormones that were causing a seismic shift in her emotional wellbeing. What the hell was Cara up to? Her phone chimed to indicate she'd received a text. She read it and replied with: *Leave me alone. I've no interest in anything you have to say.*

Cara Frost: *Give me a chance to explain. That's all I'm asking.*

Fuck off!

Cara Frost: *Please. Face to face. No strings. I promise.*

Jenkins's thumb hovered and twitched over the keypad. She closed her eyes and let out a deep sigh. 'I can't believe I'm doing this.'

Chapter 20

EDWARD COLLIER WAS UNABLE to finish his bangers and mash, served with lashings of thick onion gravy. It was his favourite meal, usually. But not on this particular evening. The earlier news broadcast was still playing heavily on his mind.

The victim was said to be female. Late-fifties to mid-sixties. Dead a week. It all fit. He switched the television on and flicked to the news channel, to be sure. The presenter was discussing another story, but there was a red banner running along the bottom of the screen. *Human remains found under a main road in Cardiff*, it said in white font. It caught him like a heavy blow to the stomach. 'It can't be Janet. Can't be.'

He was still trying to make sense of what it all meant when the house phone rang. 'Edward Collier,' he said with a dry mouth.

'Ted, it's Hannah. I've spoken to Mark, and he's adamant there's been no contact between Mum and him.'

'Have you seen tonight's news?' Collier asked.

'I don't usually watch it. All this stuff about Russia and China flexing their muscles. I'd rather not know.'

'Put the telly on and go to the news channel.'

'Ted, I—'

'Just do it.' He heard a clicking sound as the television set came to life. Then her rate of breathing increase while she read the news banner that would still be scrolling from left to right across the screen.

'You don't think...'

'What other explanation could there be for your mother's disappearance?'

Oakley didn't answer immediately. 'Maybe it *is* time to contact the police?'

Collier felt as though he'd been punched in the midriff. 'I think that would be for the best.'

'But it seems so unlikely that this would be Mum. Killed and buried under a road.'

'I know. It sounds ludicrous, but what alternative do we have?'

'*I'll* ring them,' Oakley said.

'What will you say?' Collier asked.

'What we know so far.'

'Which is?'

'Everything you told me about her coming to see us here in Aberystwyth,' Oakley said.

'But that obviously wasn't true.'

'That's what the police do, Ted. They wade through the bullshit and find out exactly what's been going on.'

'Hannah, I hope you're not—'

'Me too, Ted. Me too. You said Nathan took Mum to the station on the day she disappeared. You had a hospital appointment for your hip?'

'That's right. Why do you ask?'

'No reason.' Oakley sounded like she was deep in thought. 'I wanted to get my facts straight before I make the call.'

'Then there's something else you should know. Something I should have told you before now.'

'Here we go. Hit me with it, Ted.'

Collier went to the window and stared into the street beyond the glass. 'Your mother took an overdose recently. A mix of her sleeping tablets and my painkillers. She's very lucky to be alive.'

Chapter 21

'You're lying. Mum would never do such a thing.'

'She was lucky I came home when I did. It was only that I'd forgotten my wallet and went to pick it up sometime in the afternoon. I can't imagine what might have happened otherwise.'

'Why the hell am I only just hearing this?'

'I was sworn to secrecy. Your mother said she'd made an embarrassing mistake with her medication. That it was nothing more than a silly accident and I wasn't to make a big deal of it.'

'How does a person *accidentally* take enough medication to almost kill themselves? As well as take tablets belonging to someone else?'

'I don't know, is the honest answer. And I'm sorry for not telling you before now, but my hands were tied.'

'Was she seen by a psychiatrist? They must have got someone to see her?'

'The ward doctor chatted to us both. A consultant. He was very nice and asked all sorts of questions.'

'I don't give a shit how nice he was. Was she seen by a psychiatrist?'

'No,' Collier said,

'Why the hell not?'

'You know how persuasive your mother can be. She assured the consultant that she hadn't been trying to do herself any harm.'

'That's not the point.'

'And with the blood tests showing no signs of organ damage, they let her come home the following day – albeit with a pillbox to prevent a similar thing happening in the future.'

Jenkins stood outside The Travellers Rest Inn—a whitewashed, thatch-roofed dwelling—positioned on the mountain road to Caerphilly. Once a happy haunt during her dating days with Cara Frost, it had now lost most of its appeal.

The sensible thing would have been for her to leave before Cara arrived. The *really* sensible thing would have involved her not turning up in the first place. She took a deep breath and went inside.

The beamed ceiling was low, but not enough to trouble someone of her height. There was piped music playing through a couple of wall-speakers. It wasn't particularly loud. A few of the clientele were noisier. Two men—pints in hand—were feeding twenty-pound notes into a slot machine over in one corner of the room. Its lights flashed and its wheels spun before coming to an abrupt halt, one by one. There were more flashing lights and tunes that competed with the music coming from the overhead speakers. Then there was the sound of coins clinking into a winnings tray. The men high-fived, celebrating their good fortune, before feeding the machine another twenty.

Jenkins headed towards the bar, scouring the room for any sign of her ex.

'What can I get you?' the barman asked with a well-practiced smile. 'Cocktails are two-for-one for another twelve minutes,' he said, checking his watch. 'If you're quick, you'll still get your money's worth.'

'A soda-water with ice and a slice of lime, please.'

'Driving?' he asked.

'Something like that,' she answered, still preoccupied with her search.

When she set eyes on her ex, her first instinct was to leave right away. Dry-mouthed, she took a sip of her soda-water. The ice clinked against her front teeth. Her legs felt heavy, making it an effort to lift her feet and put one in front of the other.

Frost stood as Jenkins approached. On the table in front of her was a glass of white wine and a soda-water with ice and a slice. 'I'd already got you a drink,' she said, sweeping her arm as though she'd conjured the beverage from a magician's hat.

'No need,' Jenkins replied.

'Aren't you going to sit down?'

'Will this take that long?'

'Are you hungry?'

'No.' That wasn't true. She was ravenous.

'They do great salads here. You always said so.'

'What do you want, Cara?' Jenkins pulled a seat opposite. 'Because if it's any more of your bullshit . . .'

'Only to set the record straight before I leave Cardiff. I thought it was only right for me to do so.'

That wasn't at all what Jenkins was expecting. She'd entered the pub intending to tell her ex what she thought of her. Frost had been unfaithful in their relationship, and absent when Jenkins lost her mother. Those were things she could neither forgive nor forget. But now, on hearing the news that Frost was leaving Cardiff, she wasn't angry. She felt sick. The proper pit of the stomach type. She put her glass down and wiped her hand on the thigh of her trousers. 'Leaving for where?' She wanted to ask *for whom,* but didn't.

'I've accepted a new position in Edinburgh. Head of Department.'

'*Scotland?*' It was said far louder than she'd intended, and true to the law of Sod, came slap bang in the middle of the interval break between songs.

The two men at the slot machine turned to look at them. Both made their way over. 'Can we get you ladies a drink?' one of them asked. 'It's been our lucky night so far.'

'No thanks,' Jenkins replied. That put neither man off. One of them drew a chair and sat down. 'We're lesbians,' she said. 'Looks like that luck of yours has gone and done a runner.'

The men went away without creating a fuss. Back to the slot machine to feed it more twenties. She wished they'd made more of it. That way, she could be excused for smacking one or both of them in the face. It might help with what she was hearing. Scotland was a long way away.

'What are you like?' Frost asked, blushing. 'Did you really have to announce that to everyone within earshot?'

'Don't play coy with me, Cara. You know that game won't hold up to any real scrutiny.'

Chapter 22

EDWARD COLLIER HADN'T SLEPT well that night. Images of dismembered body parts had haunted his dreams and awoken him on several occasions. Janet was calling his name. Hannah Oakley was screaming. And all the while, that red news banner moved from left-to-right across the undersides of his eyelids.

He'd given up on sleep and gone downstairs. Sat and stared at the dome of an untouched boiled egg. Stirred a cup of breakfast tea while it went cold.

The police would be arriving sometime around nine, according to Hannah. To take more details and go through paperwork not easily completed over the telephone. He knew he'd be a suspect in their enquiries. Spouses and partners were always the first in need of a sound alibi. That's what the script writers of television dramas claimed. Real life couldn't be too dissimilar.

But would the police believe his side of the story? Had Hannah Oakley made wild claims about him? She'd always been suspicious of his motives for moving in with her mother.

Janet Allsop ran a business supplying customers with small to medium-sized marquees and seating for garden parties. It wasn't on a grand scale, but it paid the bills and turned some profit. Collier had already taken two telephone calls that morning: one from a person seeking confirmation that their order would be delivered and erected before the weekend. The other being a booking for the summer of the following year. He'd apologised, explaining that Janet would return their calls as soon as she got back from a short business trip.

He was tidying the kitchen when a car pulled up outside the house. Two uniformed officers walked away from it and towards the garden gate. One of them was carrying what appeared to be an iPad device. He met them at the front door, opening it before they were able to knock or ring the bell. 'Good morning,' he said, introducing himself. 'I've been expecting you.'

The officers removed their hats and followed him into the living room. Both declined the offer of tea or coffee, stating they wouldn't be staying long.

'Nice place you have here,' said the one with the iPad. He fired it up and inputted some preliminary details.

'It belongs to Janet,' Collier explained.

'The lady in question?' the uniform said, not looking up.

'That's right.'

The next few minutes were spent verifying information supplied by Hannah Oakley. Basic identifiers like Janet's full name, height and build, as well as distinguishing features, if present. Her full address, mobile telephone number, and employment details were also read out and confirmed.

'When was the last time you saw or heard from your wife?'

'Janet and I aren't married,' Collier explained.

'But you *do* live together?'

'Mostly. I have a place in Cowbridge that I go back to, once or twice a week, to make sure it hasn't sprung a leak or had its windows put through.'

'Unlikely to happen in Cowbridge,' the uniform said. 'Nice area, that.'

'True, but I prefer to be sure.'

'You don't rent it out?' The officer was making small talk. Collier would have preferred him to get on with things.

'No one's ever going to look after a property as well as the owner does. I've heard so many horror stories over the years.'

'You'd rather it sit empty and collect dust?'

'It isn't empty. As I've said, I use it.'

'Does anyone else use it? Janet Allsop, maybe?'

'Janet rarely went there.'

'Does anyone other than yourselves use the house?'

Collier rubbed his aching hip. 'Why the interest in the Cowbridge property?'

This time, the uniform did look up. 'I'm just trying to establish if Missus Allsop might have gone to stay there for a few days. Did you argue?'

'Absolutely not.'

'Have you checked to see if she's there?'

'Of course I have. What do you take me for? Is there someone else I should be talking to?' Collier asked. 'We don't seem to be getting very far.'

'They're all routine questions,' the officer assured him. 'We'll drive by on our way back to the station. Knock a couple of the neighbours' doors and—'

'I wouldn't bother them. They hardly know us. Janet and I keep very much to ourselves when we're over there.'

'Someone might have seen her coming or going recently. It won't do any harm to ask.'

'Whatever you think is best,' Collier said with a resigned shake of his head.

The uniform balanced several sheets of paperwork on one knee and the iPad on his other. 'Lets talk about when you last saw or heard from your partner. Her daughter said that was over a week ago.'

'It's been nine days since Janet left for Aberystwyth. That includes the two days elapsing since her planned return.'

The uniform referred to his paperwork. 'You told Hannah Oakley that her mother had gone to visit her?'

'I did. Yes.'

'And that the arrangements for the trip were made between her mother and husband. A Mark Oakley?'

'That's right.'

'And you know this because Missus Allsop told you those conversations had taken place?'

'*Yes!*' Collier took a moment to compose himself. 'I'm sorry for snapping at you. It's been a very stressful couple of days.'

'I understand, sir. We won't be much longer. The thing is, Mark Oakley denies making any such arrangements with his mother-in-law. He's adamant he hasn't spoken to her in months.'

'He's obviously lying to you.'

'Why would he do that, sir?'

'There are a few things you need to know about Mark and Hannah Oakley. All isn't as it appears.'

Chapter 23

Jenkins hadn't intended to divulge details of the previous evening. It was a private matter. Something best kept between herself and Cara Frost. But Ffion Morgan had a knack for drawing information out of a person before they fully realised what she was up to.

'The bloody cheek of the woman,' Morgan said, nursing a mug of coffee. 'Fancy her trying to blame you for everything. I'd have told her where to get off.'

'There were plenty of *"offs"* in what I had to say.' Jenkins lowered the front legs of her chair. 'Don't you worry about that.'

'I bet there were. Scotland isn't far enough,' Morgan continued. 'Somewhere like Australia would have been much better. That's on the other side of the world, if you were wondering.'

Jenkins couldn't help but smile. Her colleague could be deeply annoying at times, but was often funny without even trying. 'I did know that.'

'Or Mars,' Morgan continued. 'Yeah, Mars would be good. Because you'd never bump into one another if she went there.'

Jenkins watched out of the corner of her eye and wondered how Morgan had passed the police selection interview. It had to have been an all male panel. 'No, I don't suppose we would.'

'That's decided then. We'll have her sent to Mars, not Scotland.'

'Sounds good to me.'

Morgan gripped her mug with both hands and pressed it against her chin. 'Do you regret going last night? Wouldn't it have been better to not get into another argument before Cara left?'

'We've both said far worse. Yesterday was tame by comparison. Besides, I can't stay angry forever. It isn't good for my head.' Jenkins reached for her bottle of water and sipped it while mulling over the whys and wherefores of her latest failed relationship. She was definitely cursed in that department. Repeatedly stumbling from one disaster to another. Most recently, from a serial killer to a posh-speaking, two-timing, git.

Morgan leaned back in her seat and frowned. 'Wouldn't a job like Cara's require a long period of notice? Like six months from resignation to leaving date.'

'I don't know. Why?'

Morgan did a quick calculation. 'That means she must have applied for the position while the two of you were still together. Before your mum . . .'

'You're right,' Jenkins said. 'She'd been played for a fool yet again.'

'Don't beat yourself up. You couldn't have known.'

Jenkins stood and snatched for her coat, knocking over the bottle of water. Its top wasn't screwed on tightly; its contents escaping in a sudden rush. 'Shit, Shit. *Shit!*' she said, dancing about rescuing case files.

'What's going on?' Reece asked, entering the incident room. He wandered over to them, carrying an empty mug at his side. 'Are those wet?'

'Can you believe it?' Morgan asked. 'Cara Frost is only buggering off to Scotland for a new job. And worse than that, she never said a word to Elan about any of it. Not before last night.'

Jenkins did a double-take. 'For fuck's sake, Ffi. Go stand on a table in the canteen, why don't you?'

'That's just *brilliant!*' Reece said, throwing his arms in the air. 'As if we weren't already short enough of pathologists. When is she going?'

Morgan caught his eye and silently mouthed: *'Ssh. I think we've upset her.'*

'I *am* here, you know.' Jenkins grabbed for her coat. 'And I'm not upset. I'm pissed off with you.'

'With me? What have I done?' Reece asked.

'She means me,' Morgan said. 'Sorry, Elan.'

Jenkins rushed towards the exit. 'I can't do this. I need air.'

For a while, Reece stood there, wondering what he'd walked into. 'You'd better go with her,' he said. 'Make sure she's okay.'

'What did you think of him?' asked the uniform with the iPad.

'A bit weird,' his colleague said. 'But then again, he does live in Cromwell Street. Fred and Rosemary West,' he added, realising that it was only he who'd clocked the similarity in addresses. 'Twenty-six, not twenty-five.'

'And he was touchy when you pressed him on the other house in Cowbridge.'

Edward Collier was standing at the living room window, watching them. He raised a hand and nodded.

The uniforms mirrored him before getting into the patrol car.

'Do you believe any of what he had to say about the daughter and Nathan Turner?'

'Lets go find out,' said the driver, turning the key in the ignition. 'And then we break for a bite to eat.'

'Sounds good to me.'

They pulled away from the kerb. 'He's still watching us. Hasn't moved an inch from that window.'

'I bet he's buried her under the patio.'

They drove along the side street and slowed at the junction, both of them in fits of laughter.

Chapter 24

THEY FOUND NATHAN TURNER loading tent poles into the back of a van parked lopsidedly on the edge of the pavement. He was on his hands and knees, flashing the crack of his arse to passing traffic and pedestrians alike. He glanced over his shoulder when the patrol car pulled to a stop behind him. By the time it had parked and the engine had died, he was out of the van and wiping his hands on a grubby cloth.

'Got a minute?' the driver of the patrol car asked, once sure they had the correct address and person.

Turner tossed the cloth through the open back doors of the van. 'I don't suppose me saying *no* would make any difference?'

The uniform with the iPad walked towards him, shaking the device in the air, as though that held the answer. The other officer poked his head into the back of the van and raised a flap of a folded awning. 'We're here to ask about Janet Allsop,' he said, letting the fold of material fall.

Turner watched him. 'Why? What's up?'

'Can we go inside the house and talk?'

'Here's fine,' Turner said, checking next door's windows. 'Come over to this side of the van. She's a nosey cow.'

'Are you sure you want to give a statement out here on the road?'

Turner's eyes narrowed. '*Statement*. For what? I'm insured to drive the van. And I got my licence back a while ago. You can check with the DVLA in Swansea. And with Jan. The vehicle belongs to her business.'

'That's easier said than done,' the uniform told him, and perched on the edge of the van's loading bay. 'We're following up on a missing person's report involving Missus Allsop.'

Turner shook his head. 'None of that's got anything to do with me.'

'You sound like you already knew?'

'Nope. First time I'm hearing about it,' Turner said, looking away.

'You sure?' the uniform pushed. 'It's just that you didn't sound surprised.'

Turner tapped the toes of his boots against the back tyre of the van. 'I said I don't know nothing.'

'Do you deny taking Missus Allsop to catch her train on Tuesday of last week?'

'Who told you that?'

'Edward Collier. Do you know him?'

'Yeah. I know him. He's Jan's partner, and a troublemaker, if you ask me.'

The uniform ignored the comment. 'He says you went to the station while he attended his hospital appointment.'

Turner picked dry skin from his bottom lip. 'He's lying. I went nowhere with Jan.'

'Missus Allsop didn't arrive in Aberystwyth. Meaning you were one of the last people to see her before she went missing.'

Turner took a step closer. 'You're not listening to me.'

'Keep your distance, sir.'

'Stop winding me up, then. You lot know I've got a short fuse.'

'Is that a threat?'

Turner backed off and threw his arms open wide. 'This is bullshit, okay?' There was movement from behind the kitchen curtains of the house next door. 'There's nothing to see here,' he shouted over the low wall. 'Sod off and mind your own business for once.'

'There's no need for that.' The uniform said. 'I did suggest we do this inside.'

Turner glared at the old woman. 'One of these days you're gonna push the wrong button.'

Chapter 25

Reece hadn't waited long before phoning the hospital to find out what they were doing to replace Cara Frost. He wasn't satisfied with the answer he was given and made his views known to the Head of department. After that, he called Ruth Ellis at the university.

'Brân. Hello.' She sounded genuinely pleased to hear from him. 'What can I do for you?'

He told her about the shortage of forensic pathologists in Cardiff, and how Cara Frost's resignation was only going to make matters worse. 'I really could do with your help right now. The chief super's making promises to the press that I don't think we can keep.'

'I see.'

'It puts the entire team under a level of pressure we don't need.' He spent another couple of minutes bemoaning Ginge's vacancy not having been filled, and that policing was under threat of becoming a public joke. 'Everyone's a politician these days. All sound bites and empty promises.'

'It's the same at the university,' Ellis replied. 'We've had numerous cuts and amalgamations of departments. It's impossible to see where it'll end.'

'Down the swanee,' Reece said confidently. 'No one has a clue what they're doing these days, but don't get me started on that. Do you still think you'll be okay to help out with this case?'

'That'll very much depend on what you have in mind?' Ellis said.

That sounded better than a point blank refusal. 'I've got one of my detectives trawling through a list of current MISPER reports,' Reece said. 'But there's no guarantee of our victim being a local resident. She could even be a foreign tourist, for all we know. The labs are trying to run DNA profiles from tissue samples that Cara Frost sent them, but I'm told there's no guarantee of success when the remains are as badly decomposed as ours are.'

'I'd be surprised if they were unable to get you something to be working with.'

Reece liked the sound of that. 'I hope so.'

'Have you considered using facial reconstruction?' Ellis asked. 'The results are amazing these days. The technology has advanced in leaps and bounds.'

Reece had no personal experience with that particular field of forensic science. He was aware of it. But only from what he'd read, or seen in television dramas and documentaries. 'You mean using an artist to build up the face using modelling clay?'

'That's how it was done in the past,' Ellis said. 'Now they use a form of computerised wizardry that's well beyond my understanding.'

'There's no hope for the likes of me then,' Reece said with a brief chuckle. 'Tell me more.'

'It's achieved using three-dimensional scanning and modelling software.'

'And that's as accurate as the clay sculpting was?' Reece asked.

'Oh, yes. Much more so, in most cases.'

'Do you know someone in Cardiff who could do that for us?'

'You'd need to take the remains to the Face Lab at the John Moore's University in Liverpool,' Ellis told him.

'*Face Lab?* I've never heard of it.'

'They undertake forensic and archaeological research and consultancy work the world over. Their forte being craniofacial analysis.'

'Reconstructing what someone might have looked like, right?'

'Exactly.'

'And they'd be able to give us a result good enough to put on the tv news stations?'

'I see no reason why not.'

Reece felt like he was on the verge of making some progress. 'Let's do it,' he said. 'Are you on speaking terms with anyone working there?'

Ellis confirmed that she was. 'I've given at least one joint lecture with Professor Linaker: the lead researcher.'

'You still have his number?'

'*Her* number,' Ellis corrected. 'Sally Linaker.'

'And you'll give her a ring?'

'Just as soon as we're done here. You'll need to pay for the Face Lab's service, obviously. They're heavily reliant on research grants and charitable donations to keep doing what they do.'

'I'll get onto the bean counters at headquarters,' Reece promised. 'You phone this Professor Linaker and tell her that we can be there as soon as she gives us the nod.'

Chapter 26

Chief Superintendent Cable stood behind her office chair, gripping the headrest like she was using it as a crutch. 'How much will it cost?'

'I didn't ask,' Reece said. He was leaning against the doorframe with his hands planted in his trouser pockets. 'Does it matter?'

She glared at him. Then lowered her head and closed her eyes. '*Yes*. It matters.'

'If it helps solve this case, then it's got to be worth the cost, however much that turns out to be.'

'Is that so?'

'Don't you agree?'

Cable came around the front of her chair and collapsed into it. She rifled through the drawers of her desk and popped two aspirin tablets into the palm of her hand.

'Headache?' Reece asked, entering the office. 'I've noticed you get a lot of those.'

'You're killing me. Slowly but surely. You *do* know that, don't you?' Cable slammed the drawer shut, toppling a photo frame. She picked it up and found a new place for it. 'And Doctor Ellis believes this to be the best way forward?'

'Oh, I get it. If Ruth Ellis says it's the way to go, then you're all right with that. But if I as much as—'

'Shut up and close that door.'

He slammed it. 'There's a cost benefit to what I'm proposing, you know. It'll speed things up no end.'

'In your opinion. Look, I'm not dead set against you doing this, but we do need to secure a price before committing to the deal.'

Reece gripped his head with both hands. 'You make it sound like we're buying drugs from a South American cartel. You didn't see the state of those remains. I couldn't tell if they were male or female. Even the pathologist had to phone a friend. This Face Lab place is probably the only chance we have. Don't you think the victim and their family deserve that?'

'Are you not listening? Not once did I say anything to the contrary.'

'If you say no to this, then I'm not doing the press conference. How does that sound to you?'

'You'll do as you're bloody well ordered.'

'All right then. I'll look straight down the camera lens and tell every nutter at home that now's the time to murder someone in Cardiff – on account of the Force being too tight-arsed to spend money on catching them.'

Cable shot to her feet. 'I'll swing for you, Reece. So help me, I will.'

He wasn't listening. 'Tell you what I'll do on the weekend. I'll have a good root around in my attic. See what I can find to car boot. You never know, we might cobble enough cash together to do this.'

Cable thumbed each eyeball in turn and stood there blinking. 'You've given me a migraine.'

'That's because you're always so uptight about everything. You know you always come around to my way of thinking in the end.'

'Cost it,' Cable said, lowering herself into her chair. She didn't look at all well.

Reece reached for the handle of the door. 'See what I mean? We could have avoided all that shouting.'

'Cost it. But you do nothing until we get a number.'

Five minutes later, he was in his office with his phone wedged under his chin, shooting rolled up balls of paper into a bin on the other side of the room. 'Ruth, we've been given the go ahead.'

'Chief Superintendent Cable was happy?'

'I'm not sure she's ever happy,' Reece said. 'She's a bit highly strung, if you ask me.'

Ellis cleared her throat. 'But she'll sign off the request for payment once it's received?'

'She thought it best you send the invoice directly to my inbox,' he said, craning his neck to be sure that no one was listening.

'Excellent. I've spoken to Professor Linaker, explaining the urgency in this case.' Ellis repeated most of the conversation had between herself and her academic colleague in Liverpool. 'Sally's able to accommodate you tomorrow, as requested.'

'Tomorrow it is, then. Liverpool, here we come.'

'We're on,' Reece said, marching through the Incident Room.

Jenkins approached him. 'You convinced her?'

'She never says no to me.'

'Yeah. Right. What are you up to, boss?'

'We're going to Liverpool,' he said matter-of-factly.

'*We.* As in, *you and me?*'

'Who else do you want to take?'

'Nobody. When are we going?' Jenkins asked.

'First thing in the morning. I want you in the car park by six sharp.'

'*Six!*'

'We need to be well ahead of the traffic before it gets busy.'

'And we've been authorised to do this?'

'Not more than five minutes ago.' Reece turned to Morgan. 'Are you done yet with those MISPER reports?'

She nodded. 'Each and every one of them logged before yesterday.'

'Anything promising?'

'No one who stands out as a potential for our victim. It's mostly runaway teenagers and pensioners escaping from nursing homes.'

'Some of those might be worth looking into,' Reece said. 'Similar age as our victim.' He flapped his arms at his sides. 'We've got bugger all else to go on.'

Chapter 27

Edward Collier answered the house phone on the third ring. He'd been expecting the call ever since the police had left. 'Hello.'

'What are you playing at, Ted?' It was Nathan Turner. His manner was gruff and accusing.

Collier gripped the handset. 'Calm down.'

'The police were here earlier. Wanting a statement from me.'

'They came here, too. It's routine when someone goes missing.'

'You told them I took Janet to catch a train last week. Said I gave her a lift to the station in my van. Why would you go and do that?'

Collier scratched his head. 'Why wouldn't I tell them?'

'Because it never fucking happened. That's why. You should have kept your mouth shut instead of trying to make trouble for me.'

'It was Tuesday. I had a hospital appointment and you—'

'Went nowhere near Jan or the station.'

'Nathan, you're losing me?'

'You're up to something. Up to no good. You think we haven't got your card marked?'

'*We?*' That made Collier frown.

'Ring the police and tell them you made a mistake. I don't need them breathing down my neck again.'

'And why would I do such a thing?'

'I'm warning you, Ted. Don't mess with me. You'll be biting off more than you can chew.'

'Give me a second,' Collier said, using his other hand to thumb through the menus of his mobile phone. 'Here it is. The text Janet sent me. Dated Tuesday of last week. *All good. Nathan's just picked me up. Hope your appointment goes well. I'll text once I arrive in Aberystwyth.*'

'That's bullshit. Why would she tell you that?'

'I'm guessing it's because that's exactly what happened.'

'Did you show the text to the police?' Turner asked.

'Should I have done?'

'Stop fucking about, Ted. You keep it to yourself. There's nothing that lot wants more than to put me away for a few years.'

Chapter 28

Reece awoke with a start. Not because of any particular noise. But the complete lack of it. The earlier swarm-like buzz of vacuum cleaners was gone. Doors that had banged open and closed with annoying frequency during the night were now still and quiet. The cleaning staff were finishing off and readying themselves for going home.

'It must be morning,' he mumbled, trying to check the time on his watch. His office was dark, and he wasn't yet coordinated enough to find the *light* button on his watch by feel alone. He gave up trying and rose from his swivel chair, 'oohing' and 'aahing' until he was fully upright. He reached an arm, raised the blind and opened the window that overlooked the staff car park. Jenkins's Fiat 500 was nowhere to be seen.

He angled his wrist so that his watch caught some of the outside lighting. It was 5.25am. He'd told her to be there for a 6.00am departure. There'd be no morning run. That, in itself, would make him irritable throughout the day. Running was his safety valve – a means for him to start on the right foot. He was like a toddler without sleep whenever forced to forgo his fix. Although she wouldn't yet be aware of the fact, Jenkins was at risk of being his captive sounding board during their trip to Liverpool.

He used the staff changing room to shave, shower, and get dressed for the day ahead. A navy suit with a light blue shirt was what he had left in his locker. Although he'd recently adopted an open-neck style of dress, he wore a plain silk tie for the occasion. This was his first meeting with Professor Linaker and he wanted to give the right impression.

He stopped off in the canteen for two bacon rolls and a couple of coffees to go. Unable to recall if Jenkins had ketchup or brown sauce with her bacon, he helped himself to a few sachets of each. He thanked Doris, and was on his way again, thankful that George wasn't at his post. There was no time for chit-chat this morning.

'You've arrived at last. And look like death warmed up,' Reece said, taking the supplies into his office.

Jenkins was slouched over her desk in the Incident Room. She answered with a wide yawn. 'Because it's still the middle of the night.'

'You know I'm usually up a good two hours before now? Out running, no matter what the weather throws at me.'

Jenkins buried her head beneath both arms. 'Bully for you.'

'Did you bring your overnight bag?' Reece couldn't see one and thought she might have forgotten.

'I left it in the boot of my car. Save me having to lug it all the way up here.'

'Right, let's go,' he said, heading for the door to the landing.

Jenkins got up and staggered after him with her eyes half shut. 'What's with all the rushing about?'

'I told you, we need to beat the early morning traffic.'

'Oh, we've managed that all right,' she said, hugging herself as she followed. 'We've probably beaten yesterday's too.'

Reece stood next to the driver's door of the Land Cruiser, tapping his foot. 'Your bag.'

'Oh, yeah.' Jenkins went round the back of her Fiat 500 and opened the vehicle's tiny boot. 'This hotel better have a decent bed.'

'Will you shut up about sleep?' Reece checked over his shoulder when he heard a car entering the police station's parking compound. He checked the make and model as it approached. It didn't belong to Chief Superintendent Cable. 'Come on. We've a busy day ahead of us.'

Jenkins got in, pulled her hood over her head, and slumped against the closed door. 'Wake me up when we get there.'

'There's no time for that. We're going via the mortuary.'

'Why?'

'How the hell do you expect them to do a facial reconstruction if all we pitch up with is a couple of bacon rolls?' Reece checked all around him and couldn't see breakfast anywhere. 'Shit.'

Jenkins withdrew the hood of her coat and sat there gripping a fistful of its material. 'Wait now. You mean we're taking the head with us? In the back of this car?'

'Did you think it was going by bus?'

'Why can't a hospital van take it?'

'I'll put it in the boot,' Reece promised. 'You'll never know it's there.'

'How can I not know it's there? You've told me now.'

'You'd swear I was going to mount the thing on the dashboard like a nodding dog.'

Jenkins turned away from him and looked out of the side window. 'Great trip this is going to be.'

'Look,' Reece said, throttling the steering wheel. 'If a third party transported it to Liverpool, we'd run the risk of some hot-shot lawyer arguing that the continuity of evidence had been compromised. That the DNA of the accused got on it because of X, Y, or Z. They'd only have to plant a seed of doubt in the jury's mind, and that's it, case lost. This way, we avoid that.'

Jenkins pursed her lips. 'I'm still not happy about spending half the day in a car with you and a rotting head.'

Reece turned the key. 'Tough. That's the way it's going to be.'

There was little traffic on the roads at that time of the morning. But it would busy up within the next hour, Reece knew. He parked in one of the hospital's visitor car parks and walked towards the main building with Jenkins in tow. 'Hurry up,' he called over his shoulder. 'If we're quick, we'll get past the Brynglas Tunnels before the usual carnage starts.'

It didn't take them long to arrive at the mortuary. They knew the way, but had to be swiped through the outer door by a miserable-looking technician. Reece had some sympathy for the man. Having to get out of bed early on a cold winter's morning was bad enough. But knowing he was going into work to prepare a human head for transport must have made it all the worse.

'It's ready for you,' the technician said, no more cheerily. He went over to a bank of floor-to-ceiling refrigerators and opened one of its shiny metal doors. He reached inside and produced a white plastic box only a few seconds later. There was a carry-handle sticking out of the top of it, giving it the appearance of something a person might use for a trip to the beach on a hot summer's day.

Reece took the container and handed it over to Jenkins. 'Don't look like that,' he said. 'You'd never know what it is.'

She held it at an arm's length. 'I do know what it is, and it's bloody heavy, too.'

Reece completed the accompanying paperwork, signing and dating in more places than he thought was necessary. 'Right,' he said with that done. 'Next stop, Liverpool.'

Chapter 29

Ffion Morgan wasn't aware of Chief Superintendent Cable's presence until she appeared alongside her desk, looking none too happy. Morgan rose to her feet and fastened another button on her blouse. 'Morning ma'am. I didn't see you there.'

Cable had one eye on the detective and the other on Reece's office door. 'Where is Chief Inspector Reece?' She turned both ways, checking all desks in the Incident Room. 'And Detective Sergeant Jenkins?'

Morgan could feel an uncomfortable wave of heat spreading from her upper chest to her neck. She put her hand over it in an attempt to hide the flush. 'I'm not exactly sure, ma'am. Was there something *I* could help you with instead?'

Cable's eyes narrowed. 'It's the DCI I want.'

'I think he might be following up on something related to the case we're working on. I know he was here until late last night, going through paperwork and making telephone calls. DS Jenkins could be with him, I suppose.' Morgan reached for her phone. 'Would you like me to check?'

'That won't be necessary,' Cable said.

Morgan was unsure of what to say or do next.

Cable pounced. Morgan jumped. 'Where is he, Ffion? And no bullshit this time.'

'He went over to the hospital earlier this morning, ma'am.' Morgan lowered her head. 'DS Jenkins went with him.'

Cable circled the desk, speaking while she walked with her hands cupped behind her back. 'Let's see if any of this sounds familiar to you.' She cleared her throat with a cough that was barely worth the effort. 'Chief Inspector Reece intends to ruin not only his own career, but those of two of his most capable juniors. That'll be you and DS Jenkins. My best guess is, he's got you stuck here manning the fort while he's racing up the M6 with our evidence secured in the boot of his car.' Cable turned and circled in the opposite direction. 'I can't believe he managed to talk Jenkins into it.' She shook her head and came to a stop only inches from where Morgan was standing. 'Who am I trying to kid? Of course I can believe it.' She exhaled and visibly deflated. 'Why can't that man ever do as he's told?'

Morgan couldn't be sure if that was a question she was meant to answer. 'DCI Reece is an excellent detective,' she said sheepishly. 'Most people I know say he's the best they've ever worked with.'

'I don't dispute that.' Cable was on the move again. 'But I can't have him setting a bad example for other officers. Especially when one of them should be preparing herself for a detective inspector role.'

Reece's phone chimed in the depths of his jacket pocket. He took one hand off the steering wheel to get at it and fumbled with the handset until he had it the right way round. It was a text. He couldn't read it without his glasses and passed it over to Jenkins. 'What does that say?'

'It's a text from Ffion.'

'I know what it is. What does it say?' he repeated.

'*The chief super is onto you.*' Jenkins turned to look at him. 'What does she mean by that?' The phone chimed for a second time. Jenkins read out the new text. '*A heads-up – she's on the warpath and is about to ring you herself.*'

'Give me that,' Reece said, snatching for the handset.

Jenkins held it out of his reach. 'You said this trip was authorised.'

'I spoke to her about it,' Reece argued. 'Yesterday. You saw me when I got back from her office.'

'Did she say we could go to Liverpool?'

Reece kept his eyes on the road. 'Yes.'

'So why is she pissed off with you?'

'She's always pissed off with me. If it's not her, then it's Harris. They can't help themselves. Comes with the shoulder-pips. I told her where we were going, okay. I'm not lying about that.'

'And what was her response? Her *full* response?'

Reece gripped the steering wheel like he was trying to strangle someone. 'It's always about the money with that lot.'

Jenkins screwed her eyes shut. 'We can't pay for what we're doing today, can we?'

'I'll sort it. Don't you worry about that.'

'And what about the hotel tonight? I haven't got the money to be paying out of my own pocket.'

Reece changed down through the gears on the approach to a mini-roundabout. '*I'll* pay if it comes to that. Happy now?'

'You shouldn't have involved me in this,' Jenkins said, 'Not without being up front from the beginning.'

Reece braked before they were fully clear of the roundabout, causing the traffic behind them to come to a halt. 'If you want to go home, now's your chance,' he said, ignoring the cacophony of blaring horns. He pulled away again when Jenkins stayed put. 'Don't answer it,' he said when his phone started ringing again. 'It'll be her.'

'Good morning, ma'am,' Jenkins replied. 'Yes, Chief Inspector Reece is sitting right by the side of me.' She handed him the phone and took no notice of the angry faces he was pulling.

'I'm driving. I'll have to hang up,' Reece said, immediately doing just that.

Jenkins took the phone from him and pressed the *answer* prompt when it rang for a second time. 'Sorry about that, ma'am. We must have lost the signal just then.'

'I'll lose *you*,' Reece said through gritted teeth. 'In one of those roadside ditches on the way back.' When he refused to take the phone from her, Jenkins jammed it against his left ear and held it there. Cable was ranting. Reece wasn't listening. The head was going to Liverpool, regardless of what she threatened him with.

Chapter 30

CHIEF SUPERINTENDENT CABLE HAD since returned to her office—uttering all manner of threats—leaving Morgan alone to sort through her paperwork and online case files. Morgan didn't know what Reece had said during the telephone conversation, but judging by Cable's animated response, he hadn't been playing ball.

Reece rarely did. Many people who acted in a similar fashion, did so mainly for the shock or show value. It wasn't like that with the DCI. Morgan smiled to herself, just thinking about it. Reece lived his life like a tube amplifier. Constantly on the edge of breakup. Easily pushed into distorted overdrive. He rarely did as he was told, regardless of who was doing the telling. He was a risk taker, for sure, and a danger to himself on occasions. But he played for high stakes, fighting tooth and nail to get victims and their loved ones the justice they deserved. Morgan respected him for that. The entire team did.

Suddenly aware of another presence in her personal space, and worried that the chief super might have returned, she got up to find a uniformed officer lurking behind her. He held a sheet of A4 paper in his hand. 'Are you looking for me?' Morgan asked.

It wasn't unusual for a man to stutter over his words at first sight of her. She was as pretty as any woman out there, and completely oblivious to the fact. A trait that only served to make her all the more attractive. 'Um. Yeah. I think so.' The uniform held out the hand holding the Missing Persons report. 'I, um. I heard you were looking into these. I thought I'd bring it up here, in case it hadn't pinged on the system yet.'

Morgan took it from him and read Janet Allsop's details. The name didn't trigger anything in her memory. 'Missing for nine days.'

'Ten, if you include today,' the uniform pointed out.

'And in her mid sixties.' Morgan grabbed the officer by the shoulders and hugged him tightly. 'I could give you a big kiss,' she said excitedly. 'You might have found our victim.'

The man looked proud of himself. 'You think this could be related to the find in Mill Street?'

'Could be. Did you speak to this Edward Collier fella yourself?'

'He's a bit shifty, if you ask me. Trying to be polite and look concerned, but . . . I dunno. There was something off about him.'

'That's interesting, given the circumstances.'

The uniform was beginning to relax in Morgan's company. 'Are you familiar with a Nathan Turner?'

Morgan couldn't place the name. 'Should I be?'

'He had a reputation years ago. I think he might even have had some dealings with Billy Creed. You knew *him*, right?'

Morgan nodded. 'Everyone on DCI Reece's team knows that name.'

'Turner used to be well under the spell of drugs and alcohol until a couple of years back. He was always in trouble. Usually involving violence. Particularly towards women.'

'What's the connection between him and Janet Allsop?'

'It's all in the report,' the uniform said with a nod. 'And if I were you, I'd pull up his file and have a good read through it.'

Chapter 31

'ANY HAPPIER NOW WE'VE got Cable's approval?' Reece asked. That wasn't an accurate term for him to have used. The chief super was now aware that he was on his way to the Face Lab, but in no way had she approved it. Something she'd promised they'd be discussing on his return to Cardiff.

'You shouldn't trivialise it,' Jenkins said, watching the world go by on the other side of her window. 'It can be stressful for colleagues when you decide to do your own thing. For the chief super, as well.'

'She can handle herself.'

'She shouldn't have to. If she's seen to be incapable of managing you—'

'Who says that she is?' Reece interrupted.

'ACC Harris and others at Headquarters might think so. Cable has our backs. Yes, she toes the corporate line at times, but personally, I think she gets the balance just right.'

'What is it you're trying to say?'

'That if they believe she can't manage you, they won't think twice about replacing her with some hardliner. Is that what you want?'

'They'd move me first. Or pension me off altogether,' Reece said, waiting at a zebra crossing for an old lady to hobble past on a stick. The lights had long since changed to green, but he made no issue of it, and pulled away only when the lady made it safely to the railing on the far pavement.

'You're too good at what you do for them to get rid of you. There's not another detective at the station with a clear up rate anywhere near yours.'

Reece checked his rear-view mirror before replying and could no longer see the old lady with the stick. 'I know your generation thinks that coppers like me hail from the Dark Ages. But in those days, we didn't have to second guess what top brass might say about everything we did. They expected us to catch criminals and mostly left us alone to get on with it.'

'And look how many miscarriages of justice are now coming to light.' Jenkins twisted at the waist to face him. 'That hands-off approach to managing people gave corrupt officers carte blanche to do whatever they wanted.'

Reece's head jerked sideways. 'Bollocks it did. Some people will exploit any system you put them to work in. Take the thousand or so Met officers currently under misconduct investigation. Are you suggesting that all of them are my age?'

'No. Of course not.'

'So then, you're admitting that the current setup is no better at preventing corruption within the Force. And I'm saying that it also handicaps good coppers like us from getting proper justice for people. It's a double whammy.'

Jenkins faced the front and folded her arms. 'The point I was trying to make is: someone has to be aware and accountable for what's going on. And at our station, that someone is Chief Superintendent Cable. There has to be a hierarchy system, like it or not.' Reece's reply was interrupted by a call from Ffion Morgan. 'What's up?' Jenkins asked.

'I rang your phone because I wasn't sure if the chief super had finished with the boss yet,' Morgan said.

'She has, but he's still driving. Tell me what you've got and I'll pass it on to him.'

Morgan summarised the events of her morning. 'Shall I get uniform to bring them both in?' she asked.

Reece acknowledged her good work, but insisted they wait for now. 'Lets not give them any warning of the fact we might be interested in them. We'll put whatever we get at the Face Lab on the telly, and see how they react.'

Morgan confirmed that she understood. 'I have an address for the woman Turner threatened to kill a few years back. There's a court injunction stopping him from going anywhere near her. She's unlikely to let on if I went round there for an informal chat.'

'That might give us some useful background before we bring him in.' Reece craned his neck, trying to get a better sight of the road signs. 'And you're sure he said he'd cut her head off if she didn't give him more money for drugs?'

'It was her word against his,' Morgan explained. 'But that's what she reported to the officers attending the scene.'

'Any witnesses?'

'Afraid not.'

'How did she manage to get the injunction, if her story wasn't corroborated by anyone?'

'There was previous between them. Domestic abuse. Verbal mostly.'

Reece hated men who were violent towards women, children, or animals. He and Yanto had had plenty of conversations on the subject, over a pint or three – Yanto volunteering to *sort out* anyone Reece might want to point a finger at. He'd never taken the farmer up on the offer, but once or twice, had come very close. 'I want as much background as you can get on him,' Reece said. 'But I also want you to be careful while you're at it.'

Morgan scoffed. 'You haven't forgotten my Krav Maga skills, have you?'

'Take a uniform with you,' Reece insisted. 'And make sure it's a bloke.'

'I'm not sure you're allowed to say that anymore,' Jenkins told him.

He drew in a deep breath. 'The world around us might be going to bollocks, but a machete-wielding maniac won't be checking your pronouns before getting started. Take a man with you. And a big bugger too.'

Jenkins waited for him to hang up. 'You could get yourself in hot water for saying something like that to the wrong person.'

'I don't give a flying fuck.' Reece squinted at another road sign. They'd stopped making any sense. 'I wasn't putting women down, or saying they're not up to the job. Far from it. But ask anyone with more than half a brain – you take the biggest men you've got when there's a risk of serious trouble.'

'I'm just saying.'

'Well, don't. And keep your gob shut for the rest of the journey.'

'Whatever you say.' Jenkins squinted over her left shoulder. 'But if I *was* allowed to talk, I'd be letting you know that you're in the wrong lane. Hunter Street is over there.'

Chapter 32

Morgan knew exactly where to find the type of uniformed officer Reece had in mind. The staff canteen.

Sitting at a table made to look like it had been borrowed from a school dining room were two burly constables on their lunch break. One was dragging a slice of bread and butter through a mix of tomato ketchup and egg yolk. The other was munching on a roll of some sort and chasing it down with a mug of hot tea.

She flashed her pearly whites at them. 'Hiya, boys. Which one of you hunks fancies doing me a favour?'

The men turned their heads and grinned at one another. Both raised a hand without knowing what they were letting themselves in for.

'Don't be naughty now,' she said, pretending to be offended. She knew them well and often engaged in a bit of playful banter. They played rugby with her boyfriend, Josh, and were good friends of his. She explained what she was up to and hitched a lift over to Bridie Sparkes's house.

Morgan got the uniforms to park in a neighbouring street. There was no sense in advertising a police presence outside the house belonging to Nathan Turner's ex. 'Are you two okay to wait here for me?' she asked. 'This could be something or nothing.'

'Take as long as you need,' the driver told her. 'If we get a call to a job, we'll let you know before we leave.'

'I don't know if she'll talk to me,' Morgan said. 'She might still be too frightened of him.'

'If this Turner fella arrives, he won't be going anywhere near the place while you're in there,' said the uniform in the front passenger seat. He was hunched over but still pressed against the door, and the headliner above him.

'I'm not worried about me,' Morgan said. 'It's what happens after we're gone.'

The property was non-descript and situated towards the end of a terrace street full of other houses that looked just like it. It wasn't a bad area. The houses and gardens were fairly well cared for. There were no abandoned sofas or rusting cars sitting on piles of bricks.

No salivating dogs, or half-naked men scratching themselves while swigging from cans of cheap supermarket cider.

Morgan stopped outside number twenty-one and saw that the living room windows were open. She thought that odd, given the time of year and how cold it was outside. She knocked on the front door and waited. Knocked a second time, watching the street for signs of potential aggravation. There was a woman pushing a stroller along the pavement, while a red-faced toddler did its best to shred its own vocal cords.

Morgan was torn on the subject of kids of her own. She wanted them, definitely. But carrying a harmful variant of the BRCA gene meant there being a fifty-fifty chance of her passing it on to any child she mothered. Josh wanted a family. He was one of five boys. "*One of each would be perfect,*" he'd said before the breast cancer scares had put that possibility in serious doubt. Still, it was a conversation that needed an airing, and soon. Already in her thirties, Morgan knew that the biological clock was well on its way to striking midnight.

The mother and her fighting toddler passed by. The child, no less quiet. The mother, in a zombie-like trance. Morgan watched them. *Maybe we'll get a kitten instead,* she thought. *Or a dog. Yeah, a dog for Josh.* She was staring at the back of the mother when the front door to number twenty-one opened to reveal a woman wearing a pair of faded jeans and a plain white T-shirt.

'Can I help you?' the woman asked with the door not yet fully open. 'I don't believe in God. If you're here to save me, then you're a couple of years too late.'

'It's nothing like that,' Morgan promised and produced her warrant card as proof.

'Police?' Sparkes said, looking alarmed. She pulled on the door until only her head and left shoulder remained visible. '*I* haven't called anyone.'

'I'm here to talk to you about something that happened a good while back,' Morgan said reassuringly. 'A bit more than three years ago.'

Sparkes's look of concern increased tenfold. 'Nathan Turner?' She pushed her head further through the opening and checked the street.

'It's okay. He's not out there. This is just a follow-up, of sorts.'

'After all this time?' Sparkes frowned, the skin covering her forehead creasing momentarily. 'Has he hurt someone else? Is that why you're here?'

'Can I come in?' Morgan asked, rubbing her hands together. 'It'll be more private. And a fair bit warmer.'

Reece slammed the horn in frustration. 'Why leave it until then to tell me about the turn for the university?'

Jenkins wasn't looking at him. 'Because you told me to shut my gob.'

'Not for directions,' Reece protested. 'You've probably cost us another twenty minutes.'

Jenkins shrugged. 'You should make yourself clearer next time.' She twisted in her seat to get a better view of the road behind her. 'You need to be over there, somehow.'

'I merged onto Scotland Road like I was supposed to.'

'You still missed the left turn.'

'Only because you were winding me up.'

'Over *there!* I told you to go left.'

'I Know. I *know!* But I can't drive over the fucking pavements.' Reece saw a gap in the traffic, accelerated, and swerved violently.

Jenkins grabbed hold of the dashboard as the Land Cruiser lurched to one side and cornered with a worrying degree of body roll. 'Are you trying to kill us?'

'Just you!'

She screwed her eyes shut and wailed, '*Boss!*'

'If he flashes his lights at me one more time,' Reece said, checking the rear-view mirror. 'I'm going to stop this car and punch his fucking—'

'*Enough!*' That brought a moment of total silence to the situation. 'Pull over. There. Just pull over.'

'Why?'

'I'll drive the rest of the way.'

Reece stopped without first indicating his intent to other road users. The Audi that had been behind them was now slowing and pulling up alongside. The passenger window came down. The driver leaned across the seat to scream abuse at them.

'Don't you dare get out,' Jenkins warned. 'I mean it.'

'Did you hear what he called me?' Reece said, with one foot already planted on the tarmac.

'If you beat him up, I'll nick you for assault,' she called after him.

Reece alternated his attention between the Audi driver and his detective sergeant. 'You wouldn't dare?'

Jenkins unbuckled her seatbelt and went after him. 'Just try me.'

Chapter 33

BRIDIE SPARKES'S LIVING ROOM was cluttered with laundered clothes. There was an ironing board fighting for space between a flat-pack display cabinet and the padded arm of a chair. An iron stood upright on the board, hissing like an angry cat, while a mug of coffee cooled down at the pointy end. One half of the sofa was hidden by a laundry basket full of clothes yet to be ironed. There were three piles of neatly folded garments resting next to it.

'You'll have to excuse the mess,' Sparkes said, looking embarrassed. 'I wasn't expecting visitors.'

'No need to stand on ceremony for me,' Morgan said, noting that two of the piles were children's clothing. Both belonging to boys, if she wasn't mistaken. The other pile clearly belonged to the mother.

Leggings and coloured T-shirts, mostly. There was nothing there to suggest the presence of an adult male. 'How old are your sons?'

'Five and eight. From the amount of washing they generate, you'd think I had half a dozen.'

'I bet they keep you busy. My friend says the exact same thing. She's got one boy and he can go through three different outfits in a single day.'

'Tell me about it. I sometimes wonder if the woman next door breaks in overnight to leave me her stuff.' Sparkes's smile slowly ebbed away. 'But you wanted to talk about Nathan,' she said, stepping around a clothes horse draped with towels. She put the television in standby mode and tossed the remote control handset onto an empty armchair. There were more towels drying on the radiators, making the living room so humid that the window and emulsioned walls had rivulets of moisture snaking down them.

'If that's okay with you?' Morgan said. She handed over her coat and accepted an offer of coffee. 'White with no sugar, please.' She followed the woman into a small kitchen that was how she imagined it might look after a pair of hungry kids had breakfasted before the morning school run. It was already early afternoon, and the table hadn't yet been wiped down and tidied.

Sparkes took two half-eaten bowls of Coco Pops off the table and dropped them into the sink, returning with a wet cloth in hand. While the kettle boiled, she rubbed at a crescent-shaped puddle of spilled chocolate milk before scooping a handful of scattered cereal into her open palm. 'Is it okay if we sit here at the table?' she asked.

Morgan pulled a chair but didn't sit down. 'Can I help with the coffee?' She scanned the kitchen for the whereabouts of the required ingredients.

Sparkes took a mug from a tree of four others and pointed towards one of the cabinet doors. 'The coffee's in that one,' she said, fetching a carton of milk from the fridge. 'Do you have kids?' She looked the detective up and down and answered her own question. 'Judging by your figure, I'd say it's unlikely.'

'Not yet. But I think I'd like to, someday.'

'Don't leave it too long before you start trying. There's nine years between my sister's two. Not that there was supposed to be. It just happened that way. And now she's going through an early menopause and won't be having the third child they'd always hoped for.'

'Couldn't they adopt?' Morgan asked, deciding that an option worthy of her running by Josh.

Sparkes handed over a mug of coffee. 'I already had one somewhere,' she said, hunting for it.

'It's on the ironing board,' Morgan told her. 'It'll probably be cold by now.'

'It'll do,' Sparkes said, going to fetch it. 'It's something you get used to as a mother. Cold food. Cold tea and coffee. Cold bath water.'

Morgan brought her mug to her lips. 'You're not selling it very well.'

Sparkes joined her at the table. 'What's Nathan in trouble for this time?'

Reece hadn't assaulted the driver of the other vehicle. Jenkins had shepherded him around to the passenger side of the Land Cruiser and shut him in before he could cause more trouble than he already had. She'd then apologised to the other driver, making no mention of the fact that they were police officers. Dozy tourists from the other side of the bridge fit the bill much better, she decided.

Once inside the university grounds, she found a parking space that Reece was content with. His was a big vehicle when compared with most others, and the available parking bays had been measured out with city cars in mind.

'What's the point in them providing spaces at all?' Reece asked. 'You can't park anything wider than your arse in these?' He poked his head out of the window and saw that both wheels on his side were positioned well over the white line. His door opened only a fraction of its normal travel before knocking against the neighbouring vehicle. 'How am I supposed to get out? Swing, like a sodding chimp?'

Jenkins restarted the engine. 'I'll move it someplace else, shall I?'

'Do you see anything that doesn't already have a car in it?'

'No. But—'

'So what's the point of asking?' He inched the door open and forced himself out with some effort and a fair amount of swearing. He went round to the boot—still swearing to himself—and removed the cooler-box and its grisly contents.

Jenkins knew better than to take offence. It wasn't personal. Reece was always at his worst when he thought people were on his back. The wrong turn and the angry motorist had pushed him over the edge on what had already been a fraught morning. She'd let him blow off steam in his usual way of complaining about most things, and as soon as they made some progress, he'd snap out of it like an audience member released by a hypnotist.

Reece turned left and right, looking for directional clues. 'What do you think it'll be signposted as?'

'Didn't you say it was called the *Face Lab?*'

'That's what Ruth Ellis called it. But I think it's part of the Forensic Research Institute.'

'Let's ask someone for directions to that,' Jenkins suggested. 'Once there, it should be easy enough to find Professor Linaker's office.'

For the first time that day, Reece chose not to argue with her.

Chapter 34

'We don't know that Nathan *is* in any trouble,' Morgan said, unwilling to divulge information she didn't need to. She put her mug down and opened her pocketbook. Now that the chit-chat was out of the way, the conversation would hopefully be of more relevance to her visit.

Sparkes had since decided that her coffee had crossed the line of what was palatable and gave it a quick spin in the microwave. 'So why the sudden interest in him?' she asked, waiting for the ping to sound. 'And in me?'

'I can't tell you that right now. Not the full details,' Morgan explained. 'All I can say is that Nathan's name cropped up during our investigation of a current case. Along with several other names, I might add. It's what usually happens. We're now trying to eliminate anyone not involved.'

'Involved in what?'

Morgan gave the woman a good eight out of ten for trying it on with different phrasings of the same question. 'I really can't say.' She twisted and leaned back in her chair, and was just able to get sight of a photo frame she'd noticed on her way through the living room. The man hugging two boys didn't look at all like the dour-faced mugshots in Nathan Turner's police files. 'Is that the boys' father?' she asked, pointing towards the open-shelf of the display cabinet.

'You didn't think Nathan fathered them, did you?' Sparkes asked with a show of disbelief. 'Three months with him living here was more than enough. That's Michael in the photograph. And yes, he's the boys' father.'

'Are the two of you married?' Morgan was trying to get a handle on where Nathan Turner fit into the current family dynamic.

Sparkes was slow to answer. Her voice was barely audible when at last she did. 'Michael died not long after that was taken.'

'I'm sorry to hear that,' Morgan said. 'Was it unexpected?' She thought it must have been, given the man's age.

'He killed a child.' Sparkes was suddenly lost in the depths of her coffee. 'It wasn't his fault. Even the coroner said so during the inquest. And there were plenty of witnesses to the accident. The kid came hurtling out of a sweetshop—he'd been shoplifting—and ran straight in front of the car. Coming from behind a parked van. There was nothing Michael could do, and it was all over within a matter of seconds.'

Morgan closed her eyes. It was an all too frequent and tragic loss of a young life. Anything she might have said in response would never have been enough.

'The trolls hounded Michael until he couldn't take any more. Calling him vile names whenever they passed us in the street. They even scraped *Kiddie Killer* into the paintwork of his car bonnet.'

'Did you report any of this to the police?' Morgan asked. 'You must have done?'

'For all the good it did. Michael still took his own life. In his mind, it was the only option left open to him. A life for a life, so to speak.'

'Couldn't you have moved someplace else?'

'How long do you think it would have taken us to sell up and do that?' Sparkes asked. 'Broken windows and dog shit on the doorstep aren't on most people's wish list when they go looking for their dream house.'

Morgan imagined the family going through hell.

'Michael hanged himself from the framework of the swings in the local park. The note he left said he'd chosen the spot to be closer to the boys when they played there.' Sparkes sniffed. 'Sometimes I think I can hear him talking to me. Right next to where he killed himself. Isn't that mad? And what's even madder is that the boys have never fallen off anything since. They were always hurting themselves and ripping holes in the knees of their school trousers. Not any more. It's like Michael's always looking out for them.'

Morgan blinked tears and swallowed. 'I'm so sorry we failed your family.' She reached and rested her hand on top of the other woman's. 'Would you like me to put you in touch with someone? I know it won't change things, but—'

Sparkes withdrew her hand and sat more upright. 'Been there. Done that. The coroner was scathing in his report. Listed failing after failing. I received an out of court settlement from the South Wales Police. Something that was supposed to have been for the boys' future. I think that's what brought Nathan knocking at my door.'

'He came here looking for money?'

'Not literally. We met in a pub. But the settlement was reported in the local newspapers; which went down like a cup of cold sick around here.'

'Were you threatened?'

'Just snide comments and lots of pointing and staring,' Sparkes said. 'At first, I hid away as much as I could. Did online food shops and got my mother to do the school runs. Then I thought, *sod 'em*. They couldn't ruin my life any more than they already had. So I started going out. To the shops. School. Even the pub, every once in a while.'

'Good for you. Show them that you're made of stronger stuff than they are.'

'Then one night, this guy started giving me hassle in the pub down the road. He was really shooting his mouth off and I was getting scared because other people were joining in. Nathan came out of nowhere and floored the mouthy one. My knight in shining armour. That's what I thought at the time. Here was someone who'd keep me safe. If only I'd known the truth.'

'And what *was* the truth?' Morgan asked, the nib of her pen hovering above an empty page in her pocketbook. 'Didn't he threaten to cut your head off?'

Chapter 35

THEY TOOK DIRECTIONS FROM someone and arrived at the block housing the *Face Lab* a little over ten minutes later. No one had shown any interest in the cooler box Reece was carrying. He imagined himself taking the lid off and chasing screaming students around the campus. That would be fun. Might even get them off their phones for a few minutes.

'Why are you grinning to yourself?' Jenkins asked.

'No reason.'

'I worry about you sometimes,' she said.

He nudged her onwards. 'You don't know the half of it.'

When they found the Face Lab, Professor Linaker was there to meet and greet them. A middle-aged woman of average build and height, she wore her hair in a short, almost masculine, style of cut.

'Nice to put a face to a name,' Reece said, looking for somewhere appropriate to place the container. 'Where do you want this?' he asked.

Linaker took it from him and gave it to a member of her staff. 'Don't look so worried, Chief Inspector. We work within strict protocols that are in full accordance with the guidelines set out by the Crown Prosecution Service.'

'When will you be able to take a proper look at it?' Reece asked as the container disappeared with the acne-ridden researcher carrying it.

'What if we get something to eat?' Linaker suggested. 'You must be hungry after your early start?'

Reece would have preferred to make a start on the identification. 'Whatever you think is best.'

'And then we'll discuss your case and the process of craniofacial analysis,' Linaker assured him. 'I'll give you a full tour of the Face Lab and show you examples of what we do there. We really are quite proud of our achievements.'

'Sounds good to me.'

Jenkins nodded in agreement.

Morgan scribbled another entry in her pocketbook. They'd agreed to talk about Turner's threat after filling in more background. 'And that night in the pub was the first time you'd come across him?'

'I knew him from our school days,' Sparkes said. 'We lived a couple of streets from one another and used the same bus stop to get wherever we were going. He was someone I was aware of, but it was nothing more than that.'

'What was he like back then?'

'He had no real friends that I remember. You'd hardly know he was about.'

'A surprise then, when he punched that man in the pub?'

'Who'd have thought it?' Sparkes used her knuckles to play drums on the side of her head. 'Not me, that's for sure.'

'He'd changed?'

'And not for the better.'

'When did he first get violent with you?' Morgan asked.

'That'll be when I washed his jeans without checking the pockets. He went ballistic. Almost ripped the door off the front of the machine.' Sparkes hugged herself and rocked back and forth, fighting with the memory. 'That's when I found out he was using. He denied it, of course. Said they belonged to a friend who was in a spot of bother.'

'Did he lay a hand on you that day?'

Sparkes looked away. 'It was mostly verbal. Let's leave it at that.'

'What about the boys? Weren't you concerned for their wellbeing?'

Sparkes shot to her feet. 'Is that what this is *really* about? Has someone round here said I don't look after them properly?'

Morgan followed her through to the front window in the living room. 'Absolutely not. This is about Nathan, not you. I promise.'

Sparkes leaned against the glass, using her hand to clear a porthole in the layer of condensation. She looked up and down the street. 'I wouldn't put it past them.' Then she turned to face the detective. 'For all his faults, Nathan was always good with the boys. It was me he had the problem with. Especially after he'd lost his job at the slaughterhouse.'

Chapter 36

THEY CHATTED OVER A lunch of chicken salad and jacket potato, in Jenkins's case. Reece opted for cottage pie, vegetables, and gravy. The dessert choices were limited when compared with what Doris usually had on offer back at the station in Cardiff. Jenkins bought a small pot of vanilla yoghurt. Reece chose an orange, but threw more than half of it away, claiming it was *"drier than a witch's—"*

Jenkins had thankfully interrupted him in the nick of time.

Refreshments done with, Professor Linaker took them to the department known as *Face Lab*.

The room looked like any other he'd expect to find in a research institute. Light and airy due to the presence of several large windows. White Formica work surfaces set against the perimeter walls.

Widescreen computer monitors and keyboards. Working at several of them were people wearing everyday clothing, not lab coats, as Reece had imagined they would be.

Linaker led the detectives over to one such station and introduced them to the researcher working at it. On the left-hand side of the monitor's screen was a wide column of colourful icons available to the user, similar to those found in most commercially available graphics editing programmes. Reece had no clue yet what any of them did when selected.

The researcher briefly explained the functions of some of the icons, demonstrating in real time by clicking and dragging selections of facial structures from the *tools pallet* to the image she was working on. There were Roman noses. Pixie noses. Even noses with fractured septums, like Reece's. There were sticky-out ears. Pointed ears. Dimpled chins. And heavy-set jawbones. Skin colour could be changed however the researcher thought appropriate.

On the next screen was a three-dimensional depiction of a neck and shoulders that could be fully rotated about its axis. Floating a centimetre or so above the discontinuation of the neck was the yellow, animated skull of a man. Again, three-dimensional. Areas of yellow had been filled over with grey segments representing muscle. The mish-mash of colours gave the image the appearance of an unfinished jigsaw puzzle. Its nose and ears were already in place. As were the whites, but not the iris colour of the eyes.

Reece doubted that anyone would yet recognise the man as their missing friend or family member, but was given assurances they would once the process was complete.

To demonstrate her point, Professor Linaker took them over to a workstation not currently in use. She took a moment to logon to the system and navigated to the required page. 'If you take a look at this,' she said, encouraging them to stand close on either side of her. 'Meet Robert the Bruce.' The screen was filled with the face of a thickset man wearing a crown and chain mail neck protection.

'You're kidding me,' Reece said with a broad grin. 'Bloody hell, that's good.'

'Recognised him, did you?' Jenkins whispered.

'Then there's Robert Burns. Richard the Third. And Ramses the Second,' Linaker said, producing images, one after the other.

'Are you watching this?' Reece asked.

'Glued to the screen,' Jenkins claimed.

'Why the sarcasm?'

'Because you can't know for sure that any of them looked like that. Everyone who did know them is long dead by now.'

'Look—'

'No, it's a fair point,' Linaker conceded. She clicked on a new tab and brought up more faces. 'These are a few recent cases we've worked on with the police. On the left side of the screen, as we view it, are facial reconstructions using human remains as our only reference guide. And on the right are photographs we obtained once the victims had been positively identified by other family members.'

There was no doubting the accuracy of the technology when the results were presented in such a clear fashion. 'Are you any more convinced?' Reece asked.

Jenkins nodded. 'And ours will look as realistic as this?'

Linaker saw no reason why it wouldn't.

'And how does the full process work?' Reece asked. 'How do you know that someone had sunken cheeks or a double chin?'

'We don't. That level of reconstructive detail isn't yet available to us.'

'Ah,' Reece said, sinking almost an inch in height.

Linaker clicked a hyperlink that took them to another page. 'Each skull is meticulously scanned to produce a three-dimensional starting model. You can think of it as the underlying scaffold of the face.' She clicked the mouse three times. 'Here's such a model. A second. And this, a third. The skulls are different in shape and size; each therefore unique to its owner. Would you agree?'

Reece nodded. 'I would.'

'Our own method of reconstruction is based on one developed in the nineteen-eighties, in Texas, USA,' Linaker said. 'It involves the application of tissue depth markers at various anthropological landmarks of the bony skull.'

'Hang on.' Reece's eyebrows morphed into one straight line. 'And the layperson's version of that is?'

Linaker tried an alternative approach. 'We know what the average depth of tissue covering any given anatomical structure should be. *Tissue* being fat, muscle, and skin, mostly. But also tendons, ligaments, and blood vessels. We apply those averages to the scanned skull.' She did just that to the three examples on the screen, building the forehead, cheeks, and chin on each. 'Prior to this technology being available, it was done with moulding clay.'

'And you get three completely different looking faces,' Reece said, staring at the screen.

'But what we can't know with any certainty is whether a person was overweight and round-faced at the time of death. Or going through a lean phase and looking gaunt. The best we have on that front is hair sample analysis.'

'I'm listening.'

'Hair sample analysis can tell us what a person's diet consisted of. And from that, we can make educated guesses regarding their social class and general health. It will even tell us where in the world they've been living for the previous six months.'

'You're joking?' Reece asked. 'You can tell us if this person was a native of the UK, or in the country on holiday?'

'Not the purpose of them being here,' Linaker said. 'But we can tell on which continent they've spent the bulk of their time.'

'And all that from a hair sample?' Reece shook his head in disbelief.

Linaker ended her session on the computer and pushed the mouse to one side. 'Let's go meet your victim.'

Chapter 37

Reece had no idea where Chief Superintendent Cable was when he called her from the bar of his hotel in Liverpool. 'You didn't reply to my email,' he said as soon as she'd answered. 'I thought you'd be over the moon with the end result we got.'

'I'm at home,' she said. 'And in the shower until a few seconds ago.'

'Alone?'

'What sort of question is that?'

'I wanted to know if you could talk officially,' he said defensively. 'I sent you an image of our victim about an hour ago. Or Jenkins did. As one of those attachment things.'

'Give me a minute to take a look.'

'It'll be in your work account.' He could hear movement as Cable moved about the bathroom, scrolling to the relevant email.

'That's impressive,' she said on first sight of it.

'The whole setup was amazing. That Face Lab is worth every penny they charge.'

'I wanted to talk to you about that,' Cable said. 'You did tell them to send all payment correspondence directly to me?'

'I did exactly as you said.' Reece turned his back on Jenkins so that she couldn't pick up on what he was saying. Sitting a good twenty feet away from where he was, he knew from experience that she had a skill for lip reading. 'I'll remind Professor Linaker,' he promised. 'She might have sent the invoice elsewhere by mistake.'

'Mistake.' Cable tutted. 'I should have contacted her myself.'

'You're going to get that face straight on the news channels, right?' Reece said. 'We're already almost a fortnight behind our killer.'

'Can I get dressed first?'

'Why? Are you intending to do it over a Zoom call?'

'No. But I'd still prefer to have some clothes on.'

'Are you naked now?' he teased in a soft voice.

'Sod off, Reece.'

Edward Collier almost choked on his cheese and pickle sandwich when the face of his missing partner appeared on his television screen. He lowered the sandwich onto a plate in his lap and wiped his mouth on a paper napkin. It was Janet. There was no doubting it. A red banner scrolled across the lower border of the screen, stating: *Breaking News. Police appeal to the public for help in identifying murdered woman.*

'It can't be,' Collier said, putting the plate to one side. He was breathing heavily and breaking out in a cold sweat. At first, he didn't hear the telephone ringing next to him.

'Have you seen the news?' Hannah Oakley asked. 'It's her. It's Mum. No doubt about it.'

'I'm watching it now.' Everything in Collier's world had slowed down. Colours and sounds were muted. Nothing was making sense. He felt nauseated. 'It can't be?' he said.

'I'd know my own mother.'

Collier shook his head. 'That's not Janet.'

'I'm telling you it is!' Oakley was close to becoming hysterical. 'That's Mum.'

Collier stared at the television. However much he refused to accept it, Hannah Oakley wasn't wrong. 'Have you contacted the police and told them?'

'Not yet. Have you?'

'I'm only just seeing it,' Collier said. 'I still can't believe it's true.'

Reece was on his second glass of whisky. Not his favourite, Penderyn Sherrywood. But it was still a good single malt. He pointed at the wall-hung television. 'If that doesn't get us a result, then I don't know what will.'

Jenkins pushed her plate to one side. 'Fair play. It was worth the hassle of us coming here.'

'Told you. Ye of little faith.' Reece reached across the table. 'Aren't you eating this?' he asked, sliding the plate of food towards him. 'There's plenty of meat left in this burger bap.'

Jenkins put a hand to her abdomen. 'Go ahead. I've got an upset stomach.'

Reece let go of the plate. 'You did wash your hands before touching this?'

'Of course I did.' She looked aghast. 'The early start messed with my routine.'

'How can getting up early give you the shits?'

'Will you *please* keep your voice down. I don't want my bowel habits shared with every bugger in this hotel.'

'We all do it, you know?' Reece took a bite and wiped his mouth on the back of his hand. 'Even kings and queens spend time on more than one kind of throne.'

'But they don't talk about it over their evening meal.'

'Maybe they should,' Reece said, chewing noisily. 'It's daft that everyone's so prudish about their own bodily functions. When me and Yanto go night fishing—'

Jenkins put out her hand to shut him up. 'Spare me the gory details. How did we even start on this topic of conversation?'

Reece pointed his fork at her. 'That was your fault. You said you'd been shitting through the eye of a needle all evening.'

Chapter 38

Reece sat up straight in bed. There was traffic noise outside and not the sounds of nature he'd grown accustomed to in Brecon. His phone was ringing on the pillow next to him. 'Ffion,' he said in a croaky voice.

'You're not still in bed, boss?'

He got off the bed, went over to the window, and opened the blackout blinds. The bright light caught him unawares and made him squint. His right temple felt like someone had tapped it with an ice pick. He used his free hand to shield his eyes. It was the first bit of blue sky on show for almost two weeks. 'What time is it?'

'A couple of minutes after eight,' Morgan said. 'In the morning,' she added for clarity.

'It's gone eight already?' He'd rarely slept so late. 'I told Elan I'd meet her in the restaurant for breakfast at seven sharp.'

'She told me to let you sleep. Said you needed it.'

Reece wasn't sure what was meant by that. 'Where was she when you spoke to her?' He couldn't imagine Jenkins staying in the restaurant for a full hour without him. She was probably in her room, watching telly or surfing social media on her phone. He'd check just as soon as he was showered and dressed.

'She went over to the university to collect the head first thing.' Morgan said. 'To save you having to make a detour on the way back to Cardiff.'

Reece checked the pockets of his suit jacket. His keys weren't there. Jenkins hadn't returned them after parking up the previous day. 'She took my car?'

'And she wants to do the driving on the way home today. But I didn't tell you that.'

Reece smirked. He could use the time to sit and think without getting into arguments about lane control and the speeds he was driving at. 'Why did you ring her, anyway?'

'I didn't. She rang me, wanting to know if there was any news after last night's press release.'

He instantly regretted thinking his sergeant would have been skiving in his absence. Unlike him, Jenkins was out of bed on time and doing something useful. She was going places, and he'd better not forget that. 'And was there anything useful?'

'The Incident Room got a call from Edward Collier,' Morgan said.

'Why do I know that name?'

'He was the guy I told you about yesterday. Uniform spoke to him about a MISPER. Thought he was a bit weird.'

'I remember now.'

'He's the one who gave us Nathan Turner's name.'

'Yeah. Got it,' Reece said. 'Did you speak to Turner's ex?'

'I did. And guess what? Turner used to work at a local slaughterhouse.'

'Used to?'

'Bridie Sparkes says he got himself sacked. Something to do with equipment going missing.'

'What sort of equipment?'

'The type that would come in useful for dismembering a corpse.'

Reece waited in the hotel car park, his overnight bag gripped in one hand. When Jenkins pulled the Land Cruiser in off the road, he raised his free arm to catch her attention and waited for her to skirt around a long line of parked cars and come to a stop. He opened the back door and threw his bag onto the empty seat. 'Sorry for the no show, earlier,' he said, getting in and buckling up. 'I didn't set an alarm. I'm always up at the crack of dawn without one.'

Jenkins nodded at the glove box. 'I didn't think you'd have time to go downstairs and get yourself anything.'

Reece reached inside and removed a bun wrapped in a white paper serviette. There were two small cartons of orange juice to go with it. 'Lovely jubbly,' he said, balancing the bun on his knee.

'I got you sausage and bacon. And there should be a sachet of ketchup somewhere. I had to sneak it out without them noticing.'

'Why? I paid for breakfast with our rooms.'

'Don't ask me. There were signs everywhere saying you couldn't take food out of the restaurant.'

'Bloody Gestapo everywhere,' Reece said, biting into the bun. He used a finger to wipe ketchup from his top lip. 'Anyway, Ffion said you've already been over to the university and picked up the head. Thanks for that. You've probably saved us the best part of an hour.'

'Thought I'd make myself useful while you were topping up on your beauty sleep.'

He stopped chewing and smiled at her. 'Sorry about yesterday. You know how I sometimes get when there's a lot to organise. I'm always worried that something's not going to work out right.'

'Can't say I've ever noticed,' she said, ducking away from him. 'Happy if I drive us home?'

He put the breakfast roll down. 'That reminds me. What have you been telling Ffion about my driving?'

Chapter 39

Morgan's stomach turned over as soon as she pulled up outside the slaughterhouse. It was very industrial-looking. A collection of rectangular units assembled with some of them standing on end. There was a smaller unit annexed to one side of the main building, constructed from red brick and glass. **JAMES BROS** was stencilled above the uPVC door in large, black lettering.

Morgan jumped in her seat when a loud blast of a horn signalled the departure of an empty lorry. Another—from the same agricultural haulage company—was just arriving and came to a stop not far from where her pool car was. The sides of the lorry were fashioned with slats and narrow openings between them. She saw several pink snouts sampling the damp air. Pairs of sad eyes peering out of the crowded darkness.

She looked away and hated herself for doing such a thing. Pigs were clever. They'd know what was going on. It was another conversation to be had with Josh. Most people—herself included—tucked into their Sunday roast, or summer barbeque with little to no thought given to how such food got to their plates. She wondered how many meat eaters there'd be if everyone was made to attend the manufacturing process – from the point when the lorry was loaded at the farm, to the sausage or pork chop going up in the display window of the butcher's shop.

'Don't,' she said when one of the pigs tried to get her attention. She walked away, leaving it to its fate, and entered the small office block.

There was no sign of blood. No gutted animal carcasses hanging from the ceiling on shiny metal hooks. She'd expected the place to smell of death, but it didn't. There *was* the sound of machinery in use next door. And the unmistakable clatter of hooves on concrete surfaces.

Three people were sitting at separate desks. One of them was in conversation on the telephone. Another was checking through a delivery document with a ruddy-faced lorry driver. Morgan approached the one employee who looked less busy, and produced her ID for the woman to scrutinise.

'Is there something wrong?' the employee asked, loud enough for the man on the telephone to make his apologies and leave his desk.

'I'm Brian Swift,' he said, as he approached. 'Plant manager.'

'DC Morgan.' The ID got another airing. 'I wonder if we could talk. In private,' she added, glancing at the lorry driver who seemed incapable of dragging his eyes off her chest.

Swift ushered her through a doorway and into a smaller room. 'This okay for you?' he asked, checking his watch. 'It's used by the office staff, but no one's due a break before ten.'

That gave her thirty-five minutes to get the information she'd come for. 'This should be fine.'

'Tea? Coffee?'

She couldn't stomach anything. 'I'm good, thanks.'

'What can we do for you?' Swift asked, helping himself to a coffee before joining her on a faux-leather sofa.

With the **HUMAN TISSUE** container and its contents safely delivered to the hospital mortuary, Reece and Jenkins arrived back at the Cardiff Bay police station almost six hours after leaving Liverpool. Traffic congestion and an irritating wait for the right people to show up at the hospital were mostly to blame. It was Saturday morning and everyone wanted to be somewhere else.

'If you get there before me, mine's a strong coffee with two sugars,' Reece said, climbing the steps to the front entrance.

Jenkins followed at a slower pace. 'Why do you think I'll get there before you?'

Reece put his head to the glass and peered inside. 'I think we're safe,' he said, chancing it.

'Safe from what?' Jenkins asked.

'Not what. Who?'

'Detective Chief Inspector.' Cable appeared from around the corner next to the stairs, where she'd obviously been hiding.

Reece stopped and considered beating a hasty retreat. 'I swear she's got a tracking device on me. Ten seconds we've been in this building. Remind me to get one of the tech guys to check my phone.'

'I expected you to be here long before now,' Cable said.

'And we would have been,' Reece told her. 'Only the private jet you sent must have gone somewhere else by mistake.' He tried to manoeuvre his way around her. 'Shanks's pony always takes that bit longer.'

'It wasn't a criticism. I was concerned.'

'No need to be.' He tapped Jenkins on the shoulder. 'Sterling Moss here did all the driving on the way back. And that'll be why we're a couple of hours late.'

'That was nothing to do with me,' Jenkins protested. 'You said yourself, the traffic was a nightmare.'

'I said *you* were a nightmare.' This time, he did manage to open the stairwell door and get through it. 'See you all up there.'

Cable followed after him. From where she was, only the lower half of his legs would have been visible as he climbed the first set of steps. 'Where do you think you're going?'

'Ask your crystal ball,' he called behind him. 'It hasn't let you down so far.'

Chapter 40

'Someone get the kettle on,' Reece said, marching through the Incident Room.

Morgan swivelled in her seat. 'There you are. I was starting to get worried about the two of you.'

'Not you as well.' Reece returned from his office, minus his coat and suit jacket. Unbuttoning the cuffs of his shirtsleeves, he rolled them up to mid-forearm and made his way over to her desk. 'We'd have been back ages ago if it wasn't for the traffic and a couple of jobsworths at the mortuary.'

Cable and Jenkins walked into the room shoulder-to-shoulder, having elected to take the lift from the ground floor.

Morgan waited for them to join Reece in front of her desk. 'There's a lady downstairs claiming to be the daughter of our victim.'

'That's what I was trying to tell you,' Cable said. 'If you'd stuck around to listen, it would have saved you a trip upstairs.'

'She's been waiting a while,' Morgan said. 'Given the time, I was about to go down there and take her statement myself.'

'What kind of vibes did you get from her?' Reece asked. 'Do you think she's genuine?'

Morgan handed him a photograph. 'She gave me this when she first got here. It was taken at Christmas, last year.'

Reece needed no more than a millisecond to make up his own mind.

'I'm Brân Reece,' he said, entering the room with Morgan just ahead of him. He'd left Jenkins upstairs, chasing a few points of interest. Morgan had already met Hannah Oakley—albeit briefly—and even that minimal level of familiarity might prove useful. 'You know my colleague?' Reece said.

'Ffion, wasn't it?' Oakley asked.

Morgan smiled warmly and took a seat. 'That's right. Well remembered.'

Oakley glanced at the clock on the opposite wall. Her eyes were red and puffy. In her hand was a paper tissue held in a tight grip. 'It *has* been a long time since we last spoke.'

'Sorry about that,' Reece said, before outlining the reason for his trip to Liverpool. He still had the photograph and lay it on the table between them, face up. 'This lady is your mother?'

Oakley wiped her eyes with the tissue and then blew her nose. She nodded without studying the image. 'That's right.'

Reece watched her, taking in every verbal and non-verbal response during their interaction. In the mind of a detective, everyone was a potential suspect until the evidence proved otherwise. 'We're going to need something of your mothers,' he said. 'A toothbrush would be ideal.'

Oakley reached into a shopping bag between her feet. 'Would this do instead?' She lay a hairbrush next to the photograph. 'Mum left it at my place last time she came to stay.' She picked it up with trembling hands, put it to her nose, and inhaled. 'There are strands of Mum's hair still caught in it,' she said, descending into floods of tears.

Morgan went and crouched alongside Hannah Oakley. 'Take your time. You're doing brilliantly.'

Reece stayed where he was. Not because he lacked empathy. He always felt awkward and clumsy when called upon to show his feelings. 'That's perfect for what we need,' he said as a contribution.

Oakley looked up and swallowed. 'You said you took the *remains* to Liverpool. Is it true you only found Mum's head?'

Reece wasn't keen on divulging many of the details as yet. There were things only the killer would know, and for now, he was keeping it that way. 'I'm afraid so.'

Oakley looked like she might vomit.

'Can I get you more water?' Morgan asked, returning to her chair when the offer was declined.

'Who would do such a thing?' Oakley blew her nose in a clean paper hanky. 'And why? Why kill Mum?'

'That's what we intend to find out.' Reece took the photograph off the desk and stared at it. Professor Linaker's work was astonishingly good. If not the same person, the two women would have to be sisters. 'What we now need you to do is to tell us about your mother and who you think might have had reason to do her harm.'

Chapter 41

Reece knocked on Edward Collier's door for a second time and was about to call through the letterbox when he saw movement behind the pane of frosted glass. A dark silhouette contrasting against a lighter background, grew larger in his line of sight. There was the rattle of a security chain travelling in its catch before the door fully opened to reveal a stockily built man wearing faded denim jeans and a black and yellow lumberjack style of shirt. Despite his flat footwear, the man stood as tall as the DCI.

'Edward Collier?' Reece asked. He raised his warrant card and introduced himself and Detective Constable Morgan. 'Can we come in? I'd like to speak to you about Janet Allsop.'

'I've been expecting you,' Collier said, showing them through to the living room. It was overly warm and lit with a single table lamp and the television screen. He muted the telly and limped over to the light switch. 'That's better. We can all see what we're doing now,' he said, inviting them both to sit down.

Reece sank into a chair that almost swallowed him whole and draped his arm over the side of it. He immediately got up again and removed his jacket, placing it on the floor next to his feet. 'Did Hannah Oakley call to tell you we were on our way?'

Collier stood with his back to the fire, warming his legs like a country gent returned from a game shoot. 'Hannah and I haven't spoken since yesterday evening.' His forehead creased. 'Why would she have gone straight to the police station without coming here first?'

Hannah Oakley had said plenty to Reece and Morgan. Much of it involving Collier and his whirlwind romance with her mother. She quite obviously didn't like the man. 'I've no idea,' Reece lied. 'Anyway, how did you and Janet first meet?'

'I answered an advert for van drivers,' Collier said. 'Local business. A few hours work a week. It suited me. I met up with Janet for an informal chat and it was like we'd known each other all our lives. Have you ever experienced such a feeling, Chief Inspector? It really is quite remarkable when it happens.'

'You moved in here within four months of that meeting,' Morgan said. 'Not so long after Hannah's dad passed away.'

'*Ah*. Now I understand. Hannah's been at it again, has she? Claiming I preyed on a vulnerable widow and drove a wedge between members of the family?'

'And did you?' Reece asked. He'd never been one to shy away from asking awkward and direct questions.

'Look at me forgetting my manners,' Collier said with a loud clap of his hands. 'Can I get either of you a tea or coffee?'

'We're both good,' Reece said without consulting Morgan. 'You haven't answered me.'

'Hannah is convinced I saw her mother as an easy target. But that's nonsense,' Collier said firmly. '*Yes*, Janet was lonely. But it was *she* who suggested I move in here. She'd even recently asked me to marry her.'

Chapter 42

'THE TWO OF YOU were getting married?' Reece said. If Hannah Oakley knew, she hadn't mentioned it.

'I wasn't ready for that,' Collier said, like he was still thinking it over. 'It's a big commitment for someone to take at my time of life. At any time of life,' he quickly added. 'But more importantly, I was beginning to have concerns about Janet.'

'What sort of concerns?'

Collier went over to the writing bureau and lowered its front leaf. 'This is going to sound utterly bizarre,' he said, stretching to remove something that Reece couldn't get a good sight of. 'I've recently had reason to believe that Janet might have been living a double life.'

Reece sat forward. Not an easy feat in such a large and soft armchair. 'You're losing me?'

'I'm not suggesting for a moment that she was a government agent or anything so clandestine. But she has been keeping things from me, and I have no idea why that might be.' Collier held his hand out in front of him. 'Why would she be paying Nathan Turner such large sums of money?'

Reece took the chequebook and thumbed through the stubs. **Nathan T.** was written clearly on the first, in black ink. There was a smudge next to it, caused by a careless finger passing through the wet full stop. **£2000** was penned on the line below. He flicked through the rest and came across another two stubs for the same amount of money. Both listed **Nathan T.** as the payee. He closed the chequebook and fished an evidence bag out of his pocket using his free hand. 'We'll need to take this with us. You'll get it back once we've made a copy.'

'Be my guest, Chief Inspector.'

'You've no idea why Janet would be paying Turner these sums of money?' Reece asked. 'Could it have been for new stock or supplies he was collecting on behalf of the business?'

Collier shook his head. 'Janet would never have trusted Nathan to do anything like that. Driving from A to B to put a tent up in someone's garden was as much free rein as he got, workwise. And another thing: that chequebook belongs to her personal account. I never once saw her use it to pay for anything related to the business.'

Reece was at a loss as to what was going on, but already suspected that he wouldn't need to look far beyond the family circle to crack this case. 'Aside from payments to Nathan Turner, what else made you think Janet was hiding something from you?'

Collier looked like a man with the weight of the world on his shoulders. 'This trip to Aberystwyth wasn't the first time she'd gone away without me,' he said. 'A couple of months ago, she went to stay with an old school friend in West Wales. It was only a few days following her return that she had the mishap with her medication.'

'Hannah says yesterday was the first time she heard about that.'

'Janet's decision, not mine. She didn't want to worry the family over something she claimed was a silly mistake.'

'Did *you* think the overdose was an accident?' Reece asked.

Collier's reply was barely audible. 'I know now that there was more going on in Janet's life than I was privy to.'

'That's not what I asked.'

'I don't know if she intended to kill herself or not, Chief Inspector. I really don't.'

'I'll need the name and contact details for the friend in West Wales,' Reece said.

Collier returned to the bureau. 'This is the best I can do.' He handed Reece a white envelope that was torn open along its upper seam. 'You won't find it of much use, I'm afraid. There's a signature, but not a lot else to go on.'

Reece skim read the letter and turned it over to check the reverse side. It was blank. 'You don't know this Cynthia?'

'I never heard Janet mention her name before that long weekend.'

Reece huffed. Not intentionally. 'You don't know the woman's name, address, or telephone number? Let alone where in West Wales she might live.'

'I know you must think I'm stupid,' Collier said. 'At first, I thought Janet might have been seeing another man. That the letter wasn't what it appeared to be. I didn't wish to know the truth of that and never confronted her. Stupid, I wasn't. But a coward – guilty as charged.'

Reece wondered how he, himself, would have behaved under similar circumstances. Before he had an answer, Collier was talking again.

'I don't suppose Hannah told you why she and her mother were no longer on speaking terms?'

'She mentioned an argument in the summer,' Reece said, recalling the conversation at the station.

'It was a damn sight more than that,' Collier told him. 'The neighbours were so worried that someone might get hurt, they called the police.'

Reece turned to Morgan. 'Did you know about this?'

'It wasn't in any of the documentation I came across,' she said.

'That's probably because it wasn't taken any further,' Collier told them. 'Hannah and Mark agreed to leave—reluctantly, I might add—as did the police, a short time later.'

'Did anyone get physical?' Reece asked.

'It was verbal, mostly. And initially, between Mark and Janet. Then Hannah waded in on them both and said some awful things.'

'Like what?'

Collier clenched his fists at his sides, clearly angered by the memory of that afternoon. 'She told Janet that she'd soon be dead and buried.'

For a long while, the only sound in the room came from the carriage clock on the mantlepiece. Tick-tick, it went. Just as it always did.

Chapter 43

'Hannah used those exact words?' Reece wanted to be sure he'd heard correctly. '*Dead and buried.*'

Collier had gone back to standing in front of the fire. 'That's what she said.'

'What did you and Janet think she meant by it?'

'Not a lot at the time,' Collier answered. 'It was something said in the heat of the moment. Or so I thought.'

'You're not so sure now?'

'I don't know what to think, Chief Inspector. My head's been all over the place since I saw last night's news.'

'Tell me more about the argument that started between Janet and Hannah's husband, Mark.'

Collier went back to his seat, cradling his head in his hands. 'Where do I begin?'

'Tell it like it happened.'

He dropped his hands into his lap and raised his head. 'Hannah had a brief history of alcohol abuse way back. I think she'd also dabbled in drugs at some point. I'm not a hundred percent on that. It wasn't something Janet readily spoke about.' Collier rolled his eyes. 'Yet more secrets. There's a theme emerging here.' He took a breath. 'And Mark can be selfish. Likes to play golf and go to the gym with friends. *His* friends. When Hannah's father died, she took it really badly and went off the rails. Binge drinking. Making a fool of herself in the street. Mark was of no use to her, and used it as an excuse to spend even more time on his own. Janet had no option but to bring Hannah home for a couple of weeks, to sort herself out. As soon as Nathan heard she was back in Cardiff, he was over here like a shot.'

'There was previous between them?' Reece asked, making sure he was following the right cues.

Collier nodded. 'Happened before my time here. It was the reason Janet took him on when he lost his job at the slaughterhouse. No one else would touch him.'

'I'm familiar with his record,' Reece said.

'I guess Nathan gave Hannah the support and attention she wasn't getting from Mark and . . . they had a one-night stand.'

'And Mark found out?'

'Hence the argument at the barbeque,' Collier said. 'He blamed Janet for what happened more than he did Hannah. That's why I find it so hard to believe he'd offer an olive branch.'

'But Janet claimed he had?'

'She was adamant.'

Reece pushed a finger under the collar of his shirt. It was hellishly warm in the room. He couldn't remember Hannah Oakley saying that she and Mark had split up. 'They're still husband and wife?'

'Mostly for their daughter's sake. Lucy's doing GCSEs next year.' Collier pulled a face. 'The trials and tribulations of families, *eh*, Chief Inspector?'

Reece nodded slowly and stuck another finger under his collar. He didn't feel at all well.

'Do you have children?' Collier asked.

Reece's line of sight was drawn to the window and the street beyond. He was on fire and struggling to breathe. He had to escape the heat and get outside. When he stood, he felt faint, his legs struggling to support his bodyweight. Morgan was calling to him. Not Morgan. It was Anwen. She was screaming his name. Begging him for help. His peripheral vision darkened and blurred, tunnelling his focus down a narrowing cone of sight to where his beautiful wife was slumped on her knees, gripping her belly and bleeding onto the cobblestone road in Rome. She said his name. Repeated it once more only. Then she died in his arms.

When Reece opened his eyes, he found himself staring up at Morgan. She was crouched over him and looked beyond worried. Behind her was a tall and heavily built man. The room he was in was vaguely familiar, although he couldn't yet place it. 'Where am I?' he stuttered. 'What happened?'

'You fainted,' Collier told him. 'It's my fault entirely. I don't like the cold and keep the house stupidly warm. Janet was forever going behind me, opening windows and turning down the radiators.'

Reece waved the man off when he tried to help him up. 'I can manage.'

Collier reversed away. 'Let me get you a glass of cold water.'

'Thank you.'

'Let's call this done for now,' Morgan said. 'We can always come back if we need to.'

Reece drank more than half the contents of the glass in one go, shuddering at the feeling of cold zig-zagging its way down the front of his abdomen. He put the glass to his forehead. It helped reboot his brain. Got him back on track. But it took another forty-five minutes of questions and answers before he was fully ready to leave.

Chapter 44

Reece tossed his coat into the back of the Land Cruiser. He got in and started the engine. 'I want you on to the phone company as soon as we get back. Find out when and where Janet Allsop's phone has been used over the past couple of weeks.'

'Will do, boss.' Morgan fastened her seatbelt. 'Are you sure you're okay to drive? I could give it a go if you think you're not.'

'You won't be *giving it a go* in this.'

'You know what I meant,' she said, tapping his knee.

He moved his leg. The truth was, he often had no clue what she meant, and some days, was convinced that there was something wrong with her. 'It was like an oven in that house,' he said. 'Unnaturally warm.'

Morgan dug an elbow in his side. 'You don't think he's turned the attic into a marijuana farm, do you?'

It took Reece several seconds to realise she wasn't joking. 'Will you keep still?' he said through gritted teeth. 'It's like being out with a giant squid!'

Morgan's eyes widened. 'Are you calling me fat?'

'What? No. I don't like being touched by people, that's all. I prefer everyone to keep to their own personal space.'

'I love a good cwtch, me. When Josh gets home in the evenings . . .'

Reece turned the radio on in the hope he could drown her out with the sound of music.

Morgan instantly tuned it to another channel. 'That's better.'

'What the hell is it?' Reece asked. 'Sounds like two cats fighting.'

'Showing your age, now boss,' she said, practically dancing in her seat. 'Give it a few minutes. It'll grow on you.'

Reece turned the radio off and swatted her hand when she tried to switch it back on. 'Touch it again and I'll have you and Jenkins transferred to traffic.'

'Why are you bringing Elan into this?'

'Because the two of you are like kids in the car.'

Morgan lowered her sun visor and used the small mirror on the back of it to apply a new layer of lipstick. She licked her finger and saw to her eyebrows before brushing her hair.

'Don't even think about spraying that in here,' Reece warned.

Morgan turned the pocket-sized atomiser towards him. 'This stuff is great for a quick freshen up of clothes. There's plenty left. Go on, have a squirt.'

Reece rotated away from her, screwing his left eye shut. '*Jesus!* Are you trying to kill us?' He grabbed for the device and hurled it out of his side window.

Using the rear-view mirror, Morgan watched the atomiser bounce and roll towards the gutter at the side of the road. 'Elan's not wrong about you.'

Reece gripped the steering wheel. 'I mean it. Both of you. *Traffic.*'

By the time they got back to the station, Reece was in desperate need of some male company. He went looking for George, only to be told the desk sergeant wasn't working the early part of the weekend. Not having anywhere near the same relationship with George's colleague, he made his way upstairs, thankful that Morgan had taken the lift and given him some peace at last.

He was feeling too old for this. Everything in his life was becoming a battle. He had more than enough money to retire. Could spend his days fishing with Twm Pryce. Walk the hills and forests with Yanto and Redlar. As he made his way along the landing towards the Incident Room, he could hear Morgan in what she must have thought was a hushed conversation with Jenkins. The pair of them were like a couple of characters from the Beano. Neither did anything quietly. 'I didn't have a meltdown,' he said, surprising them both when he walked in. 'You practically pepper-sprayed me while I was driving.'

'See what I mean?' Morgan said.

'You caught me on the side of the face.'

'I was aiming for your chest. If you'd kept still . . .'

'Don't you ever apply for firearms training,' Reece told her. 'There's no way I'm putting my name to that.'

Jenkins held up her phone and pointed at its screen. 'As exciting a conversation as this is, time's getting on. What's our next move?'

'You two get off home,' Reece said. 'I'll have uniform go pick up Nathan Turner. If Edward Collier's right, Turner might well have been one of the last people to see Janet Allsop alive.'

'You're not staying behind until they do that, are you?' Jenkins asked.

Reece shook his head. 'He can wait it out in a cell overnight. I'll catch up with him in the morning.'

Chapter 45

A swathe of blue flashing lights lit up just about everything within a fifty metre radius of Edward Collier's home. There were already two patrol cars and a marked van in attendance. The loud sing-song wailing of a siren sounded the speeding arrival of a third patrol car.

Officers in hi-viz jackets swarmed across the road and over the pavements, giving the area the vibe of Saturday night in the city's *Chippy Lane*. But this wasn't the usual case of testosterone-fuelled fighting. Nor was anyone brandishing a blade or broken bottle. This was a full-on domestic disturbance. Something that could quickly get as ugly as any bar fight.

Hannah Oakley was swaying on the pathway leading up to the house, hurling verbal abuse—and anything she could lay her hands on—at Edward Collier. Several of the neighbours were out on their doorsteps, copping an eyeful. Collier wasn't saying much. Oakley wasn't giving him the opportunity.

'You're a murdering bastard,' she screamed, unperturbed by the police officers bearing down on her. 'I knew you were up to no good as soon as I set eyes on you. Get out of my parents' house. Get *out!*' She swooped to pick up another stone and cocked her arm, readying herself to hurl it in Collier's direction.

'Put that down,' came an authoritative voice from close behind her.

Enraged with temper, Oakley hadn't, until then, realised she had company. She turned, stick in hand, her face contorted by anger. 'I want him out of there.' She spat the words and wiped her mouth. 'Arrest him. He's a murderer.'

'Put that down.' Two uniforms were standing shoulder to shoulder, and only a few feet away from where she was. One male. One female. 'I won't ask you again,' the female said, slipping a baton from her belt.

Oakley turned her back on them and hurled the stone at Collier. He side-stepped, letting it ricochet harmlessly off the door to land on the hallway mat.

'Stop it!' Oakley screamed as she was wrestled to the floor. 'Get off me! That's my mother's house.' It was more difficult to speak now that she was lying on her front with the uniform's knee digging into the small of her back. 'He killed her. That *bastard* killed my mother.' She repeated her accusation over and over, pausing only when her arms were drawn behind her and shoved up her back. 'Are you deaf, bitch?' She banged her head against the hard path in a fit of frustration. Then did her best to sink her teeth into the exposed flesh of the police officer's forearm.

Nathan Turner stared one-eyed through a narrow gap between the bedroom curtains. There were two coppers on the pavement below. One of them was hammering on his front door. The other was looking up at the bedroom windows. Turner didn't think the man could see him. The lights were out. There would be no silhouette to give him away. He kept very still and watched goings on.

The officer at the door stopped with the knocking, reversed a few paces, and looked up and down the street. Turner could hear them talking. The windows were the shitty single-glazed type that let in sound and cold in equal measures. The men were discussing what to do next. One of them wanted to leave and try again later. While Door-Knocker was confident that Turner was holed up inside, hiding.

He needed to make a decision. Door-Knocker was speaking into a shoulder-radio now, no doubt calling for reinforcements. If he stayed put, they'd have him under lock and key in no time. He had to get out of there. One against two was pretty decent odds, in his opinion.

Yep, Door-Knocker was definitely summoning an army to help bring him in. Damn Edward Collier for whatever he'd told them. For pointing a finger of suspicion. Turner's mind was working in overdrive. Collier knew far too much about him. What else would he be telling the detectives in charge of the case? There was only one way to find out.

He grabbed his jacket off the bedroom floor and checked the pocket. His fingers folded comfortably around the handle of the short-bladed knife. It was time to get out of there. Time to convince Edward Collier to keep his big mouth shut.

Hannah Oakley was lifted onto her knees, with her hands still cuffed behind her back. Not the most comfortable position she'd ever been in. It hurt from where the police officer had pinned her to the floor. She'd be bringing that up whenever she got to see the organ grinder. 'Let me stand,' she said, and was no longer crying. 'There's a stone digging in my knee.'

'Should have thought about that before you started playing silly buggers,' the female officer replied. 'You'll get up when I say you can.'

'I'm *sooo* going to report you.' Oakley swung her head side-to-side in a failed attempt to get a better look at everyone present. 'All of you,' she snarled. 'Do you hear me?' It was unlikely they wouldn't have, given the noise she was making.

The back doors of the police van were already open. There was an officer standing beside them, awaiting his passenger. 'She looks lively,' he joked to a colleague.

'Pissed as a fart,' he was told. 'Turned up here and snapped the wing mirror off that guy's van. Then had a right go at him when he's tried to stop her. He's almost twice her age, poor sod.'

'That's not what happened,' Oakley argued. Two officers *helped* her to her feet by hooking beneath her armpits and pulling her upward with force. It pinched her skin. Stung and burned simultaneously. 'You're hurting. I said you're hurting *me!*' She snapped her teeth, but couldn't stretch her neck far enough to make contact with anything more solid than the night air.

'Watch yourself,' the officer warned. 'This one likes to bite.'

'Fuck you,' was Oakley's only reply.

'You too. It's been a pleasure meeting you.'

Oakley's feet were slow to get moving. She stumbled towards the van screaming protests.

'The joys of chucking out time,' the driver mused.

'I'm not drunk,' Oakley told him.

'She smells like a brewery,' the female officer said.

'And you smell like *shit!*'

'Get in and watch your head.'

'Make me, you ugly '*bitch*.'

'Have it your own way.'

LIAM HANSON

The van doors slammed shut, with Hannah Oakley kicking and punching like her life depended on it.

Chapter 46

'There's no lasting harm done,' Collier told the police constable. 'I won't be pressing charges.'

'Not even for the criminal damage caused to your van?' she asked. 'You've got the neighbours as witnesses to what went on.'

Collier shook his head. 'Hannah's been under a tremendous amount of stress lately. You must be aware of the news these past few days?' The officer showed no signs of linking the discovery under Mill Street, Cardiff, with the arrest of Hannah Oakley. 'The Janet Allsop murder,' Collier said.

'Oh, I get you now.' The officer put her hand to her mouth. 'I'm sorry. We *were* told about that in our shift briefing, but I didn't connect it to this address when we were called.'

'It's been an horrendous time,' Collier said, sinking into an armchair. 'I'm still not ready to accept it. Not before those DNA samples confirm it's Janet.' It was all too much for him. He cupped his face in his hands and broke down and sobbed.

The officer came and sat next to him. She put a hand on his nearest shoulder. 'Can I get you a cup of tea, Mister Collier? Or maybe there's someone I could contact to be here with you?'

'Look at me being a silly old man,' he said, wiping his eyes. 'I should remain positive until told otherwise.'

'You're not being silly,' she told him. 'It's the shock of it all. Tonight, included.'

Collier played with his hands. 'Each time there's a knock at the front door, I think it's Janet, stuck outside without her key.'

Nathan Turner wasn't expecting Collier's street to resemble the car park at police headquarters in Bridgend. What was the man up to this time? Hiding in the shadows, he ducked behind a green bin, all the while listening for anyone sneaking up behind him.

A police van pulled away from the pavement with its blue lights flashing. There was no siren. Not on this occasion. He'd arrived too late to know who was being held captive inside. Had they arrested Collier for Janet's murder? Turner thought about that. It posed as many potential issues as it did solutions. One of two police cars followed the van to the other end of the street before both turned at the junction and were lost to sight. The second car stayed where it was: parked with two wheels straddling the pavement.

The second car's continued presence had Turner thinking the police were either searching the house for evidence, or that it wasn't Collier locked in the back of their van. But if it wasn't him, then who was hammering on its thin panels as it sped by?

Chapter 47

ON HER PREVIOUS VISIT to the Cardiff Bay police station, Hannah Oakley had simply walked up the front steps and entered the foyer of her own volition. She'd tapped on the window at the main desk, summoning an overweight police officer sporting three stripes on his epaulets.

The desk sergeant had listened to what she had to say before telling her that the detective she needed to speak to was due back anytime soon. In actuality, that hadn't turned out to be true. DCI Reece was almost two hours later than expected.

Oakley's second visit to the station was nothing like her first time there.

For a start, she arrived in the back of a police van, rolling around in her caged seat like a dice in a metal throwing cup. Whichever way the van leaned, she lurched in the opposite direction. When it stopped without warning, she was propelled forwards and then backwards.

She complained on every occasion. Not that it did her any good; both officers ignoring her until they'd reached their destination. One of them came round to the back of the van, jangling keys and whistling something deeply annoying. Oakley was as sure as she could be that the man was doing it on purpose. She knew the sort. Every profession had their fair share.

'Stay seated,' Whistler said, unlocking the back door. 'Have you calmed down yet?'

Oakley felt suddenly nauseated and needed to get out of there. 'I'm going to throw up,' she said, belching and swallowing hot and bitter bile. 'Let me out. Let me get some fresh air.' When her abdominal muscles contracted, she lurched out of her seat, still penned inside the cage.

'Stay where you are until I've opened up,' Whistler ordered in response to Oakley's charge for freedom. 'I said sit down. If you're looking for trouble—'

She'd warned him, and so it was no fault of hers when he threw open the rear doors and exposed himself as a target at the exact moment she vomited. It was very watery and impressively projectile. A guttural battle cry sounded the unleashing of more vomit; this time mostly confined to the interior of the van.

'Stop!' the uniform complained.

The other officer came running over from where he'd been swiping them into the building, his hand reaching for the baton kept on his belt. 'What's the matter?'

Whistler was bent over and dripping vomit onto the tarmac. When he straightened, he'd turned purple and had his hand clamped to his mouth.

His colleague started laughing at him. 'Rookie mistake, that. Pissheads always puke in the back of the van. It's a given.' He caught hold of Hannah Oakley and shepherded her towards the entrance to the building. 'You've ruined his nice new uniform. He's only had it a couple of weeks.'

'Where's the detective on my mother's case?' Oakley asked, clearing her throat and spitting on the floor. All that got her was a shove in the small of her back. She spoke again, but still the officer refused to engage in any meaningful conversation.

Nathan Turner was so preoccupied second-guessing events inside Edward Collier's house, that he was deaf to the presence of the man approaching from his rear. His first inkling of there being something amiss was when the toe of a leather boot caught him square on the chin, knocking him sideways onto the pavement. He rolled onto his back but didn't recognise his attacker, who was now setting himself up for a second helping.

'You were warned not to sell your shit around here?' the man said. 'You knew what we'd do next time we caught you.'

The second kick caught Tuner in the ribs. He heard at least one of them crack and felt a searing pain spread across his chest. He screamed and curled into the foetal position, doing what little he could to protect himself. This man was intent on doing him some serious harm. When the third kick came, he caught hold of the leg, buying himself enough time to reach into his coat pocket. *Kill or be killed* was the motto of the streets. He turned onto his knees, weathering the fists that rained down on him. Then he twisted and lunged, the short blade glinting in the streetlight only briefly before losing itself in the man's belly.

'This wasn't about drugs,' Turner gasped and withdrew the knife. 'There was no need for you to get involved.'

The man patted his abdomen before examining a bloody hand in the orange glow from above. 'You stabbed me,' he said in a high-pitched voice. 'You fucking stabbed me!' He started walking away, hunched over and promising this wasn't over and done with. He stepped onto the road, waving his free hand at a passing police car.

The vehicle pulled over. The occupants got out. One of them spoke into his shoulder radio. The other attended to the bleeding man. Turner recognised both officers from earlier that evening. His night had properly gone to shit.

Chapter 48

REECE GOT INTO WORK early, intending to interview Nathan Turner first thing. Sunday or not, the team had the makings of a long day ahead of them. Once done with Turner, they'd have to go back out and speak to Hannah Oakley. Not everything she'd said fitted with Edward Collier's version of events. He could understand her reluctance to bring up the one-night stand and her previous relationship with Turner, but this was a murder investigation, and the victim was the woman's mother. He came to a halt halfway across the Incident Room. 'What do you mean, he isn't here? Didn't I tell you to have him picked up overnight?'

'And I spoke to uniform on my way home,' Jenkins said defensively. 'It was all arranged.'

'So where is he?'

'He did a runner,' Morgan said, not looking up. 'Uniform think he went out the back way when they knocked on the front door. There's an alley at the bottom of his garden, leading into a neighbouring street.'

Reece walked a few steps away, turned and came back. He couldn't believe this was happening. How difficult could it be to make an arrest? If he later found out that both idiots had gone to the front door, leaving the rear exit and garden unchecked, then someone was in for a bad day at work. 'So, they let him get away?'

'And it *really* went downhill after that,' Morgan said, still sitting at her desk. Jenkins made one of her *break-it-to-him-gently* faces, not that it had any influence whatsoever over her colleague. 'He legged it again after the stabbing.'

Reece's lower jaw fell open, but nothing came out of it.

'Flesh wound,' Jenkins said, attempting to minimise the fall out. 'The victim was lucky it wasn't a longer knife. A clean up and some stitches was all it needed.'

Reece closed his eyes. 'Tell me I haven't woken up yet. That this is only a nightmare.' He opened them again. 'Nope. No such luck.'

'Uniform recognised Turner as the perp,' Jenkins said. 'They've been looking for him all night.'

'I won't hold my breath.' Reece shook his head. 'He'll go to ground now that he knows we're after him. Make sure Border Control keep an eye out.' Morgan got up and walked away with her phone held to her ear. 'Are you listening?' Reece asked.

She raised a hand to shush him. When she'd finished the call, she apologised. 'I know where he is,' she said, collecting her coat. 'That was Bridie Sparkes. Turner's at her place, trying to get inside.'

Bridie Sparkes crouched at the far end of her hallway, wearing pyjamas and fluffy slippers. She was hugging herself and chewing her fingernails. The front door rocked in its uPVC frame as Turner repeatedly kicked it. 'Go away!' she screamed at him. 'You're not supposed to be here.' She turned to her boys. 'Off those stairs. Go to your room and shut the door.' There was hesitation from both of them. Sparkes repeated herself, this time adding: 'Push your bed up against it.'

'Who's outside, Mummy?'

Sparkes pointed towards the ceiling. 'Upstairs. Now. And don't come down again until I tell you.'

The bottom half of the door bent inwards and wasn't going to survive its ordeal for very much longer. 'Go away. Leave us alone!'

The banging stopped momentarily. Then the letterbox opened, revealing Turner's yellowed teeth and stubbled chin. 'Bridie. It's me. Open the door.'

'You shouldn't be here.'

'I'm not going to hurt you.'

'Nathan. You're frightening the boys. Go away. *Please.*'

'I said let me in.'

'That's not happening.'

Turner straightened and hammered his fists against the door, forcing his face against the small panel of frosted glass. 'Open it!'

There was more movement on the stairs. 'Mummy, why is Uncle Nathan shouting at you?'

'Bedroom. *Now!*' Oakley hadn't intended to sound so harsh, but Turner might be armed and she had no clue what he was planning to do to them once he got inside the house. 'It's going to be all right,' she told her boys 'Be good and do as you're told.'

The letterbox flapped open again. 'Let me in.'

'The police are on their way.'

'You wouldn't dare call them.' This time he kicked at the door, stopping only to catch his breath before starting up again.

Where the hell were the neighbours when she needed them? If she'd been snogging a man on her doorstep, then every curtain in the street would have been twitching. A maniac smashing his way into her house wasn't their problem. 'They'll be here any second now.' The first siren was soon joined by a second. 'I told you. Here they come.' She flopped onto the bottom stair, rocking back and forth. She couldn't stop. Not even when she tried. 'Hurry up,' she repeated in a whispered mantra.

'I'll be back. For you and those runts,' Turner promised through the broken letterbox. 'You've brought this on yourself.'

Sheer maternal instinct had Sparkes race down the hallway towards the front door. Like hell was he ever going to lay his hands on the two most precious things in her life. She didn't give a shit about her own safety. She'd fight him to the death—like a dog in the street—if she had to. Drawing the chain along its runner, she turned the Yale lock with trembling hands. 'You listen to me, you bastard—'

Turner was nowhere to be seen. Oakley checked up and down the street, but still couldn't see him. She had the uneasy feeling of being watched. Was he hiding behind one of the nearby cars, waiting to pounce if she strayed close enough? Or would he skirt the car and get into the house before she did, locking the door behind him?

That thought alone had her venture no further along the pavement. She reversed towards the front door without turning her back on the street. He *was* gone. Wasn't he?

Chapter 49

Sparkes shut the front door and reapplied the safety catch. Even the closing proximity of the sirens wasn't enough to make her feel safe.

'Best lock it. You never know who's out there.'

She spun on her heels. 'You leave those boys alone!'

Turner was sitting on the top stair with one arm draped along the shoulders of the children. The other clutched his ribs. He was breathing in short gasps and sweating profusely. 'Come away from the door and no one gets hurt.'

Sparkes did as told. '*Please*. Let them come to me.'

Turner curled his arm around the front of the boys' necks. Unspoken threats were often the loudest kind. 'You're fine where you are. Ain't that right, kids?'

'Do what you want to me,' Oakley said. 'But don't harm my children.'

'Don't hurt my mummy,' the youngest said. 'I'll be sad.'

Turner riffled the child's blonde hair. 'Uncle Nathan's not gonna hurt no one.' He made eyes at Sparkes. 'Not if Mummy does exactly as she's told.'

Sparkes throttled a fistful of her pyjama top. 'You're not their uncle.'

Turner flashed a gap-toothed smirk. 'Shame that.' He got up with a squeal of searing pain, still holding the children, still gripping his ribs. 'Everyone get in the bedroom. That includes you,' he told Bridie Sparkes.

Reece got out of his Land Cruiser with Jenkins and Morgan close behind him. There were two patrol cars already parked up, their occupants awaiting instructions. 'I want this whole area shut off,' Reece told them. 'No one is to come in or out without my say so.' He left them to it and walked across the road towards Bridie Sparkes's house. He knocked on the door. 'Bridie, it's DCI Reece. Ffion's with me. You met her on Friday.'

There was no answer from within. He knocked again, while Morgan went to the front window.

'All the curtains are pulled shut,' she said. 'Same upstairs.'

'*Bridie,*' Reece repeated. 'We can't leave until we know that you and the boys are okay. Is Nathan Turner in there with you?' There was no response. 'I don't like this,' Reece said, coming away from the door. 'I don't like it at all.'

'You think he's in there?'

Reece nodded. 'We need to gain entry, and fast.'

Sparkes was sitting on the floor of her children's bedroom, with her back against the radiator. Jack and Louis were cuddled in at her side. 'You have to let me open the door,' she said. 'They know I'm at home.'

'You're going nowhere,' Turner told her.

'They'll break it down. You know they will.'

'Shut your mouth.' Every movement he made was accompanied by a groan, at the very least. The bedroom was at the back of the house. He stood to one side of the curtains and stole a look through the narrow gap. He came away and was more fidgety than before.

'They're out the back as well, aren't they? You can't get away. It's hopeless. You must know that?'

Turner raised his fist. 'If you don't shut it, then—'

Louis threw himself between his mother and her attacker. '*No!*'

Turner grabbed hold of the boy. 'One more word from you and you're gonna get yourself a right good hiding.' He let go again and slumped against the bedroom wall.

'Did you hear that?' Reece asked, returning to the front door. 'It sounded like a child shouting. What are the boys' names?'

Morgan tried to remember. She hadn't entered the names in her pocketbook. 'Jack,' she said. 'One of them is definitely called Jack.'

Reece lifted the letter box. It had a wonk to it. Like someone had tried to rip it off its fastener. 'Jack. My name is Brân. I'm with the police. Everything is going to be okay. Is Mum in there with you?' He waited for a reply that never came. 'Jack, I heard you shouting just now. Can you see Mum? Can you see your brother?'

What are you going to do?' Morgan asked. 'This is getting a bit serious.'

They were running out of options, and Reece knew there might not be a happy ending. 'No kids are getting hurt today,' he said. 'Not if I've got anything to do with it.'

Chapter 50

Reece made sure that everyone understood their roles. 'I know you don't like it,' he said. 'But it's important you do and say exactly what I've told you.'

'You can't go in there,' Jenkins repeated for what must have been the third time. 'We have to wait for the hostage negotiator to arrive. You're not trained for that sort of thing. None of us are.'

'And how long will it take them to find us one of those?' Reece took off his jacket and handed it to Morgan. 'By the time he pitches up and gets himself briefed, Turner might have slaughtered the whole family – kids included. Is that what you want?'

Jenkins looked horrified at the possibility of a double child murder. 'No. But—'

'If he's responsible for Janet Allsop's murder—and it's looking more likely by the day that he is—then you've seen what he's capable of.'

'I know. But you don't want to—'

'But nothing.' Reece was getting fed up with repeating himself. This was the way it was going down. 'You can either do as I tell you, or find me someone who will. Which is it going to be, Sergeant?'

'Okay. Okay,' Jenkins said, looking none too pleased with what she'd heard so far. 'How will we know when you're done with him and the family is safe?'

Reece looked up at the bedroom window. 'As soon as you see the bastard come flying out of that, you'll know all's well again.'

He was only part way down the street when he saw the black Jag approach. He quickened his step and lowered his head, trying his best to look inconspicuous. The Jag slowed as it pulled alongside him. The rear window came down. He didn't take the bait and refused to raise his head to look at the occupants. He was walking in the opposite direction. Perfect. The Jag stopped and then reversed at a slow speed.

'Reece.' It was ACC Harris's voice. 'Wait where you are, man.'

'Chief Inspector.' Cable was in there too. No surprise there. Top brass always hunted in packs.

He pretended he hadn't heard them and started humming a tune in his head. Music soothed him. And drowned out the existence of other people, which was always a bonus. The Jag was still reversing up the centre of the road, parked cars preventing it from getting too close to him.

'*Reece!*' Harris bellowed from its back seat. 'I said *wait!*'

Reece sped up. 'Not now, sir. I'm busy.' He turned down a side street and headed for the alleyway that ran adjacent to the back of Bridie Sparkes's house. When he glanced over his shoulder, Harris was out of the car and standing in the middle of the road at the junction. Chief Superintendent Cable joined him only seconds later. The difference in height between the two of them was exaggerated from Reece's viewpoint. Like a pawn and king on a chessboard.

'If you take another step,' Harris warned with an angry stamp of his foot.

Reece turned to face him full on and pointed at the police helicopter circling overhead. 'I can't hear a word you're saying,' he lied. 'Jenkins will fill you in. She's round the front.' And with that, he was gone. Humming to himself as he hurried into the alleyway.

'What the fuck is he up to this time?' Harris demanded to know.

'Why don't we go find out?' Cable suggested, leading the way over to where a length of yellow tape had been draped across the road, lamppost to lamppost. Jenkins came over to greet them.

'Sir. Ma'am,' she said with a double-nod of her head. 'Are you up to speed with what's happening here?'

'Where's Reece going?' Harris asked. 'Is it true there are kids involved in this one?'

'Yes, sir. Two young boys, as well as their mother. We know that one of the boys is still alive. But there's no news yet on the other hostages.'

'*Hostages.*' Harris closed his eyes. 'And the man in there with them is a known killer?'

'His name is Nathan Turner, sir. Our line of enquiry suggests he might well be responsible for the murder of Janet Allsop.'

Harris removed his service hat and ran a hand over his Brylcreem'd hair before putting the hat back on. 'And what's he doing at this particular property? I read the briefing with Chief Superintendent Cable on the way over here. This address doesn't belong to the dead woman.'

'No, sir. This is an ex-girlfriend of his.' Jenkins outlined the events leading up to the current situation: the arrest order; Turner doing a runner; and the stabbing outside Edward Collier's house.

'What a bloody mess this is,' Harris exclaimed. 'And you still haven't told me what our very own Superman is planning to do in that alleyway?'

Jenkins toed the kerb with her shoe, unsure of how much she should let on. 'Um.'

'I don't give a shit what he told you to tell me. What's he up to, Sergeant?'

Jenkins gave him the gist, but not all of it. 'And I'm to keep Turner talking while the DCI gets into the house and makes his way upstairs.'

Harris went white. Then red. And not long after that, a worrying shade of purple. 'He's going to do *what?*'

'He says he's done it before,' Morgan piped up. 'Years ago. When he was in the Met,' she added, when Jenkins tapped her ankle.

Harris turned to face Cable. 'If anything happens to those kids . . .'

'That's what DCI Reece was most worried about,' Jenkins said. 'We heard one of the boys scream and had no idea what was going on in there. That's when his hand was forced. He had no choice but to make his move.'

'You say you've had no demands as yet from this Turner fella?' Harris asked.

'None at all, sir.'

The ACC looked around him. 'Is the hostage negotiator not here yet?' He couldn't see anyone who might fit the bill.

'They're still trying to get one to us,' Jenkins said.

'So all we have is the mighty Reece to get us out of this?' Harris stared down at Chief Superintendent Cable and shook his head.

She looked away and focused her attention on the battered front door of Bridie Sparkes's house. 'Love him or loathe him, I'd want him on my side of a fight, any day of the week.'

Chapter 51

THE PRESS ARRIVED EN masse. Predictably. There was nothing like a developing hostage situation and the potential of a young family slain to sell newspapers and commercials sandwiched between televised bulletins. Journalists were like flies attracted to a bad smell, and Maggie Kavanagh was there with the best of them.

'Where's my favourite detective?' she asked, unable to find Reece among the crowd. There was a half-smoked cigarette wedged between her nicotine-stained fingers. She brought it to her mouth and drew on it like she was trying to finish the thing in one attempt. The flesh of her cheeks sank against the bone as her shoulders lifted and her chest expanded. Then everything relaxed again, hiding the reporter behind a thick and toxic cloud. 'A fiver says he's up to no good somewhere,' she gasped when able. 'And by the look on your faces, you don't disagree.'

'I'm not at liberty to divulge the whereabouts of individual officers,' Cable said in a measured reply. 'Not when it might compromise their safety.'

Kavanagh bent at the waist, cackling. Then descended into a raucous coughing fit that came close to hospitalising her. She straightened and gripped the chief superintendent by the forearm. 'It's not Reece's safety you want to be worrying about.' She cleared her throat with a wet-sounding hack. 'It's the poor bugger who's daft enough to stand in his way.'

ACC Harris called to a pair of uniforms chatting nearby. 'You two. Get these people back. Move when I tell you.' Both officers came scurrying over, waving their arms at a throng of reporters who were getting far too close.

'I'm not just anyone, you know?' Kavanagh told the ACC. She undid the first couple of buttons on her Columbo-style coat. Reached inside and produced her press card, still attached to its lanyard. 'I'm with the South Wales Herald. I'm surprised you don't know me. You obviously don't get much time at the coalface.'

'I know who you are,' Harris hissed. 'We'll brief you along with the others when we're good and ready.'

'Who's been pissing on *his* chips?' Kavanagh asked the group, before walking away veiled in another thick cloud of cigarette smoke. 'My boy Reece, I don't doubt.'

Knock. Knock. Knock. It was coming from the other side of the front door.

Bridie Sparkes hadn't let go of her children since Turner had allowed her anywhere near them. 'There they are again,' she said. 'If you don't let me go down there and talk to them, they'll have no choice but to put that door through and come swarming in.' That was the thing she feared most. Not only would it terrify the boys, but what would Turner's reaction be to a SWAT team racing up the stairs to arrest him? She couldn't bring herself to fully imagine all the potential scenarios that might play out were that to happen. 'Nathan? You have to let me go down there.'

'You're staying right where you are.' Turner went to the window and checked the garden and alleyway. He looked as far as he could down neighbouring streets. There were police officers in yellow hi-viz jackets standing at all exits out of the area. From what he could tell from where he was, none of them looked like they were expecting anything big to be kicking off soon. He checked the garden for intruders one more time and saw nothing to give him cause for concern. He knew that would change at some point. Wasn't stupid enough to think they'd leave someone with his record cooped up with a woman and her kids. They'd be coming all right, and he'd need to be ready for that moment when it happened.

His eye was drawn upwards, towards the circling black and yellow helicopter. Its side doors were closed. No glint of a metal gun barrel as the aircraft made another slow pass of the area. He ran a hand over his chest—just to be sure—and was relieved to find no red dot marking him as a sniper's target. But there would be shooters out there soon enough. Several of them. There was no doubting it.

Knock. Knock. Knock. There it was again. Insistent and not something to be ignored. It echoed through the hallway and up the stairs into the cramped bedroom.

'Mummy, I'm scared.'

'*Ssh*, Jack.' Keeping everyone calm would be instrumental in them getting out unharmed. 'It's going to be okay.' Sparkes let go of her sons and wobbled to her feet, using the windowsill shelf to get her balance. Sitting in one place for all that time had given her pins and needles in her ankles.

'Where do you think you're going?' Turner came away from the window and blocked her escape from the bedroom. His skin was covered in beads of sweat. 'Don't make me slap you in front of them.'

Knock. Knock. Knock.

'Bridie. It's Ffion Morgan. You remember me, don't you? We had a cup of tea on Friday.'

Turner grabbed Sparkes and clamped his hand over her mouth. He forced his wet forehead against hers and stared into her eyes. 'It was you. You told them about me?'

His breath stank. As did the rest of him now that he was so close. She tried to turn her head away but couldn't. 'It wasn't like that.'

He pinched her chin and kept her head facing straight ahead. There was no escape from those threatening eyes. 'What did you tell them?'

Jack and Louis were crying again, the younger of the two grabbing for his mother's leg. 'They were here about Michael. A follow up to what happened to him and how it was handled.'

Turner nuzzled into Sparkes's neck and put his mouth against her ear. 'Lie to me once more and I'll chuck 'em down the stairs. We'll see which one bounces the furthest.'

Sparkes struggled but couldn't free herself. 'They came here asking questions about you. I never asked them to.'

'What sort of questions?'

'Bridie.' Morgan's voice echoed off the walls of the hallway and stairs. 'I need to know that you and the boys are okay. Can each of you tell me that you are?'

Turner loosened his pincer grip on Sparkes's jaw. 'Tell them all's good and make them go away.'

As if there was any chance they were going to do that. She could still feel the hot breath on her neck. 'I'm okay,' she called with a faltering voice. 'We're all okay.'

'The boys?' Morgan called. 'I need to see them for myself.'

'No way,' Turner whispered. 'They're staying put. Nobody's leaving this bedroom.'

'She just wants to see them,' Sparkes said. 'She's not asking for anything else.'

Turner cocked his arm and clenched his fist, ready to lash out. 'If you don't tell them to go away, you know what I'll do to you.'

Sparkes didn't dare lose sight of the loaded knuckles. 'Have it your own way,' she said. 'But don't say I didn't warn you.'

Chapter 52

REECE HAD NO IDEA what success, if any, Morgan might be having. He'd left his phone with Jenkins, unwilling to risk it pinging and giving him away at the wrong moment. She'd offered to disable the sounds on all alerts, but he'd refused to believe that foolproof.

He was beginning to regret that decision. What if ACC Harris had taken over the situation, withdrawing Morgan and Jenkins, waiting for the arrival of the hostage negotiator? Would Cable let him? She was a career copper making her way to the top in a male-dominated profession. She'd rock the boat only when it offered some advantage to her.

Surely the AFOs—Authorised Firearms Officers—were there by now? Another good reason for him to have had his phone. He needed to be sure they were aware of his presence and not have them shoot him when they sighted a lone male at the window. That could be the answer to top brass's troubles – having him shot and killed in error. The possibility scared him. But not for long. He had to remain positive and believe that all was going to plan round the front of the property. He had two good officers there. They wouldn't let him down.

'Have you seen anything from your position here?' Reece asked a uniform kicking his heels in the alleyway. As he listened to the officer's reply, he couldn't help but think that everyone in the job was getting so much younger. Everyone except coppers like himself and George, the desk sergeant. The reality behind that was too depressing a thought to be dwelling upon right now.

'Turner came to the window a short time ago, sir,' the young officer said with a slight stammer. 'He was looking down on the garden, sir. Like he was checking it over. Then he was watching the helicopter. He wasn't there for very long, sir.'

'And did you see anyone else in the window with him?' Reece asked. 'The woman? Children?'

'No, sir. No one at all.'

That still worried him. There was no guarantee of them being alive. Cornered fugitives—and that's what Nathan Turner was—often did awful things during their final moments of freedom. Some for the sick notoriety of their actions. Others for the sheer evil of it. *Not the kids*, Reece chanted. *You're not having those kids.*

The officer was clearly ill at ease in Reece's presence. That wasn't unusual. The DCI was one of those men who led from the front and demanded nothing but a hundred percent from himself and everyone else. People had to prove themselves. Prove wrong his preconceptions of them. Most failed and proved him right. His simplistic view of humanity was that people—in general—will let you down when you need them most. He knew that was mostly attributable to the three personality types said to co-exist within everyone's psyche.

Type One: was the individual's main and publicly shared persona. Displayed to people in the street. To a broad circle of friends and work colleagues. It was the most false of the three and the one to be wary of.

Type Two: described behaviours and fragilities shared only with those closest to the individual. Family and best friends, ordinarily. It was another to be treated with caution.

The real person hid behind the locked door of *Type Three:* living in a landscape of deeply private thoughts and secret actions not shared with anyone else. A landscape that could be viewed only by the owner and the most competent of psychiatrists.

It was therefore impossible to let go and fully trust people when everyone, including himself, was playing the same game of charades.

'Anything else to report?' Reece gave the bedroom window more attention, picturing its orientation to the front door and stairs.

'No sir. That's it.'

Chapter 53

Hannah Oakley hammered on the heavy door to her cell, and had done ever since they'd locked her in there. Her head was pounding and her mouth felt and smelled like a rat had slept in it overnight. She'd vomited twice more after being unceremoniously dragged out of the van. Not all the vomit had hit the bowl of the metal toilet. Some had dried on the linoleum floor. Some hadn't. 'Let me out. I want to speak to a detective.'

A custody officer padded over from wherever he'd been stationed and lifted a small flap covering the door's peephole. 'If it's breakfast you're harking after, you'll have to wait like everyone else. It's been a busy night and room service has been cancelled until further notice.'

Oakley gagged at the thought of having to eat something. More vodka would do, but she doubted that was on the menu. Not in this crappy one-star hotel. Three years she'd been sober. A tad longer than that, even. And now she'd lurched off the wagon in spectacular fashion. *Thanks a lot, Mum. I always could depend on you to help me screw up in life.*

Such thoughts brought with them hellish guilt. How dare she criticise her mother: a woman who'd been horribly murdered and mutilated? Oakley was in floods of tears again. Who could have done such a terrible thing? Only one name came to mind – Edward Collier. He was the prime suspect in her eyes. She'd never liked or trusted him. There was something about the man that didn't ring true. Actually, there was a *lot* about the man that didn't ring true.

'It's not breakfast I want,' she screamed at the custody officer. 'I keep telling you. I need to talk to the detective on my mother's case.'

'Can't help you with that,' the officer said. 'DCI Reece is out dealing with a serious incident. Most of his team are with him.'

'Phone him,' Oakley insisted. 'Phone him and tell him to get his arse over here. He needs to know about Edward Collier.'

Chapter 54

Jenkins came away from the front door, carrying Reece's phone. 'How are we supposed to tell him that Turner isn't falling for it?'

'Give me a second.' Morgan stepped off the pavement and headed towards a couple of uniforms busy on crowd control. 'Boys!'

Jenkins watched her speak to one of them. 'What were you saying to him?' she asked when Morgan rejoined her.

'He'll use his radio to speak to someone round the back. I've told them to let the boss know that Turner's staying put upstairs. There we go – he's giving us the thumbs up.'

Jenkins wasn't paying full attention. She nodded over Morgan's shoulder. 'Things have changed now that lot have arrived.'

A navy blue minibus with tinted windows pulled up close to Harris's Jag. The side door slid open to reveal a troop of officers dressed in black combat gear. They wore helmets and had the lower half of their faces hidden behind snoods. Each one of them carried a Heckler & Koch MP5 submachine gun and looked like they meant business.

'I'll go and let them know the boss might still have gone inside,' Jenkins said. 'The last thing we need today is a blue on blue event.'

Turner not being lured downstairs hadn't come as a surprise to Reece. The fugitive had little to lose and was unlikely to give himself up without a dirty fight. That was almost good news to Reece, as he was definitely in the mood for a good scrap – so long as he could get Bridie Sparkes and her boys out of harm's way.

He still had the element of surprise on his side. Turner wouldn't be expecting him to break into the house and make his way upstairs. Apart from Jenkins and Morgan, no one would. But that's exactly what he was about to do. Get inside. Get into the bedroom. Then ruin Turner's day.

Reece had been informed of the *cavalry's* arrival. That always made things infinitely more dangerous for everyone involved. The presence of weapons and adrenaline were a bit like gunpowder and a naked flame, in the wrong hands.

'Give us your hat.' Reece snatched it from the uniform in the alleyway. It was a black peaked cap with a narrow band of small white squares running around it. Even though the AFOs would most likely go for a body shot—the largest target—the cap would go some way in identifying him as a friend and not a foe. It was the best option he had available to him. The only option he had. That and the hope of Jenkins and Morgan highlighting his presence. Memories of the night he was shot in Billy Creed's basement flooded his mind with unhelpful thoughts. He rubbed his shoulder and tried to forget the pain he'd been in at the time.

When he was as sure as he could be that no one was lurking behind the curtains, he made his move up the garden path. He didn't zig-zag like he was negotiating a field of mines. Point A to point B was covered in a straight line, and in a head down sprint.

Point B was the back door of the terraced property. He took a look through the glass. On the counter inside were two cereal bowls. One of them had the colourful image of Daffy Duck on it. The other had what might have been Pluto. He couldn't be sure, and it didn't really matter. Next to the bowls were a box of cereal and a carton of milk. The top of the carton had been removed and was lying on the counter next to it. Bridie Sparkes had been fixing the boys' breakfasts when Turner had called.

Reece tried the door. It was locked. The window sash to one side of it was also shut. He prised at it with his fingernails, but there was no way it was letting him through. With the cuff of his jacket pulled over his fist, he checked the whereabouts of the police helicopter.

He waited for it to make its turn and pass directly overhead again, deafening everyone below it with a combination of blade-slap and engine noise. That's when he rammed his hand through the small pane of glass. He put his arm inside and turned the key in the lock.

He waited, breathing heavily and listening for movement upstairs. Then he let himself in.

ACC Harris had Jenkins and Morgan come away from the front of the property and wait with everyone else at the top end of the street. Press and public had been pushed further back from where they had originally been congregating.

'Reece's plan was never going to work,' Harris said with his usual air of arrogance. 'I don't know what he was thinking.' He turned to Chief Superintendent Cable and rolled his eyes. 'Do we ever?'

She was busy watching the AFOs take up their positions, and didn't respond. The moment of truth was nigh.

'They do know that DCI Reece is in there?' Jenkins asked. 'You have told them, sir?'

'Sir?' Morgan this time. 'Do they know about DCI Reece?'

'Of course they know he's in there,' Harris said without taking his eyes off the movements of the AFOs team leader. 'And they're none too pleased with him. Do you realise how much more difficult he's made this situation?'

Jenkins lowered her gaze. She had a sickening feeling pulling at the pit of her stomach. There was enough firepower present to overwhelm a small uprising. She hoped with everything she had that Reece knew what he was doing. Events of the next hour or so would provide the answer either way.

Chapter 55

REECE WAS INSIDE THE house, doing what he could to avoid broken glass on the linoleum floor. When he stepped on a shard he hadn't seen, it plinked under the weight of his dirty boot like a slither of thin ice. He paused. Held his breath, listening for movement upstairs.

There was nothing to suggest he'd been found out. Only muffled movements audible through the carpet and plasterboard ceiling, like someone shifting to a more comfortable sitting position. One of the boys, maybe? He hoped so.

Reece's biggest worry was Turner still having the knife he'd used to stab the man outside Edward Collier's house. He'd have limited time to fatally injure everyone in the bedroom. But even a single casualty would be one too many.

Waiting for the AFOs to smash through the front door and storm the property was no less risky. Reece had the utmost respect for them and what they did under the stark glare of the media spotlight. Theirs was a job he wouldn't do for twice his annual salary. But the fact remained; firearms added another layer of complexity and danger. Firearms and kids . . . That didn't bear thinking about.

He opened and closed a kitchen drawer, then another, not knowing what he was looking for. There was a tea towel next to a wooden chopping board. And alongside that was a loaf of sliced bread, a tub of butter, and a can of PEK. Bridie Sparkes had been doing the boys' lunchboxes.

There was more movement upstairs. This time accompanied by a few lines of dialogue. Reece listened to the man's voice. It was staccato in its delivery. He couldn't make out what was being said, but Turner was evidently getting more nervous with the developing situation.

Reece stared at the underside of the ceiling and worked his fists in preparation for what was about to go down. 'You have every reason to be scared,' he said under his breath. 'I'm coming for you, ready or not.'

Nathan Turner grabbed Bridie Sparkes by a handful of her clothing and did his best to yank her to her feet. 'Let go of her leg,' he told Louis.

'*Mummy!*'

Turner kicked the boy's arm away, which only served to make the youngster cry all the louder. 'Get him to shut up.'

Sparkes did what little she could from her standing position. She wanted to claw her captor's eyes for the distress he was causing her boys. Louis stopped crying, but didn't dare let go of his mother's leg.

'There's something up.' Turner was suddenly more tense than he had been. Gripping his chest, he shoved Sparkes over to the window and used her as a human shield while he checked the garden and sky.

There was still a heavy police presence in the alleyway and at both ends of the street. The garden below and those of the neighbours were unoccupied, as far as he could tell. The helicopter went over for the nth time. Even from inside the house, the noise it made drowned out just about everything else.

The hostage negotiator had arrived. He was no Samuel L. Jackson. Not that Jenkins had ever expected him to be. But five-feet and two inches of bespectacled, monk-cut male wasn't what she'd had in mind when imagining a candidate for saving the day.

Chief Superintendent Cable introduced Douglas Wade to the team. 'Detective Sergeant Jenkins will fill you in on what we know so far,' she said. 'And Detective Constable Morgan will give you background on the family.'

Once the detectives had finished briefing him, Wade removed his over-sized spectacles and cleaned them with a handkerchief taken from his trouser pocket. He held the spectacles up to the light, huffed on each lens in turn, and gave both some additional attention. 'And you believe that all three hostages are still alive?'

Jenkins and Morgan glanced at one another before both nodded in unison. Jenkins spoke. 'We've no reason not to.'

'Bridie's well capable of keeping him calm,' Morgan said. 'That woman's got something about her.'

'And how could you possibly know that?' Harris asked. 'Five minutes in someone's company doesn't make you an expert.'

Jenkins stiffened. 'With all due respect, sir, it's five minutes longer than any of us have had with her. I think we should value Ffion's opinion.'

'And it was far longer than five minutes,' Morgan added.

'Still,' Harris said, looking none too convinced.

Cable got in before him. 'We've wasted enough time already. Let's get on with it.'

Reece came across an open packet of Skittles on the arm of the sofa. It reminded him of a scene from a martial arts movie he'd watched many years ago. It gave him an idea. The multi-coloured confectionary would do the job quite nicely. He poured some into the palm of his hand and couldn't resist the temptation to taste one or two.

He closed his fist and waited for the police helicopter to repeat its routing over the top of the house. He didn't have long to wait. The ground beneath his feet vibrated with the change in air pressure and sound frequencies churning beneath the passing aircraft.

Now in the hallway at the bottom of the carpeted stairs, Reece's movements were completely drowned out by the flypast. He had no clue of how much fuel those things burned during each hour of flight, but from experience knew that it should be good for a while longer yet.

On the helicopter's next pass, he got onto the stairs. Not the bottom one. He stretched and managed to plant his foot on the third tread. Then he stood still, slowing his breathing, listening for evidence to suggest he'd been rumbled. He hadn't. All was good.

The helicopter went over again. Reece counted time and was almost able to precisely predict its arrival. He moved up another three stairs in one go, not having to worry about the creaking sound they made under his shifting weight. His eyes were closed. His senses piqued. He was close now. Nearly there. The helicopter would be back any second. *Come on.*

But it didn't return. The sky above the house was quiet.

He stopped counting, concerned that his internal metronome had developed a fault. The engine sounds and blade slap were way off in the distance and growing quieter by the second. The helicopter was moving away instead of making its usual pass overhead.

Reece was stuck on the stairs. He couldn't go up. And couldn't go down.

Chapter 56

Someone outside was calling to Turner, using what sounded like a loud hailer. Reece swore under his breath. The hostage negotiator's timing couldn't have been worse. One more overhead pass of the helicopter would have been enough for him to get up the remainder of the stairs and into the bedroom. Instead, he was trapped with nowhere to go.

'Nathan.' The voice sounded robotic when transmitted through the device. 'My name is Douglas Wade. I'm here to help get you whatever it is you want from this situation.'

Reece knew the man was talking the talk, but it still incensed him. *A good fucking hiding is what's coming his way.* Even the thought of bouncing Turner off a couple of walls was cheering the DCI up.

'I'm going to ring Bridie's phone in a moment,' Wade said. 'We can use that to talk. Sound okay to you, Nathan?'

Reece was listening to every word. *Who gives a shit what he thinks?*

'Make them go away,' Turner told Sparkes.

'And how do you expect me to do that?' she answered. 'You should've listened when I told you the first time. You're done for.'

Reece couldn't blame the young mother for losing some of her resolve, but making Turner give up all hope of escape was something to be avoided.

Douglas Wade went quiet. Seconds later, a shrill ringtone sounded from the living room downstairs.

'That's my phone,' Sparkes said.

Reece's shoulders rounded over in anticipation of being caught in the act. *Nice one Doug. Remind me to punch you full in the face when this shit is over.* He kept very still, assuming the worst.

'It's on the sofa, where you knocked it out of my hand,' Sparkes said. 'Didn't you hear the man outside? He said he wants to help if you'll talk to him.'

'He's lying.' Turner sounded close to the edge of losing his shit. 'He's one of them. It's a trap.'

'It might not be. Don't you want to know what he has to say?'

'It's a trap,' Turner insisted. 'They're planning something. He's in on it.'

Reece poised himself, ready to strike should Turner venture out onto the landing. He'd have the element of surprise over the other man, but sod all else was going in his favour. *Doug, if you don't shut that phone up...*

'Go fetch it,' Turner snarled when it rang for the third time. 'Any funny business while you're down there and this pair earn their angel wings. You got me?' he said, opening the bedroom window to increase the level of threat.

When Bridie Sparkes rounded the corner at the top of the stairs, Reece had a finger pressed to his lips. He used the other hand to beckon her forward. She almost froze on sight of him. Thankfully, she didn't. He nodded and winked at her.

'Make it quick!' Turner stayed where he was in the bedroom. 'And don't think I won't do it.'

'*Mummy!*' Jack's scream was loud and shrill.

'*Stop it!*'

Reece was able to distinguish a subtle difference between the two voices. It was all the confirmation he needed to satisfy him that both children were alive still.

Sparkes was at the foot of the stairs. She hesitated when her boys called out and shook her head at Reece. He waved her on. 'Mummy's coming as soon as I've got my phone,' she called.

When Sparkes got back, Reece pointed at her and pumped his arms back and forth, mimicking the actions of a runner. He raised his fingers and counted down: three, two, one. Then he charged up the stairs in synch with the returning woman. As he went through the bedroom door, he tossed the handful of Skittles into the air, just as the martial arts expert had done in the film. The fighter had used prayer beads removed from their string, not confectionary, but the effect it had on his victim was very similar.

Turner made the inevitable mistake of shifting his focus from the stranger bearing down on him and the coloured dots raining onto the carpet.

A fleeting moment was all Reece needed. His good shoulder caught the floundering Turner in the midriff, knocking the puff out of him. They both hit the wall and bounced – Turner screaming like a hog in a snare. When Reece headbutted him square in the face, it was all over. Job done. No contest.

Jenkins was as surprised as anyone present to see the front door open and Bridie Sparkes and her boys come running out. None of the three looked back until they were shepherded away by two AFOs training their weapons on the house.

'Get down on the floor,' the AFOs ordered. Not the mother and her children, but the two men exiting the property. One of them was wearing a cap with POLICE written on it. He had the other man in a tight chokehold and was practically dragging him every step of the way. 'On the floor. Face down. Arms out at your sides.' The instructions were coming rapid fire and were not up for negotiation.

Reece knew the drill and how pointless it was trying to identify himself as a serving police officer. That would come once the team had done a full recce of the building and declared it a safe zone. He got down on his knees, flopped onto his belly, and waited as someone bag-tied his hands behind his back.

'What the hell were you thinking?' Harris asked once Reece had been released from his bindings. 'You could have got that poor family killed with your cavalier antics.'

Bridie Sparkes pushed her way in between them and threw her arms around Reece, hugging him tightly. 'I don't know who you are, but thank you for what you just did in there.' She pecked him on the cheek and turned to face the Assistant Chief Constable. 'This man is a hero. I didn't see you volunteering to help.'

'I want to be like you when I grow up,' Jack said. Louis agreed and did some clumsy Kung Fu moves in the middle of the road.

Reece got down on his knees. Once he'd stopped laughing, he put a hand on their shoulders. 'Who wants to sit on a police motorbike and sound the siren in a patrol car?'

'*Me.*'

'*Me.* I do.'

'Don't think this is over,' Harris said, stomping towards the parked Jag.

Maggie Kavanagh had somehow dipped under the tape and was now only a few metres away from the gathering. 'Oh yes, it is,' she told Harris. 'And as usual, you've got my favourite detective to thank for that.'

'That's it,' Reece said. 'Wind him up a bit more, why don't you? He's already looking for something to nail my arse with.'

Kavanagh reached over and pinched his cheek. 'He wouldn't bloody dare put you on a charge. He knows I'd hang him out to dry if he even tried.' She fished a part-smoked cigarette from the depths of her coat pocket and lit it. She took a puff and made smoke rings that wobbled on the breeze. 'How does the old saying go? The power of the pen is far mightier than the sword.'

Reece wanted out of there. He had a murder suspect to charge.

Chapter 57

When the officer on the front desk gestured for him to stop and listen, he expected a warning that Harris was waiting for him upstairs. 'He can take a running jump,' Reece said before the desk sergeant had spoken a word.

The officer looked confused. 'Who can?'

'The ACC.'

'I don't know what you're talking about,' the man said. 'But the guys on the custody suite want you round there as soon as.'

'I've been lying face down on a wet road.' Reece wiped a hand over his suit as evidence of that. And when he showed the palm of his right hand, it was stained with a rainbow of colours. 'I need to wash and change.'

'Hannah Oakley's been here all night,' the desk sergeant said. 'Playing merry hell and screaming for you to go talk to her about her mother.'

'Oakley? What's she been up to?'

The officer pointed along the corridor. 'Best you go find out for yourself.'

After speaking with the people on the custody suite, Reece joined the rest of the team upstairs. The Incident Room was its usual hive of activity. There were phones ringing, people in conversation, and the sound of fingers tapping on keyboards. Over in the corner, a photocopying machine was spitting out sheets of A4 paper marked with the logo of the South Wales Police. 'Hannah Oakley was arrested last night, for public disorder, he said in a loud voice. 'She's in a cell downstairs and none too happy about it.'

'Saves us a trip over to her hotel,' was Jenkins's reply. 'There's plenty more we need to ask her now that Edward Collier's had his say.'

Reece briefed them on what he knew of the incident so far. 'She wants Collier arrested. Claims he's the killer.'

'She's still too close to Turner to recognise him for what he is?' Morgan asked.

'Or she's in this with him,' Jenkins said. 'And last night's escapade was an attempt to blindside us.'

Morgan pulled a chair over to Jenkins's desk and sat down. 'So why did Turner run? If they intended to frame Collier for Janet Allsop's murder, then why not come in quietly, answer our questions, and be on his way again?'

Jenkins shrugged. 'Because he's an idiot and didn't stick to the script.'

'You can't really think that Oakley would do that to her own mother?' Reece asked.

'Human dismemberment doesn't happen often,' Jenkins said. 'But when it does, it's usually kept to people well known by their killer. It's rarely, if ever, carried out by a stranger. Dismemberment is personal.'

Reece perched on the edge of the desk. 'You'd have to really hate someone to do something like that. And to your own mother . . .' He shuddered at the thought.

'Enter the husband,' Jenkins said, highlighting another potential line of enquiry. 'What was it Collier said about Mark Oakley?'

'But did he hate her enough to cut her into pieces and throw them in an underground canal?' Reece slid off the desk and went over to the evidence board. He picked up a red marker pen on the way and wrote four names on it. He circled Nathan Turner's. 'Lets work with what we've been told so far.' He raised a hand when Jenkins attempted to interrupt. 'I know some of it—a lot of it—will turn out to be bullshit. But humour me.'

Jenkins nodded. 'Okay, let's do it.'

'Shall I get us all a cuppa before we start?' Morgan asked. 'I spotted a packet of Hobnobs out in the kitchen. They should still be there, unless one of those vultures has had their hands on them.'

Reece declined the offer and didn't wait for Jenkins to answer for herself. '*Turner*,' he said with a loud sigh. 'Has a history of drug abuse and dealing. Violence towards women. Threatening behaviour.' He wrote each entry in list format.

'Then there's last night's wounding with intent,' Morgan said.

Reece added that to the board. 'And hostage taking, as of today.'

'Sacked for the theft of cutting equipment at the slaughterhouse.' Morgan again.

'And trained in the dismemberment of animal carcases,' Jenkins said. 'Those two facts alone put him way up there.'

Reece was running out of room and used his fingers to wipe clean an area of board. 'He's also the last person we know of to have seen Janet Allsop alive.'

Jenkins swung on the back legs of her chair. 'And it looks like he was extorting money from her.'

'Will you stop doing that. You're going to break your back one of these days.'

'Sorry, boss.'

Reece acknowledged the apology, though knew from experience that it was a habit that couldn't be easily broken. 'That gives us plenty to ask the man, just as soon as he's given the all clear at the hospital.' He drew a line beneath his final entry and turned to face the team. 'Back then, to our earlier question. Was Turner working alone, or is one of these three in it with him?'

Chapter 58

Reece tapped Edward Collier's name with the blunt end of the marker pen. 'Let's start with this guy. What do we know about him so far?'

'Not a huge amount,' Morgan said. 'Except that we're all now familiar with how and when the couple first met.'

Jenkins was already back to swinging on her chair. 'We also know what the daughter thinks of him.'

'And before all that?' Reece asked. 'What was Collier doing then? What was his occupation? Was he married? What circle of friends does he have? What do we know about them?'

There were blank looks all round. 'I don't think any of us have asked him,' Morgan said. 'He's got an accent, but I can't place it.'

Reece had an opinion. 'There's a hint of Yorkshire English in there, definitely. But then again, there's also some place further south.'

'And now he's here in Wales,' Morgan said.

Jenkins steadied her chair without having to be told. 'He's moved about then. Making him more difficult to find any background on. Deliberate or not?' she asked.

'I want everything you can find on him,' Reece said. 'Including the people he hangs out with. You never know who he might be linked to.'

Morgan nodded. 'I can make a start once we're done here.'

Reece was okay with that. 'And find out if he stands to profit in any way from Janet Allsop's death.'

Jenkins took a swig from a bottle of water. 'Wouldn't the house and business go to Hannah Oakley? Giving her more of a motive. Without Janet Allsop, Collier's out of a home and job.'

'That's why we need this information,' Reece told them. 'Including records from the mobile operator. I want to know where our victim was when she sent those texts.'

Morgan made another entry in her pocketbook. 'I'll find out everything I can.'

'And what about Mark Oakley?' Jenkins asked. 'He'd also stand to gain from his wife's inheritance. Even if they divorce, I assume he could still stake a claim to some of it?'

'A fair point,' Reece said. 'Let's also take a closer look at him.'

Jenkins volunteered for that one. 'Ffion's pocketbook must be running short on blank pages by now,' she joked.

'You're not wrong there,' Morgan said, thumbing through the last few. 'Remind me to get another one before the day's out.'

Reece came away from the evidence board and sat down. He twisted in his chair and cast an eye over the scribbles behind him. 'The answer to this case lies somewhere among that lot.'

Chapter 59

Reece was on his way downstairs to interview Hannah Oakley when his phone rang. He sent Jenkins on ahead, telling her to get things set up ready. 'Yanto, listen, I'm up to my eyes in it right now. I'll call you back as soon as I'm done.' He'd almost hung up when a dark thought changed his mind. 'Has this got something to do with the dog? Redlar's okay, isn't he?'

'It's not about the dog,' Yanto said.

Reece carried on down the stairs with his phone in one hand and a folder of case notes clutched in the other. 'Can't it wait, then?'

There was a long silence. Then: 'Those bones you were on about about the other night . . .'

For a moment, Reece had no clue what the farmer meant. Was it a reference to something the dog might have eaten? 'You'll have to jog my memory – but you'll need to be quick. I'm about to interview a murder suspect.'

'You asked if I'd ever found human bones on the farm.'

Reece stopped at the bottom of the stairwell and stood there without opening the door. 'And you said you hadn't.' Or had he? Come to think of it, Reece couldn't remember his friend saying much at all on the subject.

A person couldn't normally shut Yanto up once he got going. Today, he was reluctant to talk; even though he'd been the one to initiate the conversation. 'You caught me off guard when you asked. I was scared of what might happen to the farm if I told you the truth.'

Reece ran a hand through his hair. '*Truth?* This doesn't sound good.'

'I want to do the right thing,' Yanto said. 'It's time I came clean and told you something.'

Reece sat on the steps. His heart racing. His mouth dry. 'I'm listening.'

'I should have done this years ago. I'm sorry. I'm really sorry, Brân.'

Reece had never previously heard his friend cry. Even now, he thought his ears might be playing tricks on him. 'Yanto. Tell me. Whatever this is, we can sort it out.'

'Not this, Brân. There's no coming back from what I'm about to tell you.'

'DCI Reece is on his way,' Jenkins said, placing her phone and a notepad on the table. She removed her jacket and hung it over the back of her chair before sitting down. 'Are you sure you don't want a solicitor present?'

'Why would I need a solicitor?' Oakley asked. 'It's Ted Collier you should have in here, not me. 'Do you know what he said to me last night—?'

'Not now. Wait for the DCI,' Jenkins told her.

Oakley checked the time on the wall clock opposite. 'That's what they've been saying all night. And there's still no sign of him. If I hadn't already met him once, I'd think the man didn't exist.'

'It's just that our conversation needs to be recorded,' Jenkins said, indicating that the machine was currently in standby mode. 'For your benefit as much as for ours.'

Oakley nodded a response. She was swallowing heavily and licking her dry lips. 'My head hurts.'

'Still not feeling well?' Jenkins wondered what was keeping Reece. He'd promised to follow her down and should have been there by now. 'I heard about you initiating the station's newest recruit.'

Oakley looked away and belched. She put a hand to her mouth and belched again. 'Don't remind me. Before last night, I was like one of those people you see on Facebook, celebrating a certain number of days sober.'

'How many for you?' Jenkins asked.

'Doesn't matter. Not now.'

'We can point you in the direction of help. I can make a few calls once we're done here?'

Oakley rested her hands on the facing edge of the table. They were shaking. *She* was shaking. 'I'm going to need all the alcohol I can get hold of just to see me through this nightmare.'

Jenkins didn't want to get into any further conversation without Reece being there. 'I'll go see what's keeping the DCI.'

Reece couldn't believe what he was hearing. If someone had caught him on the chin with a heavy-fisted punch, he wouldn't have felt anywhere near as giddy as he did right now. 'Yanto, do you know how serious this is?'

'I'm not stupid, Brân.'

'Why leave it all these years? Why have you never told me any of this before?'

'I've wanted to. You've got to believe that. But—'

'But what?' Reece pressed.

'It would have been the end of the farm. No one would have bought and sold with us. We'd have gone under for good.'

Reece got up and slammed the case file onto the steps. 'For fuck's sake, Yanto. We're talking about a dead girl here, and all you're concerned about is the reputation of your business.'

'Brân, I—'

'She was only eight years old when she went missing. What about her? What about her poor parents who went to their graves not knowing what happened to their daughter?'

'I know. I know.'

'Crying isn't going to help you out of *this* shitstorm.'

'I was two years younger than her when it happened. Only a kid, myself.'

'We're in our early fifties. You've had plenty of time over the years to do the right thing.'

'What will you do now?'

'What do you think I'm going to do?' Reece was shouting, but couldn't help himself.

'You said you could sort this for me. We've been besties all our lives.'

Jenkins peered through the glass in the door, calling for Reece's attention. When she tried to open it, he used the underside of his boot to kick it closed again. He turned his back on her and waved her off. 'Yanto, I need you to do exactly as I tell you.'

Chapter 60

REECE EXITED THE STAIRWELL and stepped around Jenkins. 'I thought I told you to get things set up in the interview room?'

'I have. I did,' she said. 'There's nothing left for me to do except wait.'

'So you thought you'd go for a wander?'

'No. But Oakley keeps trying to talk to me and—'

'Tell her to wait. She's not running the show.'

'I have, but she's not listening.'

Reece started across the open foyer. 'Neither are you.'

Jenkins went after him. 'Has something happened? Has the ACC had another go at you? He has, hasn't he?'

Reece wished it were only that simple. 'It's not Harris.'

'Who then? The chief super?'

He checked his watch. Then reached into his pocket and produced a ten-pound note. 'Go fetch us a couple of coffee's from the canteen and meet me on the steps outside.' Jenkins was only a few feet away when he called her back. 'Don't skimp on the sugar.'

Reece leaned against the wall flanking the steps down to the roadside. He took a sip of his coffee. It was good. Sweet. Just as he liked it. 'I want you to hear me out.'

Jenkins squatted with her back to the wall; a paper cup of coffee held in both hands. 'I'm already getting the feeling I'm not going to like this?'

'You won't,' Reece said. 'But I'm going to get it sorted.'

Jenkins rested on the balls of her feet. 'Come on then. Hit me with it.'

Reece stared in the direction of Mermaid Quay. He couldn't see it from where he was. There were too many houses and commercial buildings in the way. Instead, he watched the gulls perform their aerial display over the water, envying them the freedom they had. 'This all happened years ago,' he said without warning. 'Yanto's father, Meurig, killed a young girl from our village.'

'You what?' Jenkins pushed herself upright; her jacket dragging against the wall as she rose to her full height.

'I had no idea,' Reece said, pinching the bridge of his nose. 'Not until a few minutes ago.'

'When you say *killed*, is it murder we're talking?'

'From what Yanto says, it was a hit and run. Only Meurig didn't run—not right away—he stopped to bury her.'

'Yanto was in the vehicle?'

Reece shook his head. 'He says he was playing in one of the fields on the farm. With his dog. He heard the squeal of a vehicle braking, skidding, and then a loud bang.'

Jenkins put a hand to her mouth. 'The girl?'

Reece took a deep breath. 'You've seen how winding some of those smaller roads are. And with the hedgerows blocking the line of sight...'

'How old was she?'

'Eight. Yanto was only six.'

Jenkins almost choked on her coffee. 'No way?'

Reece waited for a pair of uniforms to pass them on the steps. 'Yanto sees Meurig carrying the girl wrapped in a blanket. He lays her on the grass beneath an old oak and goes back to his Land Rover to fetch a shovel. Then he digs a hole and buries her in it.'

'And never reported the accident to the police?'

'Nope.'

'What was her name?'

'Megan,' Reece said without having to trawl through a memory bank full of them. 'Megan Lewis. Lived in the village. Nice family.'

Jenkins emptied the remainder of her coffee into some sad-looking bushes on the other side of the wall. 'She was never found?'

'You've seen the size of that farm. And we're talking the seventies here. There wasn't the same expertise or equipment as there is today.'

'Was anyone arrested in connection with her disappearance?'

This wasn't Reece's fault, but he somehow felt guilty by association. 'The girl's father was questioned. And the uncles. It was no different then – still a case of looking at the people closest to the victim before taking it elsewhere.'

'Tell me none of them were charged for her murder?'

'There were paratroopers in the area at the time,' Reece said. 'On exercise. Rumours soon circulated that it had something to do with them. An accident of some kind. They'd have known how to dispose of her without leaving a trace.'

'What did the MOD say?'

'It was the seventies,' he reminded her. 'There weren't the same channels of communication back then.'

'But to leave a family with so many unanswered questions . . .'

'And now it's too late,' Reece said, crushing his empty cup. He shook his foot where a few drips of coffee had wet the edge of his shoe. 'The father spent every day walking the land and died within a couple of years of Megan's disappearance.'

'I'd be the same,' Jenkins said. 'I'd need closure. If only for my own sanity. Even if that meant finding remains and not a living, breathing person.'

Reece knew he would never fully come to terms with losing his wife. But he did have the advantage of knowing what had happened to her. As awful as that was, he'd been there in her final moments, and was given her mortal body to cremate.

'What happened to the mother?' Jenkins asked.

'She never went outside the house once the local police changed Megan's status to missing, presumed dead.'

Chapter 61

Reece was verbally set upon as soon as he entered the interview room. Many hours of waiting in a sparsely furnished cell had wound Hannah Oakley as tight as a coiled spring. Her full tirade came thick and fast and was peppered with an eclectic choice of expletives. The constable guarding the door left his post, ready to step in if required. Reece assured him that they could manage and sent him back to his original position.

Oakley paused for breath, her skinny hands gripping the edge of the desk. Wearing grey marl joggers and a baggy sweatshirt, she looked like any other criminal standing there before him. And that was the purpose of the *System* providing such drab garb. Clothes were a uniform that made it easier to identify where a person might fit into society. Bankers and doctors in their suits. Tradespeople in cargo pants and logo-embossed hoodies. And the gang affiliates showing off the colours of their particular fuckwit allegiance.

Take all that away from a person, then deprive them of sleep and the comforts of home, and you got that bit closer to knowing who they really were.

In Hannah Oakley's case, Reece didn't like what he was seeing. Gone was the woman he'd met only a couple of days ago. A woman who was respectful, despite being clearly upset and grieving for her mother. This alternate incarnation was angry and now known to be violent. But was she violent enough to be involved in a crime of matricide? That's what Reece intended to find out.

'Sit down,' he said, pulling a chair for Jenkins before taking one for himself.

White spittle marked the corners of Oakley's mouth. Her eyes were red. Her cheeks were puffy and stained with smudges of black mascara. 'You've finally shown up.'

'Sit down,' he repeated. 'I'm not starting this interview until you do.'

'I'll be demanding they put someone else in charge of my mother's case.' Oakley's buttocks hovered above her chair, not yet committing her to a sitting position. 'You've blown your chance.'

Reece stifled a yawn. It wasn't contrived. He was genuinely tired after notching up a good few hundred road miles that week. 'Finished?' he asked. 'Only, we can go next door and interview your ex, if you'd prefer?' Nathan Turner's X-Rays had shown he'd bruised, and not fractured, his ribs. It was insignificant enough an injury for the hospital to release him into the care of the police with a prescription for Ibuprofen. and not a lot else.

The news clearly had the desired effect on Oakley. 'Nathan's here? I don't understand?'

Reece hit the red button on the Digital Recording Device [DIR] and waited for its *beeeeep* to run out of puff. He ran through the formalities and legalities required of him. 'We'll come back to Turner in a little while,' he said, skim-reading some of the paperwork. 'Let's start with last night and what you were doing picking a fight with Edward Collier. I'd have expected the two of you to be supporting each other?'

Oakley clawed at an area of her forehead. 'Don't let that snake fool you.' She lowered her hand enough to be able to squint through an open fan of fingers. 'He's nothing but a conman. I saw through him straight away and knew exactly what he was after.'

'Which was?'

She shifted position and leaned on her elbows, massaging her hands and examining each finger in turn. 'He saw my mother as an easy target. A widow and business owner living alone. No family or close friends nearby to keep an eye on things. It was just about perfect for him.'

'I imagine you'd have discussed this with your mother?' Reece asked.

'I might live in Aberystwyth, but I was on that phone to her most days.' Oakley lay her hands palms-down on the tabletop. 'That was before Ted convinced her to stop listening to me.'

'And how did he manage that?' Reece again. 'Your mother sounds like she was an independent and successful businesswoman.'

'She was the exact opposite,' Oakley said. Dad was the brains behind the business. Mum didn't have a clue. That's what made her such an easy target for someone like him.'

'She put an advert in the local paper, didn't she? For a van driver.'

Oakley frowned. '*Yeah.*'

'So, she sought him out. It wasn't the other way around.'

'She wasn't looking for *him* specifically,' Oakley said. 'It could have been anyone. Male *or* female.'

'But Collier was chosen as the successful applicant?'

'Because he's got the gift of the gab. Look – I'm not saying he hunted Mum down, but when their paths crossed, he recognised an opportunity when he saw it.'

'What proof do you have that he was up to no good?' Reece asked.

'I found out that he was a signatory on Mum's business account. Meaning he could spend her money whenever he liked.'

'That doesn't mean it was done under duress,' Jenkins said. 'Maybe sharing responsibility and workload took some of the pressure off running a business on her own.'

'If Mum had handed him anything, it wouldn't have been financial control,' Oakley said firmly. She lowered her gaze. 'I can't believe any of this is happening.'

Reece waited until she'd composed herself. 'Let's talk about the summer barbeque. What did you mean when you told your mother that she'd soon be dead?'

Chapter 62

Hannah Oakley's mouth moved in silence. Then her bottom jaw hung open like a sleeping cowboy catching flies. 'What the hell are you talking about?' she eventually managed.

'You told your mother she'd soon be dead. How could you have possibly known?'

She sighed and rounded her shoulders. 'Ted Collier,' she said, drawing out his name. 'That's where you got this from, wasn't it?'

Reece folded his arms. 'I'm asking the questions. And so far, you haven't answered me.'

Oakley turned her stare in Jenkins's direction. 'I'm right, aren't I? This is all Ted's doing?'

'I'm with him,' Jenkins said. 'We're both waiting on that answer.'

Oakley threw herself against the back of her seat, shut her eyes, and let her head flop back until her neck looked like it might snap. She tapped out a drum-roll on the table. 'Ted knows that's not what I said. Not what I meant, anyway.'

'What *did* you mean?' Reece asked. 'Sounds clear cut to me.'

Oakley opened her eyes and righted the position of her head. 'Mum and I were having a blazing row. Things got said that shouldn't have. On both sides, mind you. I was trying to tell her that life is short, and that she was getting on in years. It was a clumsy figure of speech on my part. Not a threat to her life. Ted would have known that. He's talking through his arse.'

It sounded plausible enough to Reece. 'You really don't like him, do you?'

'That's an understatement, if ever I heard one. When Mum was alive, I tried to be civil to him. But not now. Not after what he's done.'

'Is that why you went round there last night – to confront him?'

'Probably.' Oakley looked away. 'I don't remember much about it.'

'Why else would you have gone there?' Jenkins asked.

'It's still my mother's house, you know?' Oakley's face contorted. She put her hand to her mouth. 'Mum wouldn't have. Please tell me she hasn't signed the house over to him?'

'That's something we're looking into,' Reece said. 'I'd imagine you were expecting to inherit all of your mother's assets?'

'I'm an only child. There *is* no one else.'

'Was it a discussion you ever had with your mother?'

'She once told me where to find the paperwork in the bottom of the wardrobe in her bedroom. I said she was being morbid and moved the conversation along.'

'But as far as you were aware, everything *was* being left to you?'

Oakley's prior bullishness was gone. Her face draining of colour as she made sense of the detective's remark. 'You can't think I had anything to do with this? I made a fool of myself last night. But that wasn't the real me.' She leaned across the table. 'I can't expect either of you to understand what I'm going through right now. My mother's been prematurely snatched from my life.'

Out of the corner of his eye, Reece saw Jenkins lower her head. He had firsthand experience of losing someone well before their time. Just because Jenkins's circumstances were different, it didn't make her a stranger to heartache.

'My mother died only a few months ago,' she said. 'You don't have a monopoly on grief.'

Oakley flushed. 'I never claimed to. But I'm assuming your mother wasn't dismembered and scattered about the city like a butcher's scraps?'

'Last night . . .' Reece said, wanting to avoid a fight breaking out. There was a knock at the door. 'Yes.'

Ffion Morgan stepped into the interview room. 'Boss, can I have a word, please?'

Oakley got to her feet. 'We're not finished here. Not before I've told you everything I know about Ted Collier.'

'This can't wait,' Morgan insisted. 'There's been an important development in the case.'

'What did you find?' Reece asked once they were both out in the corridor. 'Is something back from the labs?'

'DNA results on that hairbrush confirm our victim to be Janet Allsop.'

'But that's not why you pulled me out of this interview?'

'Two things,' Morgan said excitedly. 'That dive team in the bay. They've found another body part.'

'And the second thing?' Reece asked.

'Janet Allsop's phone – it never left Cardiff during the dates we're interested in.'

Chapter 63

The path winding around the Bay's man-made lake was out of bounds to anyone not officially involved in the investigation. Regardless, there were already enough *civvies* present to field a full-on athletics meet.

Some were the usual rubberneckers; there to cop an eyeful of something they shouldn't. The rest of them were from the local newspapers and television stations. If Reece had his way, he'd poke them off the walls of Mermaid Quay, using the pointy end of a sharp sword. Unfortunately, he wasn't having his way and had to push through the crowd to get where he was going.

'No comment,' he repeated for the umpteenth time. 'You'll know when I know.'

There was a blue tent on the pathway. CSIs in white coveralls came and went. A rigid police inflatable patrolled the water with at least two divers aboard that Reece could see.

A uniform approached. 'Sir. They found it stuck in some weeds. On the side of the bank, over there.'

'Who did?'

'A couple out walking their dog, sir. They initially thought it was someone's jacket, and only realised their mistake when the fella got his hands on it.'

'That must have spoiled his day.'

'Just a bit, I'd imagine. The dive team has been out there a while now. Not that they've found anything else.'

Reece wondered how long—if at all—it would take for Janet Allsop's head to be reunited with all the other body parts. He stared out to sea, buffeted by a wind that was playing havoc with the CSI's tent, and knew that *never* was the most likely answer. 'Is that the couple over there?' he asked, indicating two people and a black lab on a lead. He went over and introduced himself. Asked a few questions and then came away again.

Jenkins was waiting outside the tent. 'It's in a worse state than the head,' she told him. 'The pathologist estimates it being about two weeks old.'

'Which fits our timeline perfectly.' Reece knew there was no guarantee the latest finding belonged to Janet Allsop. A spree, or serial killer, might well have dispatched multiple victims in a similar fashion. That was something the city didn't need. He stepped inside the tent and out of the wind.

The decomposing torso rested in an open-lidded container and smelled awful. A few remnants of black bag still clung to it, though most had been lost during its travels. Someone in white coveralls took photographs from every conceivable angle beneath the stark glare of artificial light; a rule alongside the exhibit giving it scale for future reference.

'Chief Inspector.' Dr Gareth Bagshot pulled his mask down his face and hooked it under his chin. 'Not my idea of a fun Sunday afternoon, this. I'm missing the Merseyside derby.' Snort, snort.

Reece was happy to miss any football match. He couldn't stand the amateur dramatics of grown men rolling around on the floor like they'd been shot. Rugby was his game. And boxing in his earlier years. 'Wrong shaped ball,' he said.

'You not a fan, Chief Inspector?'

'In a word – *No*.'

'I could take you to a game and—'

'I'd rather have someone strip me naked and peg me out in the desert,' Reece said, with no hint that he might be joking.

Jenkins pulled a face. 'Another image I won't be able to unsee for weeks to come.'

He ignored her and spoke with the pathologist. 'When will you be able to tell us if this belongs with the head?'

'Someone will get onto it first thing tomorrow,' Bagshot said. 'Lucky them, eh?' Snort, snort.

Jenkins delved into her jacket pocket and produced a small green vial. She removed the cap and offered some to Reece. 'Forest Glade. Should take the edge off it.'

Reece applied a couple of drops to the inside of his facemask. 'Better already.'

Jenkins returned the vial to her pocket. 'Courtesy of Twm Pryce.'

Mention of the retired pathologist's name gave Reece an idea. Pryce might well be able to help with the Yanto thing. He'd ring and speak to him when he got a spare minute.

'You still think one of the family members is responsible for this?' Jenkins asked.

Reece said he did. 'Don't you?'

'What if Janet Allsop was the money behind Turner's drug dealing? They might have stepped on someone's toes.'

'Why make an example of a woman in her sixties? Surely Turner poses more competition than Allsop ever would?'

'That depends on how deep she was into this. Maybe that business of hers was a front for moving drugs about the country. I mean, if you're throwing a party and get an offer of some coke thrown in with your tent – who's going to turn that down?'

'You, I hope. And it's a marquee, not a bloody tent.'

'Here we go again. And the difference between the two is?' Jenkins whipped her phone out before Reece could answer, and did a quick Google search. 'There we go,' she said, reading from the screen. 'There's no difference at all. The term *marquee* is used in the UK. Whereas the rest of the world calls it a *party tent*.'

'And where are *you* standing right now?'

'I'm just saying. You're always making out I'm thick. Sometimes you're the one who's wrong.'

Reece readjusted his mask. The Forest Glade was finally losing its battle against the rotting torso. The stench got up his nose and into his mouth. It was time to get out of there. 'Come on then Einstein, let's go see what Nathan Turner has to say for himself.'

Chapter 64

No sooner had Reece stepped into the building, word got to him that Yanto's wife, Ceirios, needed his help. He checked his phone, and sure enough, there were five or six missed calls from her. He gave the handset to Jenkins. 'Switch the ringer back on for me, will you? I must have turned something off in the settings.'

'You shouldn't be let loose with a phone,' she said, taking it from him. 'Even a three-year-old kid could do this.'

'Do you ever do anything without providing a running commentary?' he asked, heading for the stairwell. 'I think it's gone faulty after one of those update things.'

She gave the phone back. 'You had it set to *silent mode*. See that little button on the side? It needs to be up, not down.'

He dug at the button. 'My fingernails are too short to shift it. What a useless, sodding design.'

'Have a word with Ffion. She'll sort you out with a nice set of manicured extensions.'

Reece had stopped listening and was reading a text that had just pinged through. '*Damn!* That's not what I told you to do, Yanto.'

'Trouble?'

'Just a bit.' Reece turned back on himself with his phone held to his ear. 'I'm needed in Brecon.'

'Now?' Jenkins stood in the middle of the foyer with her hands clamped to her hips. 'Wait. You can't do that.'

'There's no time. Yanto's about to do something incredibly stupid.'

'And what about Turner?'

'You and Ffion deal with him until I get back.'

'But boss—'

'Just do as you're told.' And with that, he went running down the steps, talking into his phone.

Jenkins decided it best to divulge only part of what she knew. Morgan was a gem and a close friend, but she couldn't be relied upon not to drop them in it.

'I hope the dog's all right,' she said after Jenkins's explanation. 'It's like having kids. Especially when they're unwell.'

Jenkins knew it was a lot more serious than that. Reece should have put friendship to one side and dealt with Yanto like he would any member of the public. This really could bring his career to a sudden and unceremonious end. There'd be no coming back if he got this one wrong. And now she was involved. She considered—only briefly—going to Cable's office, to tell all. She had a career ahead of her. That's what everyone kept saying.

'What are we going to do while the boss is out?' Morgan asked, getting up from her desk. 'This coffee needs a quick spin in the microwave. Want me to do you one while I'm out there?'

'No ta,' Jenkins replied. 'Don't forget the spoon this time.' It was a reference to Morgan having recently destroyed the department's microwave.' Reece found the thing lit up like a Catherine wheel on bonfire night and had to explain the cause of the incident to the attending fire crew.

'It wasn't a spoon,' Morgan said, cupping a hand over her eyes in a flush of embarrassment. 'I was warming mince pies for everyone, remember? Only, I forgot to take the foil trays off before I put them in there.'

Reece was hammering along the A470, headed for Brecon. He'd got as far as Merthyr Tydfil and was negotiating his way through a set of roadworks that seemed to have been going on since the year dot. He glanced at his passenger. 'Ruth, I can't thank you enough for helping me out with this. Sunday afternoon as well.'

Ellis reached for the dashboard, steadying herself as the Land Cruiser swung right, then left, before accelerating up the hill. 'So you keep saying. But why the cloak and dagger approach?'

What was he supposed to say in response to that? A version of the truth generally worked. 'It's delicate,' he said. 'What if you take a look at it first? That way, you won't be influenced by anything I say. I can fill in the gaps after that.'

'And the local police are already at the burial site?'

'Yes,' he said, deciding it unwise to elaborate. He gripped the steering wheel and powered the Land Cruiser through a low cloud base that hid anything that was more than a hundred feet away.

Ellis sank into her seat 'Do we need to be travelling quite this fast?'

'I know these roads like the back of my hand.'

'I'd still like you to slow down.' She let out a breath. 'Drivers coming in the opposite direction might not have your knowledge of the area.'

Reece eased off the accelerator. But not by much.

Chapter 65

CHIEF SUPERINTENDENT CABLE WENT to the window at the main desk. 'Where is he?' she asked, propping her elbow on the counter and resting most of her bodyweight on one leg only.

George hid half a Penguin biscuit behind his back and swallowed the rest without fully chewing it. It made him cough. A slurp of tea helped a little. 'And who would that be, ma'am?'

Cable had anticipated such a response, but wasn't put off by George's bluff. 'Your pal, Reece. I saw his car earlier. Taking up two parking spaces, as usual.'

The desk sergeant wiped his mouth and turned to check a bank of flickering monitors on the wall behind him. The images were in colour and of a good quality. He pushed his spectacles along the bridge of his nose, still attached to the short length of strap behind his neck. After a thorough interrogation of the security cameras, he said: 'It's not there now, ma'am.'

Cable stretched on tiptoes but didn't grow much taller. 'I know that. I have eyes of my own.'

'Did you try his office, ma'am?'

'It's like the Mary Celeste up there. And as we've already established, his car isn't on site.'

'That's what Sundays are like, ma'am. People come and go without staying long.'

'Not during a murder investigation. And certainly not when the prime suspect is being held in a cell, awaiting interview.'

'*Ah*,' George said, his whole demeanour suddenly shifting to a more relaxed one. 'Now I remember. There was an incident over on the lake – related to the case he's working on. Maybe he's gone to have a quick gander at what's what.'

'I've spoken to him since then,' Cable replied. 'By phone, not in person, mind you. He promised me he was coming straight back here to deal with Nathan Turner.'

'He must have got caught up in traffic, ma'am?'

Cable recognised a good yarn when she heard one. Her head lolled to one side. 'We're less than a mile from Mermaid Quay and the water. A person could walk it in under ten minutes.'

George shrugged. 'It's a mystery, ma'am.'

Cable marched off. 'Thick as thieves, the pair of you.' She came to a stop in the middle of the foyer, turning to point a finger at the desk sergeant. 'But I'll have the last laugh. Don't you worry about that.'

She went looking for Jenkins next. As the saying went: *the apple never falls far from the tree?* The ambitious detective sergeant would know that she'd be jeopardising her own career prospects if she was in any way involved in Reece's shenanigans. There was no proof yet that the DCI *was* up to anything he shouldn't be. But experience alone told Cable that when he was *flying below the radar,* then he usually was.

She'd phoned him several times already; each attempt going to voicemail. He was avoiding her, and she wanted to know why.

This time she came across someone in the Incident Room. A junior member of the team. A brief conversation took her a smidgeon closer to knowing the truth. Reece had been called back to Brecon. It had something to do with a dog and a vet. Jenkins and Morgan were downstairs, interviewing Turner until Reece got back and took over.

Cable thanked the young detective. Maybe she'd jumped the gun and hadn't given Reece the full benefit of the doubt. She shook her head, dismissing the thought. Who was she trying to kid? He was up to something. Brân Reece was *always* up to something.

Chapter 66

Reece leaned across the front of Ruth Ellis, craning his neck to see through the gaps in the bare hedgerow. The landscape beyond was bleak. Punctuated with outcrops of craggy rock and dry stone walling. There were flat expanses of fields and steep slopes that swept up and into the drooping cloud base.

He had a pretty good idea where the little girl was buried—had once been buried—but was clueless as to where Yanto was planning on taking her remains. The farmer wanted her off his land. It was sheer madness on his part, and without question, highly illegal.

Reece could see three people waiting at the roadside ahead, one of them waving a red scarf at the approaching Land Cruiser. He squinted. It was Ceirios with the scarf. Dr Twm Pryce, retired Home

Office Forensic Pathologist and DCI Dylan Prosser of the Dyfed Powys Police, looked none too pleased with having their lazy Sunday afternoon ruined. Reece brought the vehicle to a full stop alongside them with the engine still running. 'Any news on where he's gone?'

Ceirios was crying. 'The daft sod's done it this time.'

Reece got out, leaving his door open. He gave her a hug and promised he'd do everything possible to make things okay again. 'And the girl?' he asked, stepping away from the farmer's wife.

DCI Prosser answered before Ceirios could. 'I don't know what you've got yourselves into, Brân, but I have to make a phone call. Friends or not.'

'You promised you'd let me see it first,' Reece said, knowing how desperate he sounded. 'I won't touch or interfere with anything. When I'm done, you can call whoever you want. Don't make me beg.'

'I've seen the remains for myself.' Prosser blew on his hands and reached into his coat pocket. His nose was blue. 'This is a police investigation now,' he said, blowing his nose in a paper hanky that was rolled up to the size of a golf ball.

'He left her where she was?' Reece asked. That was something, at least. There would be criminal charges to face, obviously. But moving and concealing a body would now not be one of them.

Prosser sneezed into his hanky. 'I'm assuming he couldn't go through with it. The guilt must have overwhelmed him.'

'I asked Twm to be here,' Reece said. 'And this is Doctor Ruth Ellis. Ruth's a forensic anthropologist at Cardiff University.'

'For what purpose?' Prosser asked with a deep frown. 'With all due respect to Twm, he's been retired for well over a year.'

The man himself nodded solemnly. 'That's very true. I don't see how I can be of any help.'

'And this is a Dyfed Powys case,' Prosser continued. 'If we feel the need to involve experts from out of area, we'll make our own connections via the appropriate channels.'

Reece was trying to imagine how he'd have reacted if Prosser turned up to one of his Cardiff crime scenes with a pensioner and a Charlie Dimmock lookalike in tow. He wouldn't have been too happy. What had he been thinking, getting Twm Pryce and Ruth Ellis involved? He'd wasted their time and made a fool of himself, asking favours of a colleague at a neighbouring police force. No one could go near that grave or the evidence it contained. Not without the appropriate measures in place.

Prosser was busy cleaning out his nasal passages with the same paper tissue. 'Now, if I was to walk a couple of hundred yards up the road to get a phone signal, I couldn't be blamed for not knowing you'd wandered over there for a peak.'

Reece grabbed his colleague by the shoulders. 'I owe you one. Again.'

Prosser freed himself and went in search of better mast coverage. 'Five minutes, Brân. Not a second longer.'

Reece pushed on the gate. 'Ruth. This way.'

The anthropologist had attended enough crime scenes to know that something was amiss. She hesitated. 'What exactly are you getting me involved in?'

Reece caught her by the elbow and steered her across the wet ground, towards an abandoned shovel and a pile of disturbed earth marking Megan Lewis's resting place. 'Take a look,' he said. 'Tell me what you see.'

'You brought me here under false pretences.'

'Would you have come if I'd told you the truth?'

'Of course I wouldn't have. Engaging in such activities could end my career.'

'Even if you're caught, it'll blow over eventually,' Reece said. 'That's how it's always been with me.'

She stared at him, shook her head, then walked away.

Reece turned his back on everyone and stared into the hole. It wasn't very deep. There, at the bottom, were the tatty remains of the blanket Yanto's father had used to cover Megan when he'd carried her lifeless body from the roadside. Once a mustard colour, it was now stained a dark brown with the fluids that would have leached from her corpse. In places, the material had rotted away like the girl it concealed.

He was about to come away from the hole when something caught his eye. He crouched to get a better look. Took a Biro from his pocket and used it to lift one edge of the blanket. What he saw had him fall back on his haunches.

Chapter 67

The chief super had summoned Jenkins from the room only minutes after she'd got started interviewing Nathan Turner. It was clearly going to be one of those times when the messenger got themselves well and truly riddled with bullets.

'And that's all I know, ma'am,' Jenkins said, coming towards the end of her account. It hadn't gone well. 'It's definitely got something to do with a dog.'

'His dog, or someone else's?' Cable wanted to know.

'His, I'd imagine.'

The viewing room was snug, poorly lit, and overly warm. 'There needs to be a senior rank present for a case of this magnitude,' Cable said. 'I know you'll soon be looking for detective inspector jobs, but right now . . .'

'Yes, ma'am. But all DCI Reece wanted was for us to establish a few facts with the suspect. We won't be talking about this case, specifically.'

'What facts?'

'Background and a few things relating to previous employment, mostly. And then there's the more recent wounding charge.'

Cable lowered herself onto the balls of her feet. 'How is the victim?'

'He's doing well, ma'am. Already discharged from hospital, in fact.'

'That's good to know. This whole affair could have been many times worse,' Cable said.

Jenkins agreed. She nodded towards the one-way window in the wall and Nathan Turner leaning on a table beyond. 'Ffion and me are just trying to speed things along while the DCI's busy with other things.'

Cable put her hands behind her back and approached the only exit from the room. 'As you were, Sergeant.'

Reece stood at the side of the grave and tossed the remnants of a leather collar onto the ground in front of him. 'It's a *dog!*' he said, belly laughing. 'Megan Lewis isn't in there. Meurig ran over and killed a dog.'

Prosser was back and came closer, gripping his phone in his hand. 'Are you sure? I didn't see it properly,' he now admitted. 'Just the blanket and a couple of ribs.'

Reece used his thumbnail to clean the metal name disc. 'JJ,' he said, holding it to the light. 'After the seventies rugby legend.'

'Yanto took that dog everywhere,' Ceirios said.

'Even to school, on one occasion,' Reece remembered. 'He hid the thing under our desk until first break.'

'Do you remember Mrs Riddiford's face when Yanto got up and walked it out of there on a lead?' Ceirios was laughing. 'I thought she was going to pee herself with shock.'

'She was a miserable so and so,' Reece said. 'Used to slap the backs of our hands with her bony knuckles.'

Ceirios said she remembered it as though it was yesterday. 'Yanto was gutted when JJ ran away. He cried for days. No one could do a thing with him.'

'He didn't run away,' Reece said. 'Meurig only told him it had, because he didn't want him knowing it was dead.'

'Are you positive it's a dog?' Prosser asked. 'People make mistakes sometimes.'

'Ruth,' Reece said sheepishly. 'I know I owe you one, but do you mind?'

'A bloody good meal is what you owe me,' she said, trudging over to the grave. 'Somewhere expensive.'

Twm Pryce made eyes at him. 'And I'll have a day's fishing licence for the reservoir.'

Reece caught Prosser's attention. 'I'll get you a nice single malt.'

Ruth Ellis moved the spade out of the way and crouched to scoop a small cardboard box off the floor. 'One of you had better take these.'

Reece took the cartridges, while a sickening feeling washed over him. 'Ceirios, this is important. Did Yanto have his shotgun with him when he left the farmhouse?'

She nodded. Then it dawned on her. '*No!*' She dropped to her knees in the mud. 'Find him, Brân. Find Yanto.'

Reece handed the box of shotgun shells to DCI Prosser. 'Promise me you won't call a firearms team in on this.'

Chapter 68

Darkness would soon be making an appearance, and Yanto could have been anywhere on the Beacons. There were hills and quarries. Fields and lakes. Woods and forests. And no shortage of them to check.

Reece's phone had no signal. 'Think,' he said, accelerating away from the field with his tyres spraying muck and grit. The others got into their cars — DCI Prosser, the last of them to get going. And then everyone disappeared from sight as Reece negotiated the first of many bends in the road.

He leaned over to his left and turned off the radio. This wasn't the time for a sing-song. He needed a clear head to think properly. A hump in the road gave him that feeling of weightlessness he remembered as a child—on the back seat of the family car, wearing no seatbelts—he and his sister shouting for their father to floor the accelerator pedal.

But this was no longer a game enjoyed in a rusting Hillman Hunter. This was a life or death situation and Reece didn't like it.

Ten minutes later, he pulled off the main road and onto a dirt track; the light thrown by the Land Cruiser's headlamps dancing an erratic jig out in front of him. The vehicle rocked side-to-side, but it was nothing the Toyota couldn't handle. Even the deep potholes that had multiplied tenfold since he'd last been there were no match for its ruggedness. The same wouldn't have been true of his old Peugeot. That would have shaken itself to death.

The National Park offered Yanto over five-hundred square miles of places to hide. Reece was working, not so much on a hunch, but on a memory. Albeit a hazy one of a drunken night spent in the woods with Yanto and Twm Pryce. After a successful day's fishing, they'd pitched down in a log cabin known to only a select few. The three had pan-fried their catch and finished off a full litre of whisky between them.

The evening had started off happily enough. The trio reminisced about their school days and the trouble they'd often found themselves in. Pryce was almost eleven years older than they were, and so they'd teased about him having to count with the aid of an abacus. And write on pieces of slate. He'd taken it well enough. Had no choice but to sit there in front of the crackling fire, glass in hand, listening to the laughter get louder and louder.

Conversation had inevitably progressed to the girls they'd fancied, but never got anywhere near. There was plenty of fighting to discuss. Sometimes with squaddies from military regiments all over the country. Yanto loved a good scrap and reckoned it was like rugby without the rules.

Then they'd attempted to put their best fifteen Welsh greats together – something they never achieved full consensus on, even after a good hour or so of trying. Yanto would inevitably have something derogatory to say about the English and why everyone in Wales, Scotland, and Ireland wanted to beat them so badly every season. Reece and Twm Pryce would sit there poking fun at his prejudices. Those were good times. Great times.

More whisky brought tired eyes and slower conversation. There were periods of quiet contemplation, punctuated with something almost philosophical. Three orange-faced men staring into the glowing embers of a dying fire.

Yanto would eventually get maudlin. Questioning every decision he'd ever made in life. Worrying about the future of the farm. Worrying about his health. Ceirios's health. The man was fit enough to last two lifetimes, but he far too often dwelled on the negatives whenever he'd had a belly full of booze. *"How do you want to bow out when the time comes?"* he'd asked them both. He was being serious and expected an answer.

The timing of the question preceded Anwen's death and was long before Reece's relationship with her had properly got going. Reece didn't regularly think about death. As a murder detective, he saw plenty, but rarely did it make him consider his own mortality.

Twm Pryce wanted to be wrapped up warm in a blanket and floated out into the middle of Llangorse Lake, in a small boat, with a fishing rod in one hand and a good single malt in the other. "*That would be the perfect way for me,*" the pathologist told them.

"*I'm not waiting for the day when I'm shitting my underpants and forgetting my own name,*" Yanto had so eloquently explained. "*When I decide it's time, this cabin is where I'm coming. Just me, a shotgun, and a single cartridge.*"

Chapter 69

Reece came to a small clearing off to one side of the dirt track. It was as far as the Land Cruiser was going to take him, regardless of its off-road capabilities. He got out and zipped up his coat. The temperature had dropped to not much above zero and the wind was picking up in the trees. He took a moment to get his bearings, then entered the treeline, twigs snapping underfoot on the thick carpet of soft moss. The air smelled of pine sap and something that was more earthy. The deeper in he went, the darker it became.

He used individual tree trunks as reference points; moving from one to the next, and always in a straight line. The thing to be avoided at all cost, was to lose concentration and wander aimlessly. That would be a death sentence.

Tree trunk to tree trunk, he went, sticking to his basic method of navigation. Had he been more tech-savvy, he'd have known that the phone in his pocket had a compass app. He could have simply pointed the arrow in the direction he wanted to travel and – hey presto. As it was, he had no clue what technology his phone possessed, and in his pocket, it stayed.

Something was watching him. He'd been aware of its presence for several minutes now. When he moved, it moved. With far more stealth than he possessed. When he stopped, it stopped. He took a good look over his shoulder, all the while pointing the index finger of his left hand in the direction of the next tree trunk. He didn't dare drop that arm. Not even when the muscles screamed for release.

There were no wild bears in Brecon. No mountain cats. And as far as he knew, no reported sightings of any *Big Foot* creature. Wales was the land of fire-spitting dragons, wizards and warlocks. Bears and large cats weren't so bad after all.

It would be a curious fox on his trail. Keeping its distance. Wondering what the daft human was up to. A couple of owls started a conversation nearby. Reece was causing quite a stir among the locals.

He'd lost track of time—estimated he'd been going a good forty minutes—but hadn't once lost his sense of direction. Ahead and just visible through the trees was the glow of a campfire. Yanto was standing over it, swaying, and swigging from a bottle of something. On his shoulder rested the barrel of a shotgun.

'Any of that going free?' Reece called.

'Stay back,' Yanto warned, and lowered the shotgun to show he meant it. 'You don't need to be a part of this.'

'That wasn't Megan Lewis's body you saw your father with,' Reece said, getting straight to the point. He went a few paces nearer. 'Meurig buried JJ in that hole. He must have run him over when he came round the bend in the road.'

Orange dancers waltzed around the shadows in Yanto's face. His eyes had a glassy look to them—something made worse by the wood smoke rising from the fire—and he clearly hadn't shaved for at least two days. 'There's nothing you can make up to change what's happening here tonight.'

'It's true,' Reece insisted. 'If it was a choice between shooting yourself or going to prison, I wouldn't stand in your way. But you're not in trouble. And you're free to go home.'

Yanto gulped more whisky and wagged the barrel of the shotgun left and right. 'Don't make me take you along for the ride.'

Six to nine months earlier, Reece might have willingly climbed aboard that bus. There were worse ways to go than bowing out with a lifelong friend. But he no longer craved death. There were plenty of things that made him happy now. Yanto being one of them. 'Meurig ran over your dog. Not the girl.'

'You're lying.' Yanto's face contorted with the pain of his memories. He wiped his eyes, spilling some of the whisky down the front of him. 'I saw her in his arms. She wasn't moving.'

'You saw something wrapped in a blanket. When you heard about the missing girl, you put two and two together and . . . You never were much cop at maths.'

Yanto lowered the barrel of the shotgun by a few inches and then brought it up again when Reece inched closer. 'I know what I saw.'

Reece tossed his phone the short distance between them. 'If you can get a signal, call Ceirios. She'll tell you.'

Yanto let it fall to the floor and pushed it to one side with his boot. 'Last chance to piss off,' he said, taking aim.

'You're not going to shoot me.' Reece reached for the barrel. 'I saw the cartridge box. Only one missing. You weren't expecting to need a second go. If you kill me, what then?'

Yanto tapped the breast pocket of his gilet. 'I've got plenty.'

Reece couldn't see a bulge in the material, but lowered his arm, anyway. 'I really need to get back to Cardiff. My boss is going to have me on desk duty as it is. Look,' he said with a deep sigh. 'I brought someone with me today. Someone who knows more about bones than the rest of us put together. She says it's definitely a dog in that grave.'

Yanto sidestepped, struggling to see past Reece and the fire that was night-blinding him. 'I don't see anyone with you.'

'Her name's Ruth. She's a doctor of anthropology at Cardiff University. Twm's giving her a lift home now that she's done giving those bones a once over.' Reece went closer and stood on the nearest edge of the fire. It was warm and felt good when he held his hands over it. 'I'm going to ask you a couple of questions. Was JJ in the field with you that day?'

Yanto swayed under the influence of alcohol and came dangerously close to the flames. 'Aye. He was.'

'Why do you think you never saw him again?'

Yanto tossed the empty bottle to one side. 'Because the bugger ran off. I don't know why, though. I was nothing but good to him.'

'He must have chased a squirrel through the hedge and onto the road,' Reece said. 'Meurig wouldn't have had a chance of avoiding him.'

'Dad killed JJ and let me think he ran off because he didn't like me?'

Reece went round the fire and closed his fist over the warmed metal of the shotgun barrel. 'He couldn't bring himself to tell you that JJ was dead.'

Yanto twisted away and yanked both barrels skywards. '*Bastard!*' he yelled over the deafening noise of the shotgun blast. He let a second shot go and only then turned to face a cowering Reece full on. 'Just as well you kept your distance when I warned you to.'

Chapter 70

Reece had already been warned that Chief Superintendent Cable was waiting for him at the station. What he hadn't expected was her to be glued to a chair in the foyer, watching the main entrance with a hawk-like stare.

'I thought you'd have gone home by now,' he said without slowing his pace. 'You're missing the *Antiques Roadshow*.'

Cable came out of the chair like a sprinter released from the blocks, spilling coffee on the floor. She thumped the mug down on a table covered with flyers for window locks and garden shed security. 'Where the hell have you been?'

'Out.' Reece headed for the door leading to the stairwell. 'Seeing a man about a dog.'

Cable went after him. 'Don't you start that cryptic bullshit with me. I asked you a straight question.'

Reece reached for the door handle. 'I was busy with Ruth Ellis. Ring her if you don't believe me.'

Cable wedged her foot between the closing door and the jam. 'That would be Doctor Ellis? Of the university?'

'That's what I said.'

'What were you doing with her?'

'I'll catch up with you later,' he said, springing up the steps and disappearing from sight. 'I'm running a bit late for something.'

He was more than only a *bit* late, as Nathan Turner's brief pointed out as soon as he set eyes on him. Reece apologised, though in truth, didn't give a damn how long he'd made the two men wait. Friends and family would always come first. Murder suspects and anyone who chose to defend them could keep their opinions to themselves. With the preliminaries over, he opened the interview as he meant to go on.

'Did you kill Janet Allsop?'

The bridge of Turner's nose was held closed with three paper *stitches*. His left eye already bruising. Both injuries courtesy of Reece's Skittles trick. Surprisingly, Turner hadn't yet threatened him with legal action over the short, yet violent assault. But that would probably come at some future point in time.

'Why would I do that?' Turner said, gripping his ribs and squirming in his seat. 'Jan's always been good to me.'

'Did Hannah Oakley ask you to kill her mother?'

Turner couldn't get comfortable, no matter how hard he tried. 'Are you nuts?'

'Not according to my last evaluation,' Reece said with a pop-eyed stare. That reminded him. Miranda Beven had texted him twice in the previous month. He hadn't yet replied. 'Did you kill Janet Allsop on the request of Hannah Oakley? It's a simple enough question.'

Turner leaned away from his brief when the man attempted to whisper advice in his ear. 'No. Is that a simple enough *answer* for you?'

Reece was reading through the full transcript of Jenkins's interview with the suspect. 'You're a man of violence,' he said, dropping the paperwork onto the desk. 'That's what it says here.'

'That was years ago.' Turner grimaced and gripped his ribs. 'I was a smack head back then. I'm done with that shit now.'

'Yeah, right.'

'Straight up.'

Reece scoffed. 'So you're admitting to be completely lucid when you stabbed that man last night?'

Turner shook his head and glanced at his brief. 'The guy came out of nowhere and started kicking the shit out of me for no reason at all. He bust my ribs.'

'Bruised them,' Reece said. 'Don't exaggerate.'

'They're still killing me.'

'My heart bleeds.'

Turner's brief cleared his throat. 'My client acted in self defence. The knife he had on his person is one he carries and uses for work on a daily basis. There was no intent to harm – rather, to warn his attacker off.'

'Keep that for the judge and jury,' Reece said. 'I'm too long in the tooth to fall for any of it.'

The brief's pasty complexion reddened. 'Chief Inspector. I'll be having a word with your superior.'

'*Senior*,' Reece corrected. 'Chief Superintendent Cable is my senior, not *superior* officer.'

'The Assistant Chief Constable then.'

Reece belly laughed. 'I don't think anyone in their right mind would class that one as superior.' He felt Jenkins's hand grip his knee. He shrugged it off. 'I'm just trying to cut to the chase here. It's already been a long day for everyone. Why eek it out any longer than we need to?'

Turner muted another groan as he shifted position. 'I didn't kill Janet Allsop.'

'You took her to the station to catch her train.'

'I didn't.'

'You're the last person we know of to see her alive.'

'Says who?'

'Says Edward Collier.'

'It must have happened then, if Ted says so.' Turner's fingernails clawed at the surface of the table. 'I wouldn't read too much into anything that cockroach says.'

'He speaks highly of you, too.'

'Bullshit is the only thing he speaks.'

'Tell us about the morning you took Janet Allsop to catch her train,' Jenkins said.

'It never happened.'

'Edward Collier had a hospital appointment and asked you to take Janet to the station.'

'You should check that appointment,' Turner said. 'Pound to a penny says he didn't have one.'

'We *have* checked. And he *did* attend.'

That shut Turner up. But not for long. 'I don't know what's going on here, but I didn't take Jan anywhere.'

'Is there any CCTV footage to prove otherwise?' Turner's brief asked.

The team had already spoken with staff at Cardiff Central Station, and were informed that the security system was on a loop that recorded over itself at the end of each week. There was nothing to show for the date in question.

'Lack of footage only means he didn't take her to catch her train,' Reece said, shifting his attention from the solicitor to Turner. 'Where *did* you take Janet Allsop?'

'Nowhere. Like I already said. I didn't work for a few days and hung around the house.'

'Can anyone else vouch for that?'

The brief cut in before Turner could respond. 'It isn't my client's responsibility to prove himself innocent, Chief Inspector. It's yours to prove otherwise.'

Reece got to his feet and collected his things. He lay a hand on the brief's shoulder as he ambled past. 'And that's why I've sent a team out to tear his place apart. See you both in a bit.'

Chapter 71

It took the locksmith no time at all to get them into Nathan Turner's property. The door had been forced open the night Turner had gone on the run and secured again with only a single security device. Regardless of how simple they'd made it, the key to said lock couldn't be found when Jenkins went to sign it out. Hence the presence of a locksmith; who was charging them one hundred and sixty quid for his services.

'Great work if you can get it,' Jenkins said, and did a quick mental calculation. 'Just under five grand an hour.'

'I've got overheads,' the man said with a cheeky wink.

'Get out of the way before I nick you for scamming.'

The hallway was littered with the usual flyers and rubbish that no one ever bothers to read. Most people would walk front door to back door and drop them straight in the recycling bin. Not Nathan Turner. He obviously preferred to use them as a doormat.

The place smelled of damp and when Jenkins flicked the light switch, the glow from above was no more illuminating than a couple of candles might have been. So much for energy saving bulbs. She let the CSI team get in front. 'Once you're given the all clear by these guys,' she told a small army of uniformed officers, 'I want some of you upstairs. Some down here. And at least one of you checking the garden and any shed he might have out there.'

The CSIs wasted no time at all getting to work; checking the walls and carpets for evidence of blood spatter. Once confident there was none present, they led the way into the living room, where there was the same damp odour, and the cloying smell of an ashtray overflowing with cigarette butts. But there was nothing bad enough in the air to suggest that a body might have been stored there for a while. There were a few empty lager cans on the floor by a scruffy-looking armchair.

'This might be of interest,' said one of the CSIs. She was standing next to a large window on the other side of the room.

Jenkins went over and joined her. 'What have you got?'

The woman held the curtains open, exposing the windowsill. 'Two dirty coffee mugs. One with lipstick round the rim.'

Jenkins had an inkling of who it might belong to. 'Can we get it straight across to the lab? I'll give Ffion a ring and ask her to take a DNA sample from Hannah Oakley.'

'You've got the mother's DNA on file,' the CSI reminded her. 'Why not work with that for now? It'll be quicker.'

It was a fair point, but Jenkins knew that any defence lawyer worth their fee would use that to plant a seed of doubt in the minds of jury members. They needed a sample from the suspect herself. That would be foolproof.

'It's routine,' Morgan said, sliding the DNA sample into its protective cover. She bagged and labelled it.

'You're treating me like I'm a suspect in my own mother's murder,' Oakley replied, once able to use her mouth. 'I can't believe you're wasting so much time chasing after the wrong people.'

'I can't discuss the case with you. Not without the conversation being recorded in the proper way.'

'Did you find something of mine at Nathan's house? Is that what this is about?'

Morgan shrugged. 'We can't have this conversation. Not here. Not now.' She let the custody officer know that she was ready to leave.

Oakley flopped back down onto the thin mattress in her cell. 'So I stayed at Nathan's the week Mum went missing. It was more than a one-night stand. There. It's out in the open now.'

Morgan about-turned. 'If you're trying to tell me something important to this case, then I need you to wait until I've organised an interview room and someone to sit in with me.'

Oakley stared at the floor between her feet and tugged at her fingers like she was trying to dislocate them. 'I didn't go away with friends. What I told Mark was a lie. I came here to Cardiff and stayed at Nathan's.'

Morgan let the custody officer shut and lock the cell door behind her. As she walked along the corridor, she could still hear Oakley banging on it.

'That's how I know Nathan had nothing to do with this,' Oakley shouted. 'You've got the wrong man.'

Chapter 72

JENKINS WAS CALLED TO one of the bedrooms upstairs. It was late in the day and she was running on adrenaline and not a lot else. 'Tell me you've found the murder weapon,' she said, entering the room. The stairs had taken it out on her legs and she was still a little breathless when she spoke. 'I can live in hope, can't I?'

The uniform grinned and moved away from an overnight bag that was wedged between a wardrobe and a wall that was missing some of its paper covering. There were patches of dry, flaking plaster. Crumbs of it littered the floor. 'That's not the only powder in there,' the officer said, standing aside.

Jenkins crouched over the aging sports bag. Its zip was half-drawn; the end nearest her, gaping open. 'If even a single spider climbs out of this, you make sure you Taser the sod before it gets anywhere near me,' she said, taking a pen from her pocket. Poking inside, she was coiled and ready to spring away at the first glimpse of a hairy leg. 'Cocaine.' There was also a quantity of pills in there. 'And *molly*,' she said, using Ecstasy's slang name.

'There's far more than he'd need for his own personal use.'

'He must be supplying the party hosts,' Jenkins said, getting to her feet. 'The million dollar question is: was Janet Allsop in on it with him – and that's what got her killed by a rival gang? Or did she stumble onto the truth, confront Turner, leaving him with no choice but to silence her?' They were questions she was asking herself. Something to be discussed more fully with Reece and the rest of the team.

'At least we've got him in custody this time,' the uniform said. 'Murder. Kidnap. Wounding with intent. And now possession and supply of Class A drugs. He'll be an old man before he gets anywhere near a parole hearing.'

'If only it was that simple. We've still got nothing to prove he's our killer.' Jenkins was alert to footsteps approaching from her rear. She turned to see a uniform so wide that his shoulders rubbed against the walls on either side of the stairs, leaving her instantly thankful that he was one of the good guys. 'You after me?' she asked.

'I am, Sarge,' the uniform said in a voice that was unbelievably deep. 'We've found a woman's bag.' He turned and started down the stairs. 'It's in the garden shed. The credit cards in the purse have Janet Allsop's name on them.'

Chapter 73

'How did you sleep last night?' Reece asked. 'Tossed and turned with worry, I should imagine?' He reached under his chair for the first of several exhibit bags. 'Look what we found round your house.'

Turner folded his arms and chewed his bottom lip. For a moment, he forgot what pain he was in. 'Shit.'

Reece had so far only shown him the haul of drugs. 'You've been a proper busy boy. Someone's going to be well pissed off with you for losing that lot. One of my colleagues from the National Crime Agency will be talking to you later. Unless, of course, the drugs angle is what got Janet Allsop killed?'

'Jan wasn't into drugs,' Turner said. 'Why would any of you think she was?'

Reece referred to a lab report in his open file. 'Analysis of hair clippings taken at post-mortem suggests otherwise. She tested positive for morphine and codeine. The pathologist said she'd been taking both substances for several months.'

Turner shook his head. 'They must have tested the wrong samples. Jan was the one who got me off drugs the first time round. Me *and* Hannah. If she'd have found out what I was back into, she'd have wiped the floor with me.'

'The two of you weren't using her business to front dealing to partygoers?'

'Why do you keep asking me that?'

'We've looked at your phone records as well as Janet Allsop's. The two of you were in regular contact.'

'I worked for her. Often, she'd ring or text me with the next job. If the pair of us were dealing drugs, do you think we'd be stupid enough to use our own phones?'

Reece had met plenty of stupid criminals. 'Nice Segway,' he said, reaching under his chair again. 'How did that end up in your shed?'

Turner stared at the clear evidence bag. 'That's Jan's phone.'

'The question I asked was, how did it come to be hidden behind a lawnmower in your shed?'

Turner's head snapped up. 'Like fuck it did.'

'Along with these.' Reece produced a handbag and purse and dropped them onto the table. 'They, too, belong to Janet Allsop. Care to explain?'

'You couldn't have found them in my shed.' Turner spoke to his brief. 'This is a windup. It's gotta be.'

'That handset hasn't been anywhere near Aberystwyth in months.' Reece said. 'Did you text Edward Collier pretending to be Janet?'

'No.'

'You wanted him to think that Janet had caught her train and was safely on her way to see her daughter.'

'No.'

'But you'd killed her by then, hadn't you?'

'This is bullshit. All of it.'

'Killed and dismembered her.'

Turner slammed a fist onto the table. Then wailed and caught hold of his ribs. '*No,*' he said, dribbling down the front of him.

His brief was on his feet. 'I demand we take a break, Chief Inspector.'

'I'm almost finished,' Reece said, placing another evidence bag before Turner. 'I'll save you the bother of looking. They're cheque stubs.'

'What's it to me?' Turner asked through gritted teeth. He was now sitting side-on to the detectives with his knees drawn up and into his body.

'Why were you taking thousands of pounds each month from Janet Allsop? Was she putting the money up front for the drugs? You paying her back once you'd shifted them?'

Turner was sweating profusely. 'I don't feel well.'

'Tough!' It was Reece's turn to slam a hand against the tabletop. 'Neither does that poor woman.'

The brief was on his feet again. 'A break, Chief Inspector. I'm not taking no for an answer this time.'

'Is that a fact?' Reece said, controlling his temper. 'Okay, I'll give you a break. But only after I've formally charged you with the abduction and murder of Janet Allsop.'

Chapter 74

'It's all go this morning,' George, the desk sergeant, said. He offered Reece a crisp from a packet that was meant for sharing with at least one other person. 'Oakley's still playing merry hell down in the cells and now her old fellar's turned up, demanding to know when you'll be letting her out.'

Reece couldn't believe his luck. He'd been spared a trip to Aberystwyth. Not that there was anything wrong with the place—it was a beautiful coastal university town—but the thought of doing a two hundred and fifty mile round trip, with Jenkins bleating driving instructions, was bringing him out in a cold sweat. 'Mark Oakley's here at the station?'

The man himself must have heard mention of his name and came wandering out of a waiting room. 'Are you the detective in charge?'

'I'm DCI Reece. And yes, I'm the Senior Investigating Officer for this case.' He led the way to an interview room that wasn't in use and pulled a seat for Oakley to sit down. 'Can I get you some water?'

'I must have had a litre of the stuff while I was waiting for you.'

Reece couldn't help but interpret that as a subtle dig. 'I've been busy interviewing a suspect,' he said as a fact and not an apology.

'Nathan Turner?'

'I'm not at liberty to say.'

'I wouldn't blame you for thinking they were in it together. Him and Hannah.' Oakley leaned against the back of his seat and left it at that.

Reece studied him. Detective work involved sifting through all the bullshit and red herrings in pursuit of the truth. What was this man's motive for suggesting his wife could be somehow involved in the murder of her own mother? 'Is she capable of such a thing?'

'All of us are capable of murder, Chief Inspector. I've read up on you. I know what happened in Rome.' He held Reece's eye. 'Don't tell me that given the opportunity, you wouldn't have taken the life of the man who killed Anwen. It *was* Anwen, wasn't it?'

Reece swallowed. Images of his dying wife flashed in quick succession on the reverse side of his eyelids. He balled his fists and focused on his breathing 'Could Hannah kill her mother?'

'Turner has a spell over her,' Oakley said. 'And he always did. When they were teenagers; after her father died; and even now.

She thinks I don't know what they've been up to.' He tapped the tabletop with a finger. 'But when Janet was murdered, Hannah was here in Cardiff with *him*.'

Morgan had already informed Reece of Hannah Oakley's admission of infidelity, and so the comment didn't come as a total surprise. But it did make him think about what the husband had to say. 'Were you aware that Collier had recently been added to the list of named company directors?'

'Ted, a director? That's news to me.'

'Did Hannah know?'

'If she did, she never let on to me. Probably told Turner though.'

'Let's talk about you,' Reece said.

'What's there to say?'

'Is it true you hated your mother-in-law?'

'Is that what Hannah said?'

'It was Edward Collier, actually.'

Oakley threw his head back and chuckled. 'I wouldn't take much heed of anything *he* has to say.'

'You're not a fan?'

'Let me tell you something. Edward Collier is one slippery fish.'

Chapter 75

'I've just been talking to your husband,' Reece said, lowering himself onto the thin blue mattress in Hannah Oakley's cell. 'Is it okay if I sit here?'

She slid a few inches further away from him, making room. 'Mark's in Cardiff?'

Reece leaned his back against the cold tiles. Police cells were designed with little regard for the creature comforts most people were accustomed to. The lighting coming from above was a stark white. He couldn't look at it for long without it hurting his eyes. He blinked and lowered his head. 'Mark knows about you being with Nathan Turner recently, and not where you said you were when your mother went missing.'

Oakley got up and paced near the doorway. Wall to wall could be covered in no more than four steps. 'He never confronted me.'

'He's saying plenty about it now. And none of it supportive. He even wondered if you and Nathan Turner had made some kind of love pact and killed your mother together.'

Oakley looked incredulous. 'He said that?' She wiped her eyes on the back of her hand. Reece gave her a paper hanky. A lucky find in his suit pocket. 'I don't blame him,' she said, sitting down again. 'I've been a shit wife. Mark never stood a chance. There's something about Nathan. Something that makes him exciting to be around. There always was. It's what attracted me to him in the first place.'

'But he got you into drugs and alcohol. That could easily have ruined your life. Or ended it prematurely.'

'Everyone was at it back then. Parties. Raves. Anything to drag you away from the humdrum of everyday life. Me doing drugs had nothing to do with Nathan. If I hadn't been getting my gear from him, it would've been from any one of a hundred other people. And he always supplied me with stuff that was safe.'

Reece had smoked a few spliffs in his time. Nothing stronger. 'There's no such thing,' he said.

'You know what I mean. He was looking out for me.'

'He was looking out for himself.'

'Aren't we all, Chief Inspector?'

Reece knew that was probably true. His thoughts drifted back to the three different personality types. There were no prizes for guessing which one they were talking about. 'Maybe.'

'Nathan may be a lot of things. But a killer, he isn't.'

Reece slid off the mattress, his backside aching after only a few minutes of sitting on it. It was time for him to get going. There was plenty to do. 'Saturday night,' he said, while waiting to be let out. 'Nathan Turner stabbed an innocent man. Sunday morning, while on the run, he held a mother and her two young children hostage in their own home. Whether you're willing to accept it or not, that's one nasty piece of work you're defending.'

Chapter 76

Reece finished updating the team and sat waiting for the questions to roll in. His wait wasn't a long one.

'You're letting Hannah Oakley go?' For once, Jenkins had all four legs of her chair safely planted on the carpet tiles. 'What's changed since yesterday?'

'I said she was someone we needed to consider. You know I always push the importance of keeping an open mind. I'm now satisfied she had nothing to do with this.'

Chief Superintendent Cable looked as confused as Jenkins did. 'And on what grounds are you letting her go?'

'On the grounds of there being nothing I can see linking her to the crime.'

'Apart from her still shagging Turner.' Jenkins nodded at the chief super. 'Sorry ma'am. It just came out that way.'

'I've heard worse,' Cable said with a subtle shake of her head.

Reece hadn't finished. 'And we've run out of time. It was either charge the woman, apply to extend her custody period, or let her go.'

'And you went for the latter,' Cable said. 'Without discussing it with me first.'

'And what would you have done?' Reece asked testily. 'Agreed on an extension from thirty-six to ninety-six hours? I didn't think so.'

'You should still have informed me of your intentions.'

'I just did. I only made the decision a few minutes ago.'

Cable's lips retracted, showing off her teeth like a terrier set for a fight. She hid them away again. 'Let's move on.'

'I've spoken to Hannah's husband,' Reece said. 'Here at the station. He's taking her back to the hotel. I've told them both to stay in Cardiff until I say otherwise.'

Jenkins tutted. 'Let's hope room service don't find his head bobbing about in the fish tank.' She didn't dare look up and make eye contact.

'What about their daughter?' Cable asked. 'She's only fifteen, isn't she?'

'Mark's parents have gone to stay with her in Aberystwyth,' Reece said. 'She can carry on with school that way.'

Morgan turned to a screen on the wall and used a handheld device to select and display the images she required. 'Here are the bank details you wanted. Apologies, but things might be getting a tad more complicated on that front.'

'Who's Arthur Potts?' Reece asked, squinting to read the name from where he was. 'Do we know him?'

'Nope,' Morgan said. 'But *his* is the account those cheques were paid into. He's not with the same bank as Janet Allsop, so it was a bit of a faff following the trail. But I got there in the end.'

Reece scratched his chin. 'There was nothing paid into Nathan Turner's account?'

'He's got no more than twelve quid in that, according to the manager at the bank. This Potts guy, on the other hand, has close to a hundred thousand.'

Reece could smell the makings of a chase. 'Did they give you an address for him?'

'That's the thing,' Morgan said. 'They did, but I haven't been able to find it.'

Reece lowered his head. 'Here we go.'

'It seems the account was set up using an address that was nothing more than a plot of land with a demolished bungalow on it.'

'Don't you need proof of identity to set up a UK bank account?' Jenkins asked. 'Like a passport or driver's licence.'

'And a recent utility bill,' Cable said. 'That's what my local branch insisted on.'

'Who owns the plot of land?' Reece instinctively knew that he wasn't going to like the answer and screwed his eyes shut in anticipation.

Morgan selected another image; this one showing a photocopy of Land Registry details. 'This man. Simon Richardson.'

Reece clamped his head in his hands. 'And where does *he* live?'

Morgan pulled a face. 'Flat Twelve B doesn't exist in that particular high-rise block. I've already checked with the company dealing with all lettings there. It's twelve, then thirteen. Definitely no Twelve B.'

Chapter 77

THE DAY WAS FLYING by. It was already getting dark. Reece had left the team preparing for Nathan Turner's court appearance the following morning while he went to update Edward Collier. It wasn't only a courtesy call. He had questions regarding the toxicology findings in Janet Allsop's hair clippings. Had Collier ever heard his partner mention the names of Arthur Potts or Simon Richardson?

Reece pulled up in front of number twenty-six and turned the engine off. There were no lights on at the front of the property. He sat listening to the engine tick and click as it cooled in the early evening air. It wasn't raining for once. That was a miracle in itself. He got out and walked up the path. Knocked on the front door and waited. He checked the living room window. Reversed a few steps and checked the bedrooms.

He went round the side of the property to make sure, but couldn't get past the tall wooden gate. Standing on tiptoe, he saw no light thrown from the kitchen onto the patio slabs or garden lawn beyond. Collier wasn't in. Absence of his van confirmed that.

Back inside the Land Cruiser, Reece had a decision to make. Should he go home to Brecon and catch up with Yanto and Redlar, or should he head out to Cowbridge on a hunch that Collier might have gone there following his visit from Hannah Oakley?

With his decision made, he swung the Toyota around in the road. Cowbridge, it was.

Reece eventually found a place to park. Having such a large vehicle did have some disadvantages. The solitary space was a couple of streets away from Collier's house, and yes, it had started drizzling again. Would it ever stop? he wondered. Would it flush more of Janet Allsop's remains into the lake on Cardiff Bay? There was no way of him knowing the answer to either of those questions.

His approach to the property brought him towards it from the street behind. And then a shorter distance alongside it. There was a light on in the kitchen. His hunch about Collier staying at the Cowbridge property had been a sound one. He was congratulating himself when a woman appeared in the window. Reece had never seen her before. She held a glass of something in her hand and was talking to someone over her shoulder.

Reece stopped where he was. A man came and rested his chin on the woman's shoulder. Brought his hand around the front of her, letting her sip from his wineglass. It wasn't just any man. Even from his vantage point outside, Reece could clearly tell that he was looking at Edward Collier. Collier was now also staring at him.

'You've got some explaining to do,' Reece said under his breath.

Collier straightened and withdrew from sight. As did the unidentified woman.

Reece sped up. He'd gone only a few yards further when someone stepped out of the shadows and struck him from behind. Everything in his line of sight coned in and went dark.

Chapter 78

'Did you arrest him?' Reece wanted to know. He was leaning on the rear edge of the ambulance, between its open back doors, holding a cold compress to the back of his head. Everything nearby was drowned in blue light.

'Arrest who?' Jenkins asked.

'Collier.'

'For what?'

Reece got up. 'For *this!*' He groaned and immediately sat down again.

'Why would Edward Collier assault you?'

'Because I caught him with a woman. Just now. Before he snuck down the garden path and hit me from behind.'

'Do you mean *that* woman?' Jenkins asked, nodding at someone in conversation with a uniformed officer. 'She's his sister. I've already spoken to her. While you were having a lie down.'

'I wasn't lying down,' Reece said. 'I was spark out.'

'She's visiting. Collier's shaken up by everything that's gone on these past few weeks.'

Reece checked the compress for signs of bleeding. There wasn't any. 'I'll do more than shake him up once I'm rid of this headache.'

'It wasn't him who hit you. He went to the front door to let you in and when you didn't show up, he came round here and found you on the side of the road.'

'He's talking bollocks. Why are you listening to him?'

'He phoned the ambulance. Why would he do that if he'd just assaulted you?'

Reece rolled his eyes. 'To deflect the blame.'

'Okay then. Why did he stop at a single blow?' Jenkins asked. 'He could just as easily have finished you off.'

'I don't know,' Reece said. 'But I do know what I saw. And if that's his sister, I'm glad I'm not part of their family.'

'Meaning?'

'Meaning he just about had his hand up her skirt when he caught me watching him.'

'Why don't you let them take you to the hospital for a proper check over?'

'You think I'm seeing things? I saw what I saw *before* he hit me, remember? Explain that one.'

'Maybe your recall of what you saw is inaccurate. You really should go and see a doctor.'

'I'm not going to hospital.' Reece jabbed a finger in Collier's direction. 'I'm having some serious doubts about that one. He's really got my paydar rigging.'

'Boss, what are you doing?' Jenkins caught him by the elbow as he walked off on unsteady legs. 'You're mixing up your words.'

'Arthur Potts sends his regards,' Reece shouted along the pavement. Edward Collier didn't react to hearing mention of the name. 'And *what's-his-face* Robinson.'

'Richardson,' Jenkins corrected. 'The man's name is Simon Richardson. Not Robinson.'

Reece sank on one knee. 'What's happening to my legs?'

Unable to support the DCI's full weight, Jenkins fell to the pavement with him. 'Paramedic!' she called. 'Paramedic – over here.'

Chapter 79

Reece had spent the night in hospital with a concussion and a raging headache. The CT imaging of his brain had returned a normal result, leading Jenkins to joke that the machine must have been faulty. Reece didn't see the humour in her comment and sent her away so that he could get some sleep prior to Nathan Turner's appearance in court the next day.

Study of all available CCTV in the Cowbridge area had provided pedestrian and traffic movements that were of interest to the police. Images that resulted in the arrest of Mark Oakley.

'What do you have to say for yourself?' Jenkins asked. 'That's you walking to and from the scene of the assault on DCI Reece. And that's your car parked only two streets away. If you look at the digital times in the top right corner, they're bang on.'

Oakley pinched the bridge of his nose. 'I didn't mean to hit or hurt him. You've got to believe me.'

'I'll do no such thing,' Jenkins said firmly. 'All you've done so far is peddle a pack of lies.'

He raised his arms at his sides. 'What have I said that isn't true?'

'What were you up to last night?' Morgan asked. 'Why were you lurking behind Edward Collier's house?'

'Your boss told me that Ted was spreading rumours about me. Saying I hated Jan. That I might have had something to do with her murder.'

'And did you?'

'I've been through this already.'

'Let's go through it again,' Jenkins said.

'How many more times?'

'However many it takes for me to believe you.'

Oakley leaned on his elbows. 'I went to confront Ted. To have it out with him, man-to-man.'

'Why?'

'Because Janet was my daughter's grandmother. What's Lucy going to think of me if she ever got to hear the rubbish he's been peddling?'

'How did you know where in Cowbridge he lived?' Morgan asked. 'I'm assuming you never got an invite to go round there?'

'Hannah had me drive past it one day. The address had come up in a conversation she'd had with Janet.'

'She never did trust Ted and wanted to know where he lived. Just in case.'

'Let's get back to last night,' Jenkins said. 'You never got as far as Collier's front door?'

'I didn't get a chance. When I came round the corner, your boss was standing only a few feet away from me. He was looking over the garden wall.'

'You hit him before he saw you.'

'I was *here* earlier in the day. I knew he'd recognise me.'

'So, you hit him,' Jenkins repeated. 'With what?'

'I panicked. Is he all right?'

'No thanks to you. What did you hit him with?'

Oakley lowered his head and was barely audible when he spoke. 'One of those metal water bottles. That's all I had with me.'

'And then you legged it?'

'I didn't have much choice.'

'Without getting even with Edward Collier?'

'I couldn't have got anywhere near Ted, as it turns out. He had company – of the female kind.'

Chapter 80

CABLE TOOK TWO ASPIRIN without water and sat staring at the ceiling tiles. 'Can someone *please* explain to me what's going on in this case? Why can't we ever have a bog-standard murder to investigate? One victim. One suspect. All over in a couple of days, and with the minimum amount of drama?'

Morgan raised her hand. 'Fingers crossed for next time, ma'am.'

Jenkins elbowed her, and not too discreetly. 'What do we do about Nathan Turner? He's due in court in just over an hour.'

'None of this calls his guilt into question,' Cable said. 'Does it?' Her eyes darted from one of them to the other. 'Am I missing something here?'

'Only that DCI Reece was right about Collier being with another woman last night. And if Mark Oakley is to be believed, their claims of her being Collier's sister are untrue.'

'Collier was having an affair.' Cable put the aspirin pot back in the drawer of her desk and closed it. 'There's plenty of that going around.'

'It does put into question the reliability of everything else he's told us,' Jenkins said. 'Maybe we should take a closer look at him?'

Cable picked flecks of fluff from the sleeves of her service uniform. 'Study the evidence. We have firsthand experience of Turner's character and what he's capable of when he thinks he's been cornered. Janet Allsop confronted him over the drugs, threatened to sack him, or to hand him in to us. That gives him several good reasons to kill her.'

Jenkins pursed her lips. 'I don't know, ma'am. I think we should—'

'Allsop's bag, phone, purse. All found hidden in Turner's shed. How else would it have got there?'

'The more I think about it, the more staged it looks,' Jenkins said. 'Why would he hide her belongings on his own property? Why keep any of it at all? The bag would have cost about a tenner, new. The phone was ancient.'

'As trophies,' Cable said.

'Not personal enough,' was Jenkins's opinion. 'He'd have taken a lock of hair, or a fingernail.'

'Who says he didn't?'

'We searched that house, top to bottom. We'd have found something if he had.'

'You did, Sergeant. In the garden shed.'

Jenkins knew when to quit. 'Are we still taking him to court on a charge of murder?'

Cable's eyes widened. 'What sort of question is that? Of course we are.'

'Ma'am.'

'He's pleading, not guilty, I'm told.'

'He is, ma'am. Obviously, the charges for the other crimes will be heard separately – not to prejudice this case.'

'We'll seek to have him remanded in custody, awaiting trial,' Cable said. 'On the grounds he poses a potential danger to family members and witnesses.'

Chapter 81

'Where's my car?' Reece's throat was dry and his voice had a croak to it. He'd snored most of the night according to several neighbouring patients. He'd apologised and then discharged himself from hospital before the medical staff had arrived to conduct their morning rounds. It was only when he'd gone as far as the exit corridor on the lower ground floor that the possibility of his Land Cruiser still being parked in Cowbridge struck him.

'I drove it back to the station last night,' Jenkins told him over the phone. 'Don't you remember giving me the keys?'

There were people talking loudly in the corridor. Then a fire alarm sounded from a red box on the wall above him. It was shrill and annoyingly insistent, and made his head hurt.

'It's Tuesday morning,' one of the porters told a worried-looking visitor. 'A routine test. It'll stop soon enough.'

'Hang on,' Reece barked into his phone. 'It's like a sodding disco in here. Let me get outside before my head explodes.'

'They've let you go home?' Jenkins asked. She sounded concerned. Worried, even.

'Not exactly. But it's not up to them.'

'Tell me you didn't sign yourself out?'

'I'm going back to Collier's house. The one at the Cowbridge address. I know what I saw last night; bang on the head or no bang on the head.'

'Mark Oakley saw the exact same thing,' Jenkins told him. 'I'm sorry I didn't believe you at the time. You were a bit mixed up. Talking gobbledegook.' She brought him up to speed with their earlier conversation. 'He was there to have it out with Collier. When you turned up, he panicked.'

'Oakley hit me?'

'He's owned up to it. At least three surveillance cameras put him in the area at the time. He couldn't really plead his innocence.'

'Did you say he saw that woman in the kitchen window?'

'His statement is typed, signed and dated.'

'You've nicked Collier?'

Jenkins's silence on the line was a clear indication that she hadn't.

Reece swung a boot at a plastic bottle as it rolled down the incline towards him. Then raised a hand in apology to the man who'd almost taken the bottle full in the face. 'This other woman changes things. Collier loses credibility as the grieving partner. It also presents another potential motive.'

'Not in the chief super's eyes.' Jenkins sped through her earlier conversation with Cable. 'Turner's on his way to court as we speak. I'm there, standing outside, waiting for the CPS solicitor to come speak to me.'

Reece stepped off the pavement, waving his arm at an approaching taxi. 'When you're done in court, come and find me in Cowbridge. And get one of the others to rustle up a forensics team and search warrant.'

Chapter 82

Reece's promise of a twenty quid tip for the journey had the taxi travelling at "*warp speed.*"

'Shame you haven't got one of those blue lights I could stick on the roof,' the driver said with only one hand gripping the twelve o'clock position on the steering wheel. He was using the other hand to reposition the mirror, so that he could see his fare on the back seat.

Reece checked his seat belt was properly fastened. 'You only get the money if we're not killed on the way there.'

'Relax,' the man told him, swerving around a kid on a bicycle. 'Today's going to be a good day. When I was back in Mumbai—'

Reece patted his chest. 'I keep a gun under this jacket. Just shut up and drive.'

With the cab driver remunerated as promised, Reece knocked on Collier's front door.

'You've not long missed him,' came a voice from across the street.

Reece went over. 'You know the man who lives there?'

The neighbour shook his head. 'He's a right miserable so-and-so. Never talks to anyone. And he comes and goes at all hours of the day and night.'

A middle-aged woman appeared in the doorway behind her husband. 'Are you two talking about *Van-Man*?'

'Edward Collier,' Reece said. 'Have you had much to do with him?'

'Not recently. I made the mistake, once, of accepting a parcel when he was out,' the woman said. 'There was no thanks. No polite conversation. He just looked straight through me and shut the door.' She turned and went inside, only to reappear a few seconds later. 'That wasn't the name on the parcel,' she said, staring across the road like she was checking she had the correct address. 'It definitely wasn't for an Edward Collier.'

Reece knew the package could have been delivered in error. Or taken by Collier as a favour to someone who didn't want a birthday surprise spoiled by prying eyes. But he couldn't stop thinking about those names Morgan had come across during her property searches.

He took a scrap of paper from his trouser pocket. 'Arthur Potts?' he asked. 'Or a Simon Richardson?'

'Nothing like that,' the woman said, looking to her husband for help. 'It was Irish sounding, wasn't it?'

The man scratched his head. 'Brady,' he said after a good think. 'Like the Moors murderer.'

'And the first name?' Reece pressed.

'It wasn't Ian.' The man's smile was short-lived. 'Um, Gerald. Gerry. That's it – Gerry. Gerry Brady.'

'You've got it,' his wife said. 'You joked about him being a member of the IRA.'

'Is that what this is about?' the man asked, looking decidedly less chirpy. 'He hasn't got a bomb factory on the go over there, has he?'

Reece was already on his phone to the station. 'Gerry Brady,' he told Morgan when she answered. 'Look him up using anything you can get your hands on. Election rolls, population census. I want an address for him.'

Chapter 83

THERE HAD BEEN A sudden change of plan. Reece was no longer waiting in Cowbridge for Jenkins and the forensics team to arrive. According to Morgan's hurried enquiries, Gerry Brady owned a second property: a flat in Raglan House, Westgate Street. It was directly across the road from the castle.

As soon as he got the news, Reece recalled his wet and muddy conversations with Huw Jones. The ground under Westgate Street was riddled with tunnels and hidden waterways. Could the dismembered body parts have been disposed of in a storm drain, then flushed onwards by the torrents of water generated by more than a fortnight's downpours?

'Do you know a Gerry Brady?' Reece asked the person who let him into the building. 'He's got a flat here. Up on the third floor.'

The woman might have been a Chinese national. Or Nepalese, perhaps. It didn't matter. She couldn't understand a word of what he was asking of her. He gave up trying variations of what he'd said and made his way to the third floor in search of Brady's flat.

He found it within minutes and put his ear to the door. There were no noises on the other side to suggest that anybody was at home. What he *could* hear were vehicles drawing up outside the building. Car doors slamming shut. People talking in loud voices. Jenkins being the loudest of all of them. He went downstairs again and let everyone inside.

'Uniform checked Collier wasn't hiding at Janet Allsop's property,' Jenkins told him. 'Ffion's got traffic keeping an eye out for his van. If he makes a move, we should know.'

'Good.' Reece led the way upstairs. 'How did it go in court?'

'As we expected. Turner pleaded not guilty to the abduction and murder charge. He was remanded in custody, awaiting trial.'

They made their way along the narrow corridor towards the flat belonging to Gerry Brady. 'Even if Nathan Turner is innocent,' Reece said, 'getting him off the streets for a while is still a result.'

Jenkins came alongside him. 'By your turn of phrase, you still have him in the running for Janet Allsop's murder? Isn't Collier our main suspect now?'

'It's this one.' Reece stopped next to the flat door. 'My honest answer is, I don't know yet. It might be that all Collier's guilty of is possession of multiple aliases.'

'For what purpose?'

'Fraud. Tax evasion. He could be running away from someone or something. The list is as long as you want to make it. But what makes him of particular interest to me is that one of those aliases links him to this building. And Raglan House gives him access to the tunnels and waterways beneath it.'

Chapter 84

'Is the search warrant in order?' Reece asked. 'If he's guilty, I'm not risking him getting off on a technicality.'

Jenkins handed it to him and waited while it was checked. 'It was straightforward enough getting it.'

Reece knocked loudly on the wooden door. 'Police. Open up.' Several doors along the corridor did, but not the one he was interested in. He knocked again and then got out of the way of the *Big Red Key*.

The door splintered along its length and flew inwards, striking against the wall with an echo. 'That's going to need a new lick of paint,' Reece joked and stepped inside. 'Remind me never to get into an argument with you,' he told the uniform.

The flat was small, but functional. Reece went over to the window and stared at the view outside. To his left was Cardiff Arms Park. Home to the national squads before the Principality Stadium was constructed next to it. He'd known great times at the Arm's Park. Particularly in the seventies, standing shoulder to hip with his dad, singing hymns and chewing on his leak while the likes of Phil Bennett, Gareth Edwards, and JPR Williams conjured magic on the hallowed turf.

Directly below Reece was the flat expanse of the Castle Court car park. He scoured every inch of it, searching for an access chamber in the concrete.

'We've got evidence of blood spatter just here,' one of the CSIs announced.

Reece spun on his heels to find the woman examining the wall above the microwave. 'Show me,' he said, following the trail of the blue light she was using.

'There's more here. Near the bathroom door.' A second CSI was crouched and using a similar lighting device. 'Blood absorbs light that's within certain bandwidths,' she told one of the more junior uniforms. 'Blood spots will usually show up black against lighter surfaces. Like on this laminate flooring.'

Reece studied the area of floor between the two finds. 'Let's shift this coffee table and rug.' The surface beneath the rug looked pristine to the naked eye. When the blue light passed over it, there was another story to be told. Reece stared at a dark smudge that trailed an arc from the kitchen area to the bathroom. 'He's hit her with something over there and then dragged her body this way.'

'The bath and toilet are covered in blood spatter,' the CSI said. 'As is the washbasin.'

'I want this flat and the area outside protected as a crime scene,' Reece told Jenkins. 'Get uniform knocking on doors. If anyone saw or heard anything, you bring them to see me.'

Chapter 85

Reece had since been summoned to a flat one floor above and two doors to the right of Gerry Brady's. He'd left the forensics team to dismantle the waste traps in the kitchen and bathroom, in search of fragments of human tissue. Some lucky soul would soon be checking the sewer outlet. Not him, thankfully.

The uniformed constable introduced Reece to a young couple. 'This is Natalie and James, sir.'

Reece smiled politely. 'I'm told you saw or heard something the other night? Something that might be of interest to us.'

James nodded and took Reece through the flat and out onto a small balcony. It was a bleak retreat given the time of year and weather, but he could see its appeal during the warmer months.

There were two plastic chairs and a matching circular table. A clay flowerpot pushed into one corner contained dirty sand, dead insects, and evidence of a few burned down joints.

Reece had a quick look over the balcony and then came away to stand in a safer spot. He felt giddy. A height thing. 'If you lived in the next building along, you'd get a free view of all the games going on in the Arms Park,' he said with more than a hint of envy.

James glanced at the stadium. 'I'm happy where we are. Neither of us follow the rugby.'

Reece instantly lost some respect for the man. 'Don't tell me. You're into *Wendy-ball* instead?'

James looked at Natalie for help, and when she shrugged, he tried Jenkins.

'He means football,' she said. 'He hates the game.'

'Ah. Right. I'm an Arsenal fan,' James said proudly.

Reece winced. 'You know you can get medicine for that sort of thing?' He clapped his hands together. There was work to be done. 'What is it you want to tell me?'

'We come out here for a cigarette,' James said. There was no mention of weed, and Reece wasn't going to make an issue of it. 'Even when it's raining, the balcony above shelters us from the worst of it. A couple of weeks ago. I can't remember when exactly. It might have been a Tuesday. Yeah, it was definitely a Tuesday, because I'd been playing five-a-side footie and Nat was at her Pilates class.'

For a fleeting moment, Reece imagined himself shoving the guy over the railings. Why could so few people ever make their point without describing every breath and fart they'd taken throughout the day? 'Just the bit you think I need to know,' he said, doing his best to remain civil. 'Only, I'm a bit preoccupied downstairs.'

'I let this woman in downstairs,' James said. 'She asked if I knew where someone lived. It was an Irish name.'

'Gerry Brady?'

'Could have been. I'm not great with names. Then she said he was a big guy who walked with a limp.'

Reece caught Jenkins staring at him. 'Had you ever seen the man she was describing?'

James shook his head. 'Not before that conversation.'

'And since?'

'Well, that's the thing. I could be wrong but—'

Reece balled his fists. 'Just tell me.'

'I was having a cheeky smoke the following night. I couldn't sleep and came out here with a cuppa. Must have been about two in the morning. I saw him down there by the wall, next to the car park. The big guy, walking with a limp like the old lady said.'

'What was he doing down there?'

'Coming and going. Carrying things.'

'What things?' Reece asked, clenching his toes.

'Couldn't tell you. They were wrapped in black bags. Different shapes and sizes. He must have made four or five trips in total.'

Natalie joined in. 'You said at the time you thought he looked cagey.'

'He definitely looked like he was up to no good. Keeping to the shadows. Constantly looking up at the building like he was checking he wasn't being watched.'

'He didn't see you?'

'I hadn't lit up at that point. And it was raining and dark.'

'What else did he do?' Reece asked.

'There's a metal cover in the path. About that big,' James said, measuring out twelve to eighteen inches between his open hands. 'I couldn't see him lifting it. But I could hear metal scraping against metal. And the cover dropping down again when he closed it.'

'You didn't see him put those black bags down the drain?'

James shook his head. 'Nope. But he never brought them back into the building.'

'And you went down there the next day,' Natalie said.

James looked like he hadn't intended to bring that up. 'I was curious,' he told the detectives. 'There were no dumped bin bags that I saw. I thought he must have put the lot down that drain.'

'Did you see any evidence of blood?' Jenkins asked.

'It hadn't stopped raining all night,' James told her. 'There was nothing to see except puddles.'

Chapter 86

THE FORENSIC TEAM HAD found remnants of human hair and skin in the waste trap of the bath. And a splinter of bone located behind the toilet pan. Positive indicators of someone—Janet Allsop in all likelihood—having been killed and dismembered in Gerry Brady's flat.

'I need a favour,' Reece said into his phone.

Maggie Kavanagh sounded like she was trying to turn her lungs inside out. When she'd finished hacking, she said: 'When this morning's horoscope reckoned I was going to be whisked off my feet by a dark and handsome man, never in a million years did I expect that fella to be you.'

'Shut up and listen to what I'm trying to tell you.'

Kavanagh cleared the phlegm in her throat and spoke with a raspy voice. 'I love it when you get all mean and masterful with me.'

Reece ran his fingers through his hair. 'I'm trying to have a serious conversation here.'

'Conversation is all I ever get these days,' the reporter said. 'What I really need is a good old-fashioned—'

'*Maggie!* I'm losing the will to live.'

'I'm listening. I'm listening,' she said in a high-pitched whine. 'What is it you want from me?'

'I need you to run a story in this evening's paper. Front page. Big, bold headline. Get on to anyone you know in television. Tell them to run it as their main news feature.' He spent the next few minutes explaining exactly what he wanted.

'You're trying to flush Collier out,' Jenkins said once he'd ended the call.

'It's either that or wait weeks to locate him. This'll hopefully make him run to someplace where he's not making the news.'

'Outside of Wales?'

'Maybe.'

It was still raining when they got round the back of Raglan House. Reece raised his collar and walked with a hunched posture. 'Get those lights over here,' he said once he'd located the metal cover. He went down on a knee and clawed at it with his bare hands. It was heavy and rusted and wouldn't budge. He jammed his house key down the slither of a gap, but only succeeded in bending it out of shape. 'Any minute now, one of you is going to bugger off and find me something to lift this with,' he said, shaking his head at a pair of uniforms. He got up and blew on his numb fingers while he awaited their return.

Surprisingly, that wasn't too long. 'Got you a flat chisel, sir,' one of them said, and handed it over. He looked proud of himself, standing there like service staff awaiting a tip.

'Open it then,' Reece told him. 'Your knees are younger than mine.' The chisel made short work of the job. The officer lifting and sliding the cover to one side with the minimum amount of fuss.

The environment seemed instantly colder now that the subterranean waterway had been exposed. The tunnel was like a gateway to a frozen version of hell; all souls swept along into the impenetrable darkness.

'All yours, sir,' the uniform said, getting out of the way.

Reece was on both knees; his head pushed through the hole in the floor.

'You'd never get a body in there,' Jenkins said.

'Not a whole one,' Reece agreed. 'Bloody hell.' He examined his hand in the torchlight. 'Please tell me that's not rat shit.'

One of the CSIs used a small pair of forceps to peel away something resembling a shrivelled slug. 'I'd say it's more likely to be a piece of Janet Allsop.'

Chapter 87

With the flat at Raglan house secured with a crime scene guard, they'd gone back to the station to warm up and wait for Edward Collier to panic and take the bait.

In Reece's case, a shower and a change of clothes were required. The piece of human tissue squashed by the palm of his hand hadn't been his only find of the afternoon. Concealed in a black bag, and wedged wall-to-wall as it had rotated in the water, was a human arm and hand, missing its ring finger.

Morgan was sipping from a mug of coffee and staring at the evidence board. 'I wonder what his real name is?'

'Does it matter?' Jenkins said.

'Suppose not. I was wondering what makes someone like him tick?'

'Greed. Arrogance. A complete disregard for the rest of us.'

'Any news?' Reece asked, towelling his wet hair as he made his way through the Incident Room.

Morgan told him that there wasn't any. 'There's a nice hot coffee on your desk,' she said.

'With sugar?'

Jenkins clucked her tongue. 'We've given up trying to help you.'

'Good. I'm glad.'

Morgan had something else to say but was robbed of the opportunity by a member of the support staff.

'Boss,' the woman called from her position behind one of the desks. 'Edward Collier's van just triggered ANPR cameras in Newport. Looks like he's headed for the M4, eastbound.'

Reece tossed the towel to one side, leaving his hair looking like he'd been plugged into a mains socket. 'He's making a run for the Prince of Wales Bridge.'

Chapter 88

'MAKE SURE THEY CLOSE the bridge before he gets there,' Reece said from the passenger seat of the fast-response vehicle.

Jenkins was in the back, gripping hold of Reece's headrest. 'Gwent Police have shut it off on both sides.'

The BMW was nudging ninety miles per hour whenever traffic conditions permitted such speeds. On a few occasions, it slowed for vehicles that dithered to move out of its way. For once, Reece wasn't hanging out of the window, berating anyone.

He turned his head to the driver. 'You've obviously done this before.'

The traffic officer sped up the windscreen wipers and kept his eyes on the road ahead. 'Once or twice, sir.'

There was the background noise of radio chatter. Mostly updates on the whereabouts of Collier's van, together with other police business. Reece loved this part of the job. The chase. The final showdown.

The lights of the bridge were only a mile or so further on, blinking against the night sky. There was a heavy police presence on the Wales side. And the Highways Agency had at least a half-dozen vehicles attending. They were flagged down by an officer in hi-viz gear waving a torch.

The driver pulled alongside him and lowered the window. 'This is DCI Reece.'

The torch bearer came around the other side of the vehicle. Reece got out to talk to him. 'Tell me you haven't lost him.'

'No, sir. We used the Stinger when he came racing through. All four tyres are flat.' The officer pointed along the bridge. 'He made it as far as the hump and came to a stop against the side-barrier.'

'You've already made the arrest?'

The officer shook his head. 'He's on top of the van and won't let anyone go near him. Says he's going to jump over the side if anyone tries.'

Reece stared at the wet road ahead. 'Here we go again,' he said, beginning his trudge up the hill towards the lop-sided van.

Chapter 89

THE WIND FORCED ITS way through the gaps between the baffle plates, slapping Reece's face as he walked by. The salt in the air made it sting all the more. He had no clue how this was going to end, but it wouldn't be with him clambering onto the roof of Collier's van. Even the thought of that had him yearning to lie on his belly and claw the tarmac for safety.

He didn't know how high the bridge was above the mud flats and water. He'd once read that the Severn Estuary had the second highest tidal range in the world and a wave that swept along it with little regard for anything that got in its way. Knowledge wasn't always a good thing, he decided, while trying to put all thoughts of drowning out of his head.

'Stay where you are,' Collier shouted at him. 'I'll jump over the side if you come any closer.'

There were several ways for Reece to play this. He kept walking towards the van with his hands shoved inside his trouser pockets. 'If that's your decision, do it sooner rather than later. It'll save us all having to hang around in the cold.'

Collier inched closer to the abyss. 'I mean what I say. Stay where you are or I'm going to jump.'

Reece was now close enough to touch the van. 'If you don't hurry up, I'll come and throw you off myself.' He wouldn't have wanted to get his bluff called on that.

Collier looked ready for the plunge. 'I'm not letting you take me in. I'd rather be dead than go to prison.'

'It might not be that easy to kill yourself,' Reece said. 'If we were having this conversation an hour or so earlier, you'd probably have had your wish. Splat on the mud flats. Lights out. As it is, there's plenty of water down there now. And a couple of police boats. You might still snap your spine when you hit the surface, but they'll fish you out of there alive. I'll make sure they do. You're going to prison. With or without the use of your legs.'

Edward Collier made his decision. Jumping to his death was one thing. The risk of him having to spend the rest of his miserable life wearing a nappy was a step too far. 'Fuck you,' he said, slipping over the windscreen of the van and onto the road.

Reece forced Collier's hands behind his back and cuffed him. 'Edward Collier. I'm arresting you for the murder of Janet Allsop.

LIAM HANSON

You do not have to say anything. But, it may harm your defence if . . .'

Chapter 90

Cardiff Bay Police Station. Two hours later.

'You were born Jonathan Wilson, in ninety sixty-two,' Reece said. 'Son, and only child of Mary and Reginald Wilson.' He was reading from an official document held at arm's length. He'd left his reading glasses in his office upstairs, but wasn't prepared to halt the interview to go get them. 'The family home was in Darlington, County Durham. England.'

'You *have* been doing your homework. Chief Inspector.' Collier's manner had changed from the abrasive stance encountered by Reece on the Prince of Wales Bridge, to one of almost nonchalant compliance. It was as though the man knew the game was up and had accepted his fate.

'I can't take all the credit,' Reece said, lowering the document for a moment. 'But I agree with you. My team has been very thorough. A few of them are still beavering away upstairs, tearing your past apart.'

Collier's grin lacked any sincerity. 'In that case, I suggest you enrol more than only *a few.*'

Reece ignored him. 'Aged eighteen, you left home and settled in Pudsey, a market town in West Yorkshire.'

'Those were the best years of my life,' Collier said. 'Selling fruit and veg out of wooden crates,' he told Jenkins. 'Not a care in the world.'

'And that's where you first met Annie Brown,' Reece continued.

Collier's eyes narrowed. There was no clever quip this time.

'Annie was an elderly widow. An arthritic woman. When she could no longer get to the markets, you did her shopping. Her garden. You even did odd jobs around the house. Imagine her friends' surprise when you moved into that cottage after her passing.'

'It certainly got tongues wagging,' Collier said. His accent had changed. Only subtly. Hinting at his Yorkshire roots. 'But a will's a will, in the eyes of the law.'

'Better than selling cabbages for a living,' Reece said. 'Preying on old women. Taking what you could from them.'

'I did Annie no harm,' Collier said. 'On the contrary. She'd have ended up in a nursing home if it hadn't been for me,'

'She died in her sleep.'

'A perfect way to go, don't you think?'

Reece knew he'd never prove that Collier had smothered the old woman. Not now that the best part of forty years had elapsed. 'Let's move on. As you did only a couple of months later. That was the first time you changed your name. Am I right?'

'Guilty as charged. London deserves more than the likes of Jon from Darlington.'

'You sold the cottage and used the sale fee and Annie Brown's savings to—'

'They were *my* savings,' Collier corrected. 'But yes, I invested them.'

'In an antique stall on Portobello Road,' Reece continued.

'And named myself Pierre Legrand.' Collier raised his arms at his sides. 'Do you like it, Sergeant?'

'Far too pretentious,' Jenkins said.

'I had aspirations of grandeur in those days. I obviously hadn't fully matured.'

'You were fronting stolen goods,' Reece said. 'A common criminal. There's nothing grand about that.'

'Those charges were never proven.'

'But you did shut up shop and disappear from the area?'

'Relocated is the term I'd prefer to use.'

'To con your way through Wales. North to south.' The conversation continued for another ten to fifteen minutes, describing what the police so far knew of Collier's travels and name changes. 'Let's talk about your wife.'

Collier shifted in his chair. Another raw nerve exposed. 'Why would you want to talk about Rosalind?'

'How did she die?'

'I don't see how this is relevant?'

'Humour me,' Reece said. 'How did your wife die?'

'She suffered a series of unrelenting seizures. I believe the proper name for it is status epilepticus.'

'That's not what killed her. I've seen a copy of her death certificate.'

Collier massaged his forehead. 'The coroner's finding was one of *accidental death by drowning.*'

Reece nodded. 'Your wife drowned while you were in the house.'

'Technically, I was in the garage, working on my car.'

'You were at home, though.'

'I was.'

'Leaving an epileptic woman all alone in a swimming pool?'

'Rosalind knew the risks and refused to live her life in a protective bubble.'

'There were no post-mortem findings to confirm seizure activity on the day your wife died.'

'Equally, there were none to prove otherwise.'

'She drowned, all the same.'

Collier spread his fingers on the tabletop. 'That was the conclusion of the coroner.'

'So,' Reece said. 'We have Annie Brown. Your wife, Rosalind. And now Janet Allsop. Tell us what happened there.'

There was no reason for Collier to clam up and not do so. The evidence amassed against him was overwhelming. 'Where do I even begin?' he asked.

Chapter 91

Reece sat down with Hannah and Mark Oakley. Also present in the meeting room were Elan Jenkins and Ffion Morgan. Chief Superintendent Cable had returned to her office to update ACC Harris.

'I wanted to thank you for finding my mother's killer.' Hannah Oakley wore outdoor clothes and a full face of makeup. She barely resembled the wreck she'd been only a few hours earlier. 'I know I've been a total nightmare, but I really do appreciate everything you've done. All of you.'

'And thank you for not pressing charges against me,' Mark Oakley said. 'I wouldn't blame you if you had.'

'Just this once,' Reece told him. He turned his attention to Hannah. 'You were right about Collier all along.'

'Jonathan Wilson,' Jenkins corrected. 'We should probably refer to him by his real name.'

Hannah Oakley dabbed her eyes with a ball of sodden paper hankies. 'If Mum had only listened to me, she might still be here today.'

'You mustn't blame yourself. Wilson made a career of preying on vulnerable women.'

'Enter *Mum*,' Oakley said theatrically. 'The well-off widow, with the dysfunctional family living hours away.'

'You being in Aberystwyth meant he didn't have to worry about you calling in for a cuppa whenever you fancied.'

Oakley blew her nose. 'Making it far easier for him to hide what he was up to – like lacing her food with sedating drugs and making out she'd taken an overdose.'

'I don't think we'll ever be able to prove that,' Reece was quick to say. 'It's best we stick to what we've got him on.'

'Mum didn't try to kill herself,' Hannah Oakley insisted. Ted poisoned her. Messed with her head and made her doubt herself. She had no choice but to give him extra responsibility within the business, just to keep it going.'

'That's how confidence tricksters operate,' Jenkins said. 'They find a way in and exploit it.'

'How did Mum find out about the Gerry Brady identity? I'd never heard her or anyone else mention that name.'

Reece answered. 'Wilson told us that your mother lost an earing and went looking for it in the van while he was taking a shower. She didn't find the jewellery, but came across an envelope that must have fallen out of his pocket. The Brady name and Raglan House address were printed on it.'

'Why would that raise suspicion?'

'Because she'd seen the same name and address on a letter at the Cowbridge property only days before,' Reece said. 'Wilson liked to collect his mail and take it there to read. He wasn't banking on your mother coming across any of it.'

'And she'd have known how unlikely it was for the post office to make the same mistake twice,' Jenkins said. 'Given how different the names and addresses were.'

Oakley nodded, deep in thought, and asked for more tissues. Morgan obliged. 'Is that when Mum joined the dots? The grogginess; overdose; cheques she couldn't remember writing. And finally, the unfamiliar name and address.'

'On the day of the murder, she went to Raglan House to confront Wilson,' Reece said. 'And told him that she was going to have him removed as a company director and wanted him out of her house by the end of the week.' Reece didn't intend to elaborate. The gruesome details of the crime would be aired fully in court. They would have to prepare the family for that. But not now.

Hannah Oakley was reading from a different page. She *did* want to know. 'How did he kill her?'

'Hannah, look . . .' Reece tried.

'It's my right to know what happened to my mother. How was she killed?'

'She tried to ring you and apologise for not listening. When she turned her back on him, he picked up the nearest thing—a kitchen pestle—and struck her on the back of the head.' Reece instinctively put a hand to his own head injury and glanced at Mark Oakley, who, in turn, looked away.

'Did she die instantly?'

Reece knew that blood splatter caused by blunt force trauma didn't usually occur from a single blow. The initial impact would cause the vascular scalp to bleed. Subsequent strikes would send droplets of that blood flying towards horizontal and vertical surfaces, much like a toddler stamping in a puddle. 'Wilson admitted to hitting her three times.'

'The post-mortem examination findings corroborate that,' Jenkins said.

'Why did he have to mutilate her body?' Hannah Oakley asked. 'Wasn't it enough for him to take her from us?'

'It was the only way to get her out of the flat,' Reece said tentatively. 'Wilson had seen the metal cover in the floor below the balcony. He knew that if he used it to dispose of her body, there was a strong possibility of her never being found.'

'I still don't understand?'

'A full size person would be difficult to remove from the flat without him being seen by other tenants. And even if he did manage it, that opening under the metal cover would have been too small.'

Hannah Oakley drew more paper hankies from the box Morgan had put on the table. 'So, he cut her up and flushed her away like . . .'

'And that was his downfall,' Reece said. 'The body parts were far easier to dispose of, but there was always the risk of them travelling under the city, only to turn up somewhere.'

'Like Mill Street.'

'Like Mill Street,' Reece repeated.

'And those texts my mother sent – saying she was on the train, and then in Aberystwyth with us?'

'Wilson had her phone all along. He sent the texts and then planted the evidence in Nathan Turner's shed when he knew he was out on a job.'

'And that woman in Cowbridge? The one who claimed to be his sister?'

'She went along with whatever he told her to say. She had no part in your mother's death,' Reece said. 'We've probably saved her life.'

Mark Oakley took his wife's hand. This time, she didn't pull away. His arm snaked around her shoulder and he hugged her close to him. 'Hannah—'

'I've been a fool,' she sobbed. 'And selfish.'

Mark was crying as much as Hannah was. 'So have I.'

Reece and the others got up and left the couple to begin a conversation that would determine their future as husband and wife.

'I've got your telephone number,' Reece said when he got to the doorway. 'Once we've spoken to the Crown Prosecution Service, I'll be in touch.'

Chapter 92

'It goes to show,' Jenkins said. 'You never can tell what's happening in other people's lives.' She reclined in her seat and put her feet up on her desk. 'You see people with nice clothes and big houses and flash cars, and naturally assume all's good. Truth is – a lot of them are living a shit show despite all of that.'

Morgan agreed. 'You're not wrong there.'

'I've sold Mum's house,' Jenkins said, staring at the yellowed ceiling tiles. 'Had a text come through when we were downstairs with the Oakleys.'

'That's brilliant.'

'Is it?' Jenkins wasn't so sure.

'Just over three hundred thousand pounds, wasn't it? You've never had that sort of money.'

'True, but I'd take one more evening watching the telly with my mother over any amount of cash.'

'Is DCI Reece in his office?' It was Chief Superintendent Cable. Come to do a final check before going home for the evening.

Jenkins swung her legs off the desk, knocking over a pot of pens in the process. 'He's showering, ma'am. He's running a tad late.'

'For what?'

'He's got a hot date, ma'am,' Morgan said with a wide grin.'

Cable sat down. 'Who drew the short straw? Miranda Beven?'

'He likes her, ma'am, but says she knows too much about him.'

'So, who does he have a date with?'

'I keep telling you,' Reece said, limping through the Incident Room wearing only one shoe. His shirt was unbuttoned all the way down, and his tie trailed along the floor behind him. 'I'm not going on a sodding date.'

'You could play a tune on that six-pack,' Morgan joked. 'Hang on where you are. Let me get a photo for Maggie Kavanagh.'

'You put that phone down,' Reece ordered, tripping on a wayward length of shoelace. He reached out and used a desk to prevent a fall.

'So, where *are* you going?' Cable asked. 'If not on a date.'

'To see Ruth Ellis, if you must know.' He was still short of that second shoe. 'She did me a favour the other day. Tonight, I'm going to do her one.'

Jenkins went to the other side of the room, to be sure that she could sprint along the landing without the risk of him catching her. 'You best take these with you then,' she said, lobbing a three pack of condoms in his direction.

About the Author

Liam Hanson is the crime and thriller pen name of author Andy Roberts. Andy lives in a small rural village in South Wales and is married with two grown-up children. Now the proud owners of a camper van nicknamed 'Griff', Andy and his wife spend most days on the road, searching for new locations to walk Walter, their New Zealand Huntaway.

If you enjoy Andy's work and would like to support him, then please leave a review in the usual places.

To learn of new releases and special offers, you can sign up for his no-spam newsletter, found on his Facebook page:
www.facebook.com/liamhansonauthor

Printed in Great Britain
by Amazon